Lessons from My Alma Mater

Diana Bartol

Published by Diana Bartol, 2023.

LESSONS FROM MY ALMA MATER

First edition. February 28, 2023.

ISBN: 979-8224859795

Written by Diana Bartol.

For my Sweetpea

"No, I never saw an angel, but it is irrelevant whether I saw one or not. I feel their presence around me." Paulo Coelho

1

Whispers

The news of their arrival floats upon the whispers of town gossip. A caravan of cars and trucks pulling faded travel trailers has been spotted driving down County Road D, our road. Their destination, we know, is the vacant lot a mile past our farm at the intersection with Reed Road.

The grapevine has been buzzing all morning like it was earlier in the week when the stranger made his inquiry about the empty lot. This is their first visit to our town. Although we've heard of visits to nearby towns in the past.

The news doesn't stop Mama from beginning her outdoor chores, much to the frustration of our neighbor, Sharon.

Her eyes darted from us to the road. "It will only be a matter of minutes until they reach our end of the road, Evelyn," Sharon exclaims, her hands flapping wildly above her head as if she's trying to ward off a swarm of angry bees.

We are used to her excitable nature, warned by my grandmother of Sharon's "sky is falling philosophy of life" when we learned that she and her husband bought the farm across the road from ours.

My grandmother, you see, is admired for the keen sense of observation she shares in the weekly social column she writes for the *Girdham Free Press*.

So we ignore Sharon's hysterics and return to our tasks as she hurries to the safety of her home. Mama takes aim with the hose at the row of thirsty yucca plants that line our driveway. The watering can intended for my use lies abandoned along with my cherished new glitter jelly sandals, freeing my toes for their attack upon the puddles forming from the runoff.

I pay no attention to the mud-speckled polka dots decorating the backs of my legs, soothed by the feel of the cool water on my sun-hot body. The braids that I begged Mama to weave this morning have escaped their bindings, helped by summer's humidity. The copper coils spring from my head in their true nature.

As an only child, I am used to creating my own entertainment. Today, it's the radio I've set up outside to listen to while we do our chores.

"Keep the volume low, Ginny, so we don't bother Sharon," Mama warns glancing across the road.

I obey, lost in my daydreams, unconcerned about everything around me except for the sound of the music and the feel of the cool water, until the lyrics of my favorite country western song begin to play.

Mama looks in my direction. "They're playing your song, Ginny." We share a smile as we remember how dad helped me learn the words to the song, "Little Bitty," his nickname for me.

I spring from the puddles onto the parched grass, and dance in her direction, bellowing a hearty duet with Alan Jackson. But the appearance of approaching vehicles stops me mid-step.

Mama's aim with the watering hose remains steady when the Ford truck pulling a turquoise travel trailer enters our driveway, creating a cloud of dust on the hard packed earth. But I take one giant hop into the protection of her shadow, and peek from behind.

The truck's door gives an ancient creak as the stranger steps out and removes his worn ball cap, but he remains standing behind the scarred door.

His workman's boots have seen much wear, as evidenced by their scuffed and worn appearance. He rests his muscular tanned arms casually in a crisscrossed fashion on the doorframe in a sociable manner. I venture to Mama's side to get a better look.

He reminds me of the popular caricature portraits I watched Miss Louise draw at the annual art fair.

With great passion, she twirled the paintbrush in the air, using broad black strokes on the white canvas background to capture and exaggerate each person's unique features.

"That's my secret," she told me with a wink, "to accent the positive no matter the number of negatives one might see in a person. A good way for one to approach life in general," she said.

Miss Louise would enjoy drawing this unique-looking man with his wavy dark hair and charcoal black eyebrows that appear as one long line scrunched together as he squints into the bright sunlight. A matching bushy mustache droops over his lips, hiding them from view until a gentle smile appears on his handsome face.

He informs us that his name is Vano, an unusual-sounding name, but not surprising, for it fits his character. He tells us that their destination is the empty lot at the end of the road.

We pretend this is news to us, not wishing to offend him with our knowledge of the local gossip.

He smiles, nodding his head in an accepting way, and shares that we are the only folks they have seen along our country road. I pray that Vano won't notice Sharon's shadow lurking behind the sheer curtains that cover her living room window.

Mama comments that it's an unusually hot summer's day, and she suspects that's why most folks are inside. She's a kind and caring person, you see.

While they continue their conversation, my attention is drawn to the passenger side of the truck where a lady has remained.

The bright sunlight reflecting off the dust-coated glass of the windshield makes it difficult to get a true glimpse of her. She leans her arm against the window frame, creating a faint tinkling sound through the open window.

I attempt to get a better look by standing on my tiptoes, but the sound of the truck door slamming catches me off guard. I turn to see Vano approaching with his right arm raised.

I yelp, remembering the story about kidnappings Sharon shared with me earlier in the week, and topple into Mama. She places her arm gently around my waist and offers her other hand in greeting to Vano.

An expression of sadness passes over his kind face, but my face burns scarlet. I know it's my behavior that has caused his reaction.

Vano hurries to explain that he asks only for the favor of replenishing their water supply for camp that night.

Most folks would refuse even though our water is as free as the air we breathe, coming from well water as it does, but I know that my mama will not refuse; she's known for her generous nature.

Vano returns to the truck to retrieve two large containers from its bed. He stops at the open window to share a smile with the lady and then turns in our direction to retrace his steps.

But my attention remains fastened on the lady. Fate has placed this moment within reach, but how can I grasp it?

I reach for the coil of hair bobbing from the center of my forehead and twist it around my finger, a habit I have when pondering a solution to a problem. My gaze shifts to the pitcher of iced tea we placed on the wicker table, and an idea pops into my head.

Casually, I stroll to the side of the table, attempting to disguise the jitters creeping down my backbone. I fill a glass with tea, and make sure that a couple of ice cubes plop inside.

Balancing the sweating glass between my two hands, I slowly step my way to the side of the truck, encouraged by the smile on the beautiful lady's face. Silently, I raise my offering. The ice cubes clank noisily against the sides of the glass, through no purpose of my own.

Her eyes follow my movements. "Hello, little girl. You read my mind, yes?" A smile forms on her lips. "That is very kind of you." She reaches her arm delicately out of the window, causing a collection of golden bracelets to tumble down her arm as her fingertips meet mine.

A trickle of perspiration meanders down my spine. I raise the offering higher to meet her grasp. A feeling of panic fills my thoughts as I realize I have no next step in my plan to meet her face to face.

Never known for a loss of words, I experience for the first time the sensation I have heard others refer to as cottonmouth. My mouth feels parched, like the Mojave Desert has invaded, and I sputter a choked, "You're welcome, ma'am."

Her smoky brown eyes peer in my direction as she sips the tea. An uncomfortable silence settles over me. I stutter to fill the void. "F-f- folks say that you're planning to camp at the empty lot down the..." My words hang suspended in the air as I realize that I've confessed to my part in the town gossip.

I stumble forward. "Um, you'll like it there, lots of big shade trees and grassy spots to spread a blanket out and share a picnic. We, my mama and me, do that sometimes on our walks." I swipe at the perspiration forming on the ridge of my forehead, threatening to overspill as I search for the words I want to say. An eternity ticks by.

In silence, I study her unique features. She's like no one I've met before. She's very beautiful, but in an uncommon way—different from the pretty ladies in my community who look the same with their pale skin and identical hairstyles. Instead, her thick black hair tumbles in waves beyond her shoulders, held back on one side by a shimmering rhinestone barrette revealing a golden-hoop earring reflecting the morning sunshine.

She rests her hand on the windowsill revealing beautiful rings on many of her fingers. Her painted nails match the ruby color of her lipstick; I hide my own chipped nails behind my back.

At last, the silence breaks when she asks, "But you do not come to talk to me about picnics. You have a special request, something you would like to ask me, yes?"

Taken by surprise, I strain to find the words to the questions I've been wanting to ask since we heard the news of their visit to our town.

I mumble a soft reply. "I, um, some folks say that you might—that you can tell people's fortunes and that you can look into the future and tell what's ahead in a person's life." My words collide as my brain searches for the words to explain my true purpose.

Sensing my distress, she softens her gaze. "Perhaps. What is your name, little one?"

Encouraged by her kindness, I reply. "My name is Geneva Evelyn Ellis." I wrinkle my nose. "But everyone calls me Ginny. I'm named after my great-aunt and mom." I sigh.

"You are not happy with this name?" she asks.

I squirm at the thought of admitting my dislike for my great-aunt's name and try to explain. "It's just that Geneva sounds like an old lady's name, but I guess I'm stuck with it!"

I change the subject, then, and share that my mom and dad are the local veterinarians. My face beams with pride, and I'm unable to stop the words tumbling from my mouth, like a water spigot turned on full force. "We call our business 'Country Critters,' after all of the different kinds of animals we treat."

"I see that you are very proud of your family business. It is a worthy profession, yes?" She nods her head, encouraging me to continue.

I straighten my posture, honored to be considered a part of the family business in her view, and eager to share more. "Yes, ma'am.

It takes the whole team to run the operation. Mrs. Johnson, our neighbor," I point to the farm next door, "works in the office scheduling and greeting customers. Her name is Rita, but I'm not allowed to call her by her first name." A frown forms on my face. "She thinks she's the boss of me when my parents aren't around, but I'm pretty self-sufficient."

A wide grin spreads across her face, and she chuckles and replies, "Yes, I see this about you."

I hesitate for a moment and wonder what it is she sees, but I realize it would be impolite for me to ask, so I continue. "I help wherever I'm needed, feeding the animals, cleaning the cages, sometimes going with my dad when he makes a farm visit. I've seen lots of baby animals born." I smile at the thought.

I boldly raise my eyes to hers, realizing I've gotten off-track and ask, "So, is it true that you can tell people's fortunes?"

She avoids an answer. Her expression becomes serious, and she asks, "I wonder what it is you think and why you ask this question?"

"Well, in answer to your question to my question," I stall for time as a smile creeps across her lips. "I do think that sometimes you can figure out things about folks, like where they're heading in life, by observing things about them." I take a brave step closer to the open window.

"What kind of things do you look for in a person?" she asks, encouraging me to continue.

I study her question and reply. "Like, for instance, Old Johnny, who owns the convenience store on the corner where you turned down our road. You might have noticed the big house sitting behind his store. The paint is peeling, the roof is falling in, and the ivy is beginning to cover it all. He built it for his true love." My voice fills with emotion at the thought.

"Yes, I see the sad old house," she says with compassion.

"It is sad, isn't it? He built it for a bride who never lived in it, and neither did Johnny. He lives in a little apartment above his store." I lean closer and whisper in confidence behind my raised hand, "She left him standing at the altar in front of the whole town and ran away with another man."

"I see." She nods her head in understanding.

"I think Johnny is a lot like his house, all broken in spirit. That's what I mean about being able to figure out where some people are headed in life."

"You are very wise, very observant for someone your age."

I consider her words. "I have a very wise teacher. I spend a lot of time with my grandmother, my dad's mom, who lives in town. Sharon, our neighbor, thinks I spend too much time with her. She says it has turned me into a precocious child. I think Sharon is jealous because my grandmother is so popular for the column she writes in our local newspaper. It's called 'News from Your Alma Mater.'"

"She writes about the university?" she asks with a puzzled look on her face.

I laugh, happy to share my story. "No, no. Alma is her first name, and Mater is the middle name she gave herself—" I stop to consider this discovery, realizing maybe I, too, could invent a new name for myself. "Ah, when she found out that her mama and daddy never gave her a middle name when she was born.

"Grandmater. That's my special name for her, chose her own middle name when she overheard two ladies talking about their cherished alma mater. She decided that was the kind of lady she wanted to grow up to be. Then, later in life, when she discovered the real meaning of alma mater, she knew she had chosen the perfect name, loving learning as she does. She's the smartest person I know. She teaches me lessons about life and love," I explain proudly.

I move forward, rest my hands on the door frame, and ask with pleading eyes, "Please, would you consider telling my fortune?"

Silently, she studies my upturned face, then nods. "You do me a favor, sharing your tea with me, yes? So, I return the favor to you."

She passes the empty glass to me, which I quickly place on the ground, fearful of losing this chance, and step away from the door as she opens it. She turns to place her feet on the ground and arranges her colorful skirt over her tan legs. Then, she holds her hands out to me. I step forward and offer my hands to her reach. She lifts my sweaty palms into her cool grasp, gently brushing away the grime as I gaze into the dark pools of her eyes.

A tiny gasp escapes from her lips as she raises my right palm for a closer look.

"Is there something wrong?" I ask, staring anxiously at my hand.

"No, no. Nothing is wrong," she hurries to assure me. "It is a beautiful palm to read. The lines, they are very deep and clear, you see?" Her voice rises in encouragement as the tips of her fingers trace a pathway across my palm.

"It's just that there is one line that is not often found. It matches the line in my own hand."

She holds her palm out for me to see as she traces a line that starts below her little finger, curves inward toward the center of her palm and then curves down, to make a perfect moon shape.

"It is called the Line of Intuition. Do you know the meaning of this word?" she asks.

Amazed, I stare at the matching line on my hand, unable to respond. With a wrinkled brow and scrunched eyes, I stammer, "It's sort of hard to explain." I twist the lock of hair dangling from my forehead. "I think it's got something to do with knowing a truth or having a feeling about something or someone that just pops into your head without being given any clues. You just know it!" I shrug my shoulders, unable to offer more.

"Perhaps," she wonders aloud, "you have had this experience of intuition. That is truly what bothers you?"

I drop my eyes from hers and confess. "It's all very confusing, these feelings I get. I was hoping that by watching and listening to you tell my fortune, I might find some clues, you know, to understand how this all works."

"I can see this concerns you." She gives my hand a reassuring pat. "It was very confusing for me at your age, too, but I have come to understand it to be a special blessing we share. I know this about you from the moment we meet. I see it in your eyes. The eyes, they are the windows of the soul. I see it when you tell your story about Old Johnny. You have been blessed with a special gift like me. We hear the whispers of the angels guiding us about matters of the heart."

"The whispers of the angels?" My voice rises as I question her meaning.

"Yes, messages carried to us by the angels if we are open to hearing them."

A puzzled look covers my face as I try to grasp her meaning.

Seeing my confusion, she explains. "It is more like an awareness about something or someone that comes over your whole being. I tell you about my first time, okay?"

I nod my head eagerly.

"When I was a little girl growing up in Romania, we lived in the country, too. One day, I come home from school to find my mama so upset, she is crying. She has lost her wedding ring and looked everywhere but cannot find it."

"Oh no. That would make my mama very sad. Her wedding ring is very precious to her."

"Yes, one of the most precious of all your treasures. So, I give my mama a big hug, and just like you say, a thought pops into my head. I ask my mama if she had been working in the garden today. She answers that she had, but she searched the garden and the tool shed many times during the day. "Let's try one more time," I say and race to her garden basket where she keeps her tools. I reach my hand deep into her garden glove—" She imitates her actions.

"And you find your mama's ring!" I shout with a wide smile lighting my face.

She claps her hands in delight. "Yes. It must have pulled off her finger when she removed her glove. Some people will say this was by chance or a good guess, but I know it is the whispers of the angels who helped me find my mama's ring. I have had too many experiences like this in my lifetime not to believe." A gentle smile fills her face as she continues speaking softly in confidence. "I know you have had similar experiences of compassions of the heart. That is why you are drawn to me today. You feel the need to speak to me to learn the truth, for it is troubling you, these feelings you have, yes?"

I attempt to offer a reason. "My mama says that people like to talk to me because of my friendly disposition."

She grins. "Ah, true, but these feelings go deeper than that, like when you meet someone for the first time, and you see into their hearts. You have an understanding about this person that others do not. That is the reason you ask so many questions."

In awe, I listen to her words, confirming my own suspicions. It's true, I think to myself, and not my nosy nature, like Sharon tells Mrs. Johnson.

"Is it a good thing?" I ask.

"But, of course, it is a gift. That is why our paths cross today so that I may help you and you, in turn, may help those whose paths cross yours. It is a serious responsibility, this gift you have been given."

She pauses and looks deeply into my eyes. "You must treasure it and use it as intended. It is not by accident we meet today." She squeezes my hand gently.

"Geneva!" My mother calls for me to return to her side.

She places her hands over mine in prayer-like fashion and asks, "Before you go, I pray to our saint for a special blessing for you, okay?"

I nod and follow her lead, bowing my head as she prays. "Kind and loving Saint Sara, bless this child. Guide her journey and make loud the whispers of the angels." She gives my hands a final pat, and I step away from the truck as she whispers the final word, "Believe."

When I return to Mama's side, I overhear Vano telling her that they live in a Roma community near Cleveland. This summer, he and his family are following the sweet corn harvest across Ohio working in the fields.

"We help to sort and pack the corn to make extra money to visit our family in Europe." Excitement fills his voice as he explains. "Next year, we all meet in southern France for the annual pilgrimage to Saintes-Maries-de-la-Mar to honor our patron saint, Sara al Kali. It will be a big family reunion." He smiles broadly.

It's then that I realize how silly I've been to listen to the town gossip and Sharon's stories all week. Vano raises his hand to Mama in thanks. This time, I do not flinch. Instead, I join Mama in offering our good wishes to him and his family.

Vano balances the full containers, one in each hand, and stows them into the truck bed. He climbs into the truck and shares a loving smile with the beautiful lady and then guides the truck and trailer out of our drive. He leans from the open window with a wide smile on his face and waves a friendly goodbye. Mama and I wave goodbye in return as the sheer curtains in Sharon's living room flutter in response.

I watch until the truck disappears from sight, my thoughts remaining with the beautiful lady and her promise of the whispers of the angels.

Later that day, jumping rope, I can't stop thinking about my visit with her. If this is to be my future, maybe it's time for a new identity.

My mind wanders as I try out one idea and then another with each skip of the rope. "Geneva." Hop. "Veneva." Hop. "Ginny." Hop. "Minny." Hop. "Neva." Hop. "Deva." Hop. "Nevy." I drop the rope from my hands and whisper, "Nevy." It's a perfect fit. And so, I christen my new self "Nevy Evelyn Ellis" and begin a new chapter in my blessed life.

2

Blessings

My blessed life is what Mrs. Johnson reminds me of whenever I've done something that displeases her, like slipping off into the piney woods that surround our property.

"Geneva Evelyn Ellis!" Her shrill voice and use of my full given name warns me of the coming "Blessed Life Lecture."

"Do you know what a blessed life you have growing up on the farm at Country Critters? You need to be more responsible when you go traipsing off into the woods without first telling me!" she exclaims, puffed up like one of Mama's prized Sumatra roosters.

You see, Mrs. Johnson is a city girl at heart and frightened of the piney woods, even after all these years of living in the country where her husband first brought her as a young bride. So I know that she's never going to give me permission, even though I know the trails like the back of my hand, as my dad likes to say.

In answer to her question, I do understand and appreciate how blessed I am. Growing up at Country Critters is like living in a magical storybook adventure.

It's our own private kingdom surrounded by a state park of pine-tree-filled woods dotted with dunes, meandering streams, and trails blazed by Dad and me. Since the moment he could strap my carrier onto his broad shoulders, Dad has taken me on hikes into the piney woods while entertaining me with tales of his boyhood adventures.

Our property consists mostly of farmland containing two man-made ponds, Big Pond and Little Pond, where the wild geese and mallard ducks vie for fish and swimming space. The deer that live in the woods sometimes venture out to nibble on the corn crop. Farmer Johnson owns the farm next to ours, and we lease the acreage to him so he can grow more corn and soybean crops. He just can't get enough of farming, I guess.

Many of the family pets and animals on the farm have been orphans brought to Country Critters by strangers or someone needing help raising them.

This is how we got Lulu, the little runt piglet given to us by Mr. Johnson. The runt is less likely to survive in a litter of competing piglets. That's what I learned listening to my dad and Mr. Johnson talk.

"We'll be her foster family until she's big enough to fend on her own, Ginny," my dad explains.

I know this is his gentle way of telling me that we can't keep her.

She was so tiny when we first got her that I could hold her in the palms of my two hands, but she's grown a lot since then!

She loves to soak in the plastic pool that I've outgrown. She has also taken over Lucky's doghouse. Except now, I'm most often called to rescue Lulu, who can be seen running across the yard with the doghouse attached like a saddle to her back.

Soon, she'll leave and return to Mr. Johnson's farm, where she'll live happily ever after as a brood sow raising her family of piglets, my dad tells me, his sweet way of preparing me for her going away.

Most of our puppies and kittens have been strays found abandoned along the country roads. That's where Lucky, our beautiful collie with a forever smile on her furry face, was found. I believe she smiles because she recognizes her good fortune of joining our family.

Because we live next door to a state park, it's common for uninformed city folks out for a country hike to bring us a wild animal they think has been abandoned. Little do they realize that most times, the mama is hiding among the pine trees, waiting for them to leave, so she can rescue her young one.

Over the years, we had quite a menagerie of animals brought to our doorstep: baby bunnies, birds, and squirrels, mostly. We've raised them to adulthood and released them into the woods.

My favorite wild pet will always be the little red fox we named Brick for the deep reddish-brown color of his fur. We raised him with Lucky's puppies. He became so convinced that he was a dog that he copied their bad habits of chasing cars down our country road. In truth, I think he was just joining in the fun of running with the others.

Of all the wild pets released back into the wild, Brick's leaving was the toughest on all of us, including Brick. I remember the day my dad carried him far into the woods. That was one hike that I could not join.

That rascal Brick found his way back to us, though. For days, he would return to sit at the edge of the woods and our property. I think he was heartsick, too, and trying to figure out what path he was supposed to follow.

The call of the wild became too strong, and one day, Brick stopped coming. I called and called his name with tears streaming down my face until Dad took my hand and walked me to the house. He explained that, like Lulu, it was time for Brick to start his own family. Dad was sure that Brick had found a lady fox, and soon they would have their own babies to raise. That's the image I keep in my mind when I'm missing Brick.

My mom and dad treat all kinds of animals. Dad handles the big farm animals, cows, horses, and sheep, often driving many miles to doctor them on-site. Mom treats the animals brought to the office—dogs, cats, hamsters, guinea pigs, turtles, birds and such. It's not a big operation, but we have a steady customer base, Dad likes to say. It's a good life, a blessed life.

3

Alma Mater

The biggest blessing in my life besides my mom and dad is my grandmother, Alma Mater Ellis. Each day after school, I walk to her grand Victorian, located across from the town square, where we share magical times.

Some kids tease me and call me old-fashioned because I like spending time with Grandmater, my name for her, rather than playing games with them. As an only child, I've been surrounded by adults my whole life. So, I think it's only natural that I like spending time with someone I can learn things from rather than playing kid games.

People say that I'm a lot like my grandmother. I'm not sure what they mean, but I'm honored by this comparison. Maybe it's our shared physical likeness, but even there, I'm no match for her. She wears her hair in the latest style, restored to its natural auburn color every four weeks by Bella at Bella's Hair Salon, unlike the unruly copper curls that spring in wild abandon from my head. She's known for her sense of fashion, unlike my "bohemian style" of clothing described by Sharon.

Like her, I have the same trace of freckles across my cheeks and nose, but unlike my grandmother, mine are exposed for all to see instead of disguised beneath expensive cosmetics.

I'm fortunate to have inherited her rare shamrock green eyes. But whereas her gaze is described as wise and observant, I'm most often teased about the ornery twinkle of my own. I certainly didn't inherit her well-endowed body or regal bearing. Instead, I'm often called the family jokester, known for the laughter that booms from my petite body.

She was born and raised in Girdham, Ohio, a town that hasn't changed much since she was a girl. Her writing career began in 1981 when my dad left for college and Beulah Bishop, who was retiring from writing the social column for the *Girdham Free Press*, convinced my grandmother to take her place. Today, it's one of the last society columns to survive in rural Ohio. I believe that it's only because of Grandmater's popularity that it continues to thrive. Each year, she swears will be the last, but interest in her column doesn't seem to be slowing down.

Grandmater is known by all the locals, though no one is a stranger to her. She has a natural way of making friends with each new person she meets with a genuine welcoming and trusting nature.

Most days you'll find her seated in the antique oak rocking chair placed before the large bay window, where she can observe the comings and goings at the stately limestone courthouse on the town square.

Whereas the courthouse is the place where the records of the important events of the lives of the residents are recorded—the births, deaths, marriages, divorces, and all other sorts of legal matters— it is to the Victorian where they turn to share the personal details of those joys and sorrows.

She places her finger to her lips as a reminder for me to remain silent as I sit at the foot of her rocking chair, perfecting my listening skills and learning some of the most valuable lessons about life.

Invisible to the eager adult intent on sharing a bit of confidential news, I listen to the stories told by each of her visitors, sprinkled with the often-repeated phrase, "Remember, Alma, this part is off the record."

Over the years, I've come to understand that it's not so much the personal news they share with Grandmater for her column, although they love seeing their stories in print, but, instead, it's the chance to share their deepest concerns with their loving and wise Alma Mater.

It's during these sessions that I learned the valuable lesson of being trustworthy as a keeper of shared secrets and confidences. For this, she is revered.

"Always respect the privacy of others, and when someone confides in you, never betray their confidence," Grandmater instructs.

These shared conversations and what Grandmater and I call "The Cookie Tin Game" help sharpen my skills of observation and teach me what Grandmater calls "matters of the heart."

The Cookie Tin Game was Grandmater's idea after listening to my story about the visit with the beautiful lady and my special power of intuition.

She replied, "Just as I suspected."

It began on a rainy afternoon. Grandmater suggested we try something new she had been thinking about that would help my skills of observation. "We will call it 'The Cookie Tin Game' to be played on rainy afternoons," she declared.

"Cookie Tin day!" I shout with excitement. Raindrops pitter-pattered against the windowpanes.

Grandmater chuckles as I race to the locked china cabinet across the room and pull the brocade footstool from the side to the front. Carefully, I stand on the footstool under the watchful eyes of Grandmater, reach inside the carnival glass bowl atop the cabinet to remove the hidden key, then slide the stool aside to unlock the glass door.

I deliver the round cookie tin decorated with a brightly colored winter scene of Santa and his sleigh to Grandmater, who waits in the rocking chair. I settle with my legs crossed on the braided rug, and together we recite our mantra: "Cookie Tin, Cookie Tin, reveal your secrets."

Grandmater removes the lid and lowers the cookie tin into my hands. I lower it to my lap, close my eyes, and scoop my hand into the collection of old photos, choosing only one.

The challenge of the game is to describe everything I can detect from the scene in the photo, with Grandmater guiding my observations and filling in the blanks.

"Remember, Nevy, there is often a hidden story not always obvious in the photograph," Grandmater teaches.

During these Cookie Tin Games, I've learned the life stories of some of Girdham's most colorful residents, and the lesson each of their lives teach—Johnny and his story of lost love, Pine Tree Tammy, and her sad lot in life, and sweet Nanny Tate, and her example of the way a good life should be lived.

I was surprised to discover a photo of Johnny as a young boy. He was dressed in a baseball outfit and stared directly into the camera with a proud smile on his face. Now, his eyes are downcast, and his conversation is limited to the business at hand. There is no small talk with Johnny.

The lesson of Old Johnny's story, Grandmater sighed, is that you must be open to forgiveness in your heart and accepting of help from others. She described how everyone in town tried to cheer him and include him in their activities after his true love ran off. Instead, he chose to live a solitary life of heartbreak and shame. I think I would rather accept help from others than live a sad life like Johnny's.

I hardly recognized Tammy Carson the day I discovered her photo in the tin. I couldn't believe my eyes. She was stunning, a real beauty, so different from the Tammy I know today.

In the photo, she stood beside a shiny new car, playfully blowing a kiss to the unseen photographer. Her golden hair flowed to her shoulders in the sunlight. She was slim and tan and full of joy.

Grandmater shared that Tammy's parents bought her the car as a gift for her high school graduation. She had worked very hard to earn a scholarship to the university to pursue a degree in journalism. They were filled with hopes and dreams for their only child. Tammy's future looked bright and beautiful.

But that summer, she met up with a bad boy. Her parents couldn't persuade her to break up with him. Soon, baby number one was on the way, with more babies to follow.

Today, she lives in a ramshackle house bursting at the seams with a houseful of children and a mean-spirited husband, who drives a long-haul truck and is gone for days on end.

It's well-known that Tammy sometimes leaves the oldest child in charge of the other children while she sneaks down the road to the pine forest where she cries her eyes out, huddled under a pine tree, while sipping a bottle of Nanny Tate's dandelion wine. That's how she got the nickname of Pine Tree Tammy.

When I asked Grandmater what the lesson in Tammy's life is, she explained that sometimes in life, you must make a choice between momentary happiness and long-term goals. The decision you make can determine the direction your life takes forever. I think Tammy cries in the forest because she is sorry she made the wrong choice.

Grandmater has the only photo I've seen of Nanny Tate. Like Tammy, she's younger in the photo, but unlike Tammy, she hasn't changed much over the years.

Her miniature body matched the tiny cottage she stood in front of, holding a wicker basket overflowing with the day's collection of wildflowers, plants, and herbs.

She wore a belted flowered dress, garden gloves, and a pair of black rubber boots. Her fly-away hair was a salt and pepper gray, unlike the snowy white hair we are familiar with today. On her face she wore the same sweet smile we've come to know and love.

Nanny can name every herb, flower, and plant native or common to our area and the medical purpose of each. She's in her nineties now, but back in the day, Grandmater tells me, she was known for her concoctions of teas, tonics, and tinctures.

It was Nanny who the locals turned to when they were in need of a medical cure, when dollars were few, or when the remedies of modern-day medicines failed to meet their needs.

Nanny can no longer practice her trade, restricted by age and the laws of the state. But a visit to her cottage at the end of Red Clover Lane is worthwhile for the stories she tells and the wisdom she shares.

A visit to Nanny's cottage is like entering a secret garden bursting with colorful paintings of flowers and herbs adorning the walls of her kitchen, her workstation of days past. Written in precise lettering below each painting is the common and botanical name of the plant, and a list of healing uses for each. I have mastered two of my favorites.

The first is the golden dandelion, *Taraxacum officinale, which* graces the east-facing wall to catch the morning sunshine. Nanny's dandelion wine was a favorite of the old-timers who swore by its miracle cure for digestive problems, or that is the excuse they used in order to secure a bottle of this popular wine.

The other is the Lily of the valley, *Convallaria majalis,* with its delicate white drooping head and green leaves. I think it hangs its head in sadness because of its past use as a remedy for heart ailments and difficult childbirths. Who would believe that such a lovely little flower was so poisonous from leaf to stem to flower and berries?

Nanny's stories always include a stern warning to each visitor to beware of using these plants without a full understanding of their dangers as well as their cures.

Like Grandmater, Nanny Tate is a walking, talking institution of learning in her own right. She is loved by all for her history of helping anyone who comes knocking at the door of her cottage. I think the lesson of Nanny's life is that we should all be more loving and giving like her.

4

James

Now grown and remembering the stories I heard at the foot of Grandmater's rocking chair, I realize how magical my life's path has been. Guided by the lessons I learned and my gift of intuition about compassions of the heart, I have lived a charmed life absent the sadness shared "off the record" with Grandmater and uncovered during the Cookie Tin Games. I have secured my dream job and will soon marry the man of my dreams.

I met James during my sophomore year of college. I heard the whispers of the angels the day the English professor asked me to choose a partner for a cooperative writing assignment. I peered into the blue eyes of the quiet, handsome guy who always chose to sit in the last row, and without hesitation, picked him. Science-minded, James struggled with the creative writing assignments, and chemistry was proving to be a challenge for me. Jamie, my name for him, was destined for med school, and a teaching degree was my goal. We agreed to collaborate. Our academic collaboration grew into friendship, and our friendship matured into true love.

I'll never forget the day Jamie proposed to me. It was a Sunday morning in May at the end of our senior year. We shared breakfast together at our favorite pancake house restaurant. Jamie paid the cashier, who returned a handful of change to him. He grinned at me as I nodded my head. As was our custom, we turned to the vending machine at the exit door and deposited the coins. We watched the colorful plastic eggs roll and bounce together, fascinated like two little kids. My eyes latched onto an egg the color of Jamie's forget-me-not blue eyes. I watched as it bobbed among the others and disappeared out-of-sight, dropping out seconds later for Jamie's reach. In that moment, I knew it contained a special treasure. He opened it to reveal a huge imitation diamond ring that sparkled in the sunshine.

Spontaneously, Jamie dropped his tall, lean body to one knee, his eyes reflecting his love for me, and asked me to marry him.

His words are imprinted in my memory. "One day, Nevy, I will replace this with a real diamond ring. But until then, will you accept my humble offer of marriage? I love you and cannot imagine a life without you." His face filled with the endearing crooked little smile that never failed to melt my heart.

"Yes, yes, yes!" I exclaimed, my feelings matching his. He placed the oversized diamond ring on my finger and sealed the proposal with a kiss, surrounded by an admiring crowd who gathered to watch.

Later, as we planned for our future together, we reached the unhappy conclusion that it would be best for each of us to finish our degrees before marriage.

Upon graduation, Jamie would be heading for med school in Detroit at the Henry Ford Hospital, but I would remain at Miami University to obtain my masters of education. We were confident that our love for each other was strong enough to endure the challenges ahead.

Our goal had been proceeding as planned. After graduating from graduate school, I was hired for a third-grade teaching position at my hometown school, Oak View Elementary.

It wasn't easily achieved, with so many others applying for the position. I have no doubt that a recommendation placed on my behalf by Grandmater helped move my name to the top of the list.

I also accepted her offer to move into the Victorian with her, which was a short walk to the school. My move was a great relief for my parents, with Grandmater entering her eighties and living alone in the huge house.

The teaching job is my dream come true. I awake each morning filled with excitement and looking forward to the new experiences that await each day.

This year, however, I'm as excited as my students for winter break to begin. I've been counting down the days until my reunion with Jamie. He can't join me for Christmas, but he promised to be home for New Year's. Our New Year's Eve celebration will launch the year of our marriage and put an end to this marathon engagement.

I'm awakened before dawn to the rattling of windowpanes. A fierce wind has blown in off Lake Erie sometime during the early hours. I take refuge under the warmth of the heirloom quilts that decorate the lovely antique queen bed, dreading the walk to school that I must soon take.

A feeling of uneasiness creeps down my spine, no doubt caused by my concern over the day's events. It will be a day full of activities culminating in a party organized and chaperoned by the parents. My job, I've been informed, is to simply sit back and enjoy myself.

The shriek of the alarm clock breaks the silence. I hurry to shut it off, but in the darkness, I don't see the fragile porcelain figurine placed too close to the edge of the bedside table.

My hand sideswipes the treasured bride and groom that Jamie and I discovered at an antique shop one fall day. The sound of shattering glass echoes in the darkness.

I slide off the bed onto the cold wooden floor. "No, no, no," I whisper, tears streaming down my face. I cradle the broken porcelain pieces in my hands, creating bloody little slits on my fingers.

The figurine has become a part of our nightly ritual. Jamie and I exchange a simple text with each other each night as I climb into bed. "Good night, my groom."

"Good night, my bride." He never fails to answer, no matter how busy he is.

The figurine was supposed to be our wedding cake topper. How will I tell Jamie? Tears cascade down my face.

Drooping my head in resignation, I already know what his loving response will be. He'll tease me about my clumsy habits and claim that it's my way of getting him to join me on another antique outing, which is not one of his favorite pastimes.

But I'm devastated. I snap at Grandmater as I hurry to escape her questioning about the commotion coming from my room this morning. I skip breakfast, rushing out of the door with the lame excuse of needing to get to school early to prepare for the day's events.

I'm oblivious to the howling wind and bitter cold as I trudge the few blocks to school, so caught up in my personal misery of the broken figurine and the absence of Jamie to make things right. I miss him so much.

"Get a grip, Nevy," I mutter between clenched teeth, silently reminding myself of the busy day ahead.

The children are wild with excitement about the end of the year party and the looming winter break, ignoring my warnings to settle down. It's so out of character for my students. No doubt the changing barometer signaling the approaching snowstorm is partially to blame.

The party is more frenzied than I anticipated, aided by a marshmallow snowball fight planned by unwitting parent helpers. Why is it that your angels turn into demons the moment a visiting parent enters the room?

At last, I usher the remaining students and parents out of the classroom and collapse into the teacher's chair so rarely used in my classroom. I cradle my splitting head between my hands.

I've tried calling Jamie throughout the day to confess my crime and to hear his reassuring voice, but, like my recent experiences, I've been unable to reach him. After several attempts at composing a text, I give up trying.

"I need to hear your voice, Jamie," I plead to the empty room.

Voices of my peers filled with laughter and holiday wishes echo from the other classrooms, but I'm in no mood for holiday cheer. I grab my coat from the rack, sneak down the hallway, and exit the building.

I try to shelter myself from the blowing wind and snow by burying my head into my coat, and regret forgetting my mittens and knit hat in my hurry to leave.

The Christmas decorations and seasonal scenes that decorate the buildings and shop windows usually bring a smile to my face and warmth to my heart, but right now, they fail to warm my shaking body.

My attempt to enter the house quietly through the back door is unsuccessful as the wind catches hold and slams the door with a loud thud.

"Nevy?" Grandmater calls, her voice drowsy with sleep. I've awakened her from a catnap in her rocker.

I peek around the corner, hoping to avoid a conversation.

"Are you okay?" she asks with concern, her look melting my heart.

"I think I may be coming down with a cold or something," I choke out a cough. "I don't want to get too close to you," I say with guilt slithering down my spine. "I'm going to fix a cup of soup and some tea and head to my room, if that's okay with you?"

"Sure, sweet girl, you go ahead. I had a hearty late lunch with Sophie, who stopped by. She brought us some yummy homemade Christmas cookies. They're on the kitchen table if you're interested. I'm sorry you're not feeling well. How was the party?"

"Beyond crazy!" I grimace. "It ended with a marshmallow snowball fight!"

"Oh my!" Grandmater tsks.

"I think I may just be suffering from party overload. It's bitter cold outside too. The wind has picked up, and the snow is blowing sideways. See you in the morning."

"Good night, Nevy. Love you." She blows a kiss my way.

Her solitary figure huddled in the oak rocker is more than I can bear. She seems smaller and frailer these days. I tiptoe to the rocking chair, tuck the blanket around her shoulders, and kiss the top of her head. "Don't stay up late," I whisper.

She pats my hand lovingly. "No worries about that," she assures.

Balancing a cup of soup and a steaming cup of tea in my hands, I trudge up the stairs. My feet feel like they're each encased in lead.

Maybe I am coming down with something, I reason. This feeling of melancholy is so uncharacteristic of my usual joy this time of the year. In truth, I know it's my missing Jamie that's at the root of these feelings. But why? I question, knowing that I'll be seeing him soon.

Alone in my room, at last, I don my flannels, turn on the TV, and burrow into the nest of quilts. The early evening newscast is just starting with the forewarnings of the approaching storm. Night comes early in the winter in northwest Ohio, and darkness envelops the room.

I must have fallen asleep in the middle of the weather forecast. It's the last thing I remember hearing before being awakened by the chiming of my cell phone. The bowl of soup sits congealed and cold on the bedside table, and the cup of tea is untouched as well.

I wonder now what it was that the beautiful lady truly saw that childhood summer day as she peered into my sweaty palms. I remember the surprised gasp she uttered and, in hindsight, how she chose to divert my attention to the Line of Intuition and away from the broken Heart Line foretelling of lost love.

How innocent and promising my life seemed, the future so bright and beautiful. Why couldn't I see the turn it would take?

They tell me he never saw the out-of-control truck sliding on the black ice in his direction. He was trying to help a stranded motorist whose car had slid off the road and into a snowdrift only six miles from the Ohio border.

It was to be a surprise visit. My Jamie had been working extra shifts in order to get the Christmas holiday off. That was why my phone calls went unanswered. They say his death was immediate.

They found the black velvet box tucked into the inside pocket of his winter coat. I wear the diamond ring on a delicate gold chain close to my heart and out of sight from others.

5

So Magical

My life has been so magical. I had a childhood untarnished by loss and was surrounded by loving adults who encouraged and praised my every effort.

Grandmater understands the depth of my sadness. She wraps me in her loving arms and doesn't offer advice, like everyone else trying to smother me with their sympathy.

So magical. Three months after losing Jamie, Grandmater passed away in her sleep. Like Jamie's death, there was no forewarning to soften the sudden loss of her. Her passing has secured my financial future, but at the moment, I cannot envision what that future might be.

The world, my world, is stopped on its axis. Time is suspended, and life as I know it will never be the same. Grief enshrouds my being. I am filled with blackness, no light of hope, of future, or dreams to fulfill. It's a void so deep it seems bottomless.

Weeks and months pass. I've taken an extended leave of absence after Grandmater's death. I couldn't face my students and peers a second time, while so deep in my sorrow. My leave is followed by the summer break.

The Victorian provides a fortress to hide behind. I've been spared from seeing Jamie's parents who live many towns over. The bond that I shared with them has disappeared. There are no words left to say to each other, no purpose for a close relationship.

The Cookie Tin Games and stories I remember hearing while sitting at the foot of Grandmater's rocking chair now have personal significance for me. I understand the depth of some of the storytellers' heartbreak.

I huddle in the rocking chair, wrapped in the heirloom Ellis quilt that was my Grandmater's favorite. My fingers trace the faded red roses she loved, and my other hand clutches Jamie's diamond ring.

His words echo in my thoughts. *One day, Nevy, I will replace this with a real diamond ring, but until then, will you accept my humble offer of marriage? I love you and cannot imagine a life without you.*

"What am I to do without you, my Jamie?" I tremble at the reality of these words.

In response, I hear my Grandmater telling me that I must move forward. In an attempt to appease her, I dug out an old journal left with a few empty pages, hidden away in my hope chest.

"My hope chest!" I spit out the words with a cynical laugh. Such an old-fashioned tradition, but I can't erase the memory of when Mom and I found the painted wooden chest at the annual flea market in the town park. She insisted on purchasing it and enlisted Dad's help transporting it to the foot of my bed in the Victorian.

Mom's words flutter through my thoughts. "We'll have such fun finding treasures for your life as a new bride, my Nevy!" she exclaimed, ending with a hug.

In a fit of despair, I emptied the contents of the chest into a plastic bag destined for Goodwill and filled it with the personal journals I collected over the years.

Each journal was a gift from Grandmater. She promised that they would help generate ideas for my college writing assignments. There was always a fresh supply waiting for me.

The journal rests on the wide wooden arm of the rocking chair like Grandmater's notebook all the years I watched her writing the weekly news article, pen poised between her fingers, her hand hovering over the blank page, as she gathered her thoughts.

I've been sitting for over an hour, the blank page daring me to write the words that scream in my thoughts. Grief consumes my being, and I stab at the page with the pen like a dagger. The bold black scratch desecrates the white page, unrecognizable from my teacher-trained perfect D'nealian print.

"Help me, Grandmater." I pray for her to give me inspiration for a new direction in my life. But instead, a list of words appears before my eyes, beginning with "WHY!" and ending with "WHAT NOW?" The depth of my feelings, my hurt, is beyond words. It's all so futile, I think.

"Why, why, why!" I scream aloud to the empty room and fling the journal violently across the room, narrowly missing the china cabinet.

"What am I to do, Grandmater, without Jamie and you in my life? You were my world." My words fade into a whisper.

6

A New Beginning

Another day passes. I have become a great escape artist, dodging well-doers except for my parents, and it's only then to soften their worry. They protect me by keeping Sharon at a distance. She means well but is filled with advice that she's eager to share.

They think I'm planning to return to my teaching job when school resumes. I deceive them by remaining silent when the conversation turns to the subject of the coming school year. I'm not ready to share my true plans. I can't because I don't know them myself.

It's a rainy Sunday afternoon, a Cookie Tin Game kind of day. "Grandmater," I call softly and wistfully look at the cookie tin resting untouched on the shelf in the china cabinet.

Absently, I glance through sections of the Sunday paper, scattering the pages on the floor around the rocking chair when I spot the words, "Writer/Photo Researcher," while looking through the help-wanted ads. A description of the job requirements follows: "Prepare draft from raw research, accurate, creative, and able to work with minimal supervision." But it's the last sentence that catches my full interest. "Locate historic photographs and write captions for a book project for a best-selling author of historical fiction based in Chicago."

"What do you think, Grandmater?" I whisper. "Those years of Cookie Tin Games should count for something, don't you think?"

The job would offer a new beginning, I reason, an escape from my current situation to a new location far from the sympathetic eyes of others. It would be a job with little interaction, where I could bury myself in research away from memories of my past.

I reach for my cell phone, my heart pounding, and call the number listed before I can change my mind.

Someone answers on the first ring, a great booming voice that announces, "Louise Lerner at your service!" She shouts so loudly that I have to hold the phone away from my ear.

"Oh, my goodness, I'm so sorry." I cast a guilty glance at the Sunday newspaper scattered at my feet. I forgot that it was Sunday afternoon. My days were running one into the other.

"I—I'm calling about the ad in the paper. I'll be happy to call tomorrow during business hours," I apologize silently scolding myself for blowing this chance.

"No worries, my dear. I often forget the day of the week. "So, you're calling about the ad?"

I don't remember my jumbled responses to her questions, but I was shocked at the end of the conversation to receive an invitation for an interview later in the week.

Mother is not pleased when I share the news along with my plans to drive to Chicago and spend the night at the Drake Hotel.

"But, Nevy," she pleads, "you've never driven to Chicago on your own..."

"I could borrow your SUV with the great GPS system you're always praising," I respond, hiding the guilt I'm feeling.

Momentarily stymied, she pauses with a look of frustration. "How about if I go with you? It would be such fun and—"

Gently I interrupt, reminding her, "Mom, that would be great, but you've been telling me about the busy week ahead with Dad away attending the veterinary conference." I say a silent prayer of thanks to myself, for remembering Dad's plans as an excuse for going solo on this trip.

I can see the wheels spinning in her thoughts as she considers her response. "Well, yes, I was hoping that you would help out at the office while Dad is gone." She looks defeated. "I don't know why you want to interview for a job when you already have your dream job here." She twists the knife of guilt ever so gently.

Seeing her distress, I realize it's time to confess. "Mom, it breaks my heart to tell you, but I gave the principal my official notice that I won't be returning to teach school this year. I gave him the okay to find my replacement," I murmur and watch sadness and disbelief cover her face. I brace myself for the barrage of questions to come.

"You did what?!" she exclaims, hands on hips, face furrowed into a deep disapproving frown full of concern. "Geneva Evelyn, why on earth would you do that? Your whole support system is here, your friends, your family. You won't have anyone there," she pleads, swiping away tears.

I wince at her words, unaware of reverting to my childhood habit of twisting the wayward coil of hair around and around my finger. "But, Mom, that's the problem. I need to get away from the sad faces and the sympathy. It would be pitiful walking into the school and my classroom again, and it wouldn't be fair to my students. They're always so filled with happiness at the start of each school year. My heart is just not in it."

I pause to allow her to consider my argument. "I need a change, Mom. Let's see what this job in Chicago has to offer, okay? It's the first time that I've felt a glimmer of hope for my future."

My mother reluctantly surrenders when I promise to keep her updated on my whereabouts throughout the trip.

I wrap her in a hug, brush away her tears, and whisper, "I need to do this, Mama."

With the rising sun behind me, I exit my parents' driveway the next morning and head west with a feeling of anticipation and hope for the first time since Jamie's passing.

The GPS works like a charm, just as Mom boasted. Four uneventful hours later, surrounded by corn and soybean fields, the towering skyscrapers of Chicago emerge like a shrouded mythical kingdom enveloped in a fog bank rolling in off Lake Michigan.

I miss the morning rush hour, which is a blessing as I navigate across the Chicago Skyway toll bridge, stopping to deposit a small fortune of coins and blessing Mom for the baggie filled with quarters she tucked into my hand when I stopped to switch cars this morning.

The navigation system gives me a feeling of confidence as I maneuver the city streets and locate the vintage duplex on Elm Street with time to spare, but finding a parking spot becomes a challenge. I circle the one-way streets, around and around, looking in vain for a place to park.

Perspiration slides down my back, soaking through my silk blouse even in the comfort of air conditioning as my parking dilemma becomes dire.

I use my peripheral vision, while keeping an eye on the traffic, to search for Ms. Lerner's phone number on my cell phone. A young mother carrying an infant in a car seat with a trailing toddler exits a brownstone down the block. I stalk their progress, slowing to a crawl toward a parked SUV, and try to tune out the beeps of a horn from the cab two inches from my bumper.

An eternity passes until she succeeds in buckling her babies and herself into their seats, then cautiously exiting the parking space. Miraculously, I manage to parallel park the SUV into the vacant spot as the cab zips by, filling the air with expletives ending with the words "woman driver!"

I take the steps two at a time leading to the massive wooden doors of the brownstone, now late for my appointment. I grab ahold of the ornate iron door knocker, banging it with more force than intended.

It's a blessing that I'm out of breath as it disguises my surprise when the door is opened. My eyes travel up from the Birkenstock sandals, flowing skirt, and voluminous peasant's blouse to the nest of golden woven braids and the jovial round face filled with warmth.

"Welcome, Geneva!" She extends her hand as she introduces herself. "Louise Lerner, but my friends call me Lou."

I place my hand in hers and feel myself propel forward by a hearty grasp into the ornate portrait-lined foyer.

"Don't let them scare you." She waves her hand at the somber-faced portraits lining the hall. "All Lerner clan but not as formidable as their paintings portray. Well, at least most of them, that is. I leave them up as an homage to my late father. I follow in her wake. "Did you drive in this morning? The traffic can be merciless!" She turns to me with an expression of mock horror.

I try to catch my breath as I answer, "I am so sorry that I'm late for my appointment. The challenge was finding a parking space."

Lou holds her hand up to silence me. "No worries. It's the reason I don't own a car. I rent one or use a limo." She ushers me through another pair of stately carved doors leading into a wood-paneled study. "Here we are. Come sit." She pats the richly brocaded sofa and turns to a serving table across the room containing a crystal pitcher and matching goblets. "I bet you could use a cold glass of lemonade. I know I can!"

I accept the much-appreciated icy drink and wait in anxious anticipation while Miss Lerner settles her large frame into the elegant leather wingback chair across from me.

She crosses her legs at the ankles, leans in my direction, and says, "I have been looking forward to meeting you and hearing more about your Cookie Tin Games and wonderful Alma Mater!" Her voice booms.

"Oh, I don't remember mentioning all that." I squirm as I feel a slow blush cover my face.

"Ha!" Lou laughs heartily. "That's the qualification I liked the best." She smiles and nods her head. "I'll tell you, Geneva, I've had

lots of inquiries about the job and several interviews. But, I swear..."
She places her hand on her heart. "I have yet to find one person who
has demonstrated the amount of sincerity in person as I heard from
you over the phone."

My heart flutters with renewed hope as Lou continues. "I know
you lack experience," she shares a consoling wink, "but I can tell
you've got the smarts. I know you will catch on quickly. I've checked
your references. You received rave reviews from each person I
contacted." She nods her head in approval. "My main concern is
finding someone I can work with and trust. This is a two-person
operation. You and me, kiddo, that's it." She arches her eyebrow in
my direction as I nod my head in understanding.

"I can teach you the skills you'll need, and I have a gut feeling
that we can form a pretty good team. So, let me tell you a little about
myself and the job."

She settles into her chair and takes a sip of lemonade. "When
I retired from teaching—you see, we have something in common
already." She chuckles and continues. "I decided to pursue my dream
of writing a novel of historical fiction. By then, my father was living
alone in the brownstone, my childhood home, but his health was
failing. I decided to move home and try my hand at this writing thing
while being close by for Dad."

I can't believe my good fortune as I listen to Lou with thoughts
about the possibility of a future in Chicago swirling through my
mind.

"Well..." Lou slaps her thigh jolting my attention back to her.
"Can you believe I discovered I'm not half-bad at this writing thing,
kid! I already have a couple of best sellers. I just love it. The downside
is the book tours I have to attend." She frowns. "The bane of
becoming a successful author, at least for me. That cuts into my
research time for my next book. Also, my office is here, so I need
someone I can trust in my home while I'm out of town." She pauses

to take a great gulp of lemonade. "Your job duties would include doing research for me, locating archival and historic information, photographs, and captions that I can incorporate into my writing. That's where your Cookie Tin Games come in, don't you see? The years of analyzing and describing those photographs are a learned skill, yes indeed," she explains, nodding emphatically.

I offer a silent thank you to Grandmater as Lou continues describing the duties that go along with the job.

"You'll be spending time at the libraries, the Harold Washington and Newberry, for sure, as well as doing most of your research on the computer in the office." Lou shifts her body leaning closer and giving me a searching look. "So what do you say?"

I'm caught off guard in this one-sided conversation and hasten a stunned reply. "You—you mean you are offering me the job?"

Lou beams a smile in my direction. "Kid, it was yours after the first phone call and reinforced by your friends and co-workers."

I'm overcome with joy and relief. "I absolutely accept your offer!"

"Good, that's settled. We'll work out the details then, and I'll draw up a contract for you to sign."

She holds the crystal goblet high. "A toast to good fortune and friendship." And I follow her lead. "Now, your turn to entertain me. I want to hear more about your Alma Mater and the Cookie Tin Games. By the way, how did she come by that name of hers?" She encourages me to share, and for the first time since her passing, I find myself eager to retell the stories about my beloved Alma Mater.

I'm fortunate to locate a studio apartment a few blocks from Lou's brownstone. It's small and will accommodate only a few of my furnishings. I don't mind as long as there's space for Grandmater's oak rocking chair and china cabinet. The rest of my furnishings will remain shrouded in cover at the Victorian under the loving care of Mom and Dad.

I end the day with the dreaded call to my mother. I can hear the distress in her voice over my decision, but there is no doubt in my heart that this is the right choice for me.

7

Whispers Return

A few weeks into the job, I embark upon a new challenge. Although it's a short walk from the brownstone on Elm Street to the "L" Red Line, I decide to walk to my destination and take in the sights and sounds of the city.

There is no need for a GPS today since the directions are simple: west on Elm, left on State Street, and continue to 400 South State Street.

Alone at last, I exhale a deep sigh, relieved to be free from making excuses to loved ones wanting to comfort me. They mean well, but space is what I need.

I consider the irony of that as I observe the vehicle-clogged streets. I'm surrounded by pedestrians filling the sidewalks and serenaded by a cacophony created by all. Space in a city filled with people will give me the anonymity I yearn.

An enticing aroma wafts through the air and guides me in the direction of a bakery door wedged open by an exiting customer. The smell of brewing coffee lures me inside.

I emerge with a steaming cup of latte in one hand and a flaky pain au chocolate in the other, a smile of contentment spreading across my face, a forgotten expression these past months. I hear the whisper of approval from Grandmater, "Chicago is the right decision, Nevy, my love."

Guardedly, I have allowed the whispers in. I had shut them out, believing that the idea of having intuitive powers or the ability to hear whispers from the angels to have been a cruel hoax played on a gullible little girl. There had been no forewarning of the tragic events that would take place in my life. Proof enough, I reasoned.

But recently, this proof has begun to crumble, beginning with the subtle appearance of the first dance song Jamie and I had chosen for our wedding reception. "At Last," by Etta James was the perfect choice, summing up our feelings about our long-awaited wedding date.

I had stopped at Madison Street Books in the West Loop in search of a book of photographs containing old-time Chicago scenes. Bookstores have always been one of Jamie's and my favorite places to visit, even though we never spent time together there. His interest in children's books maxed out after a few minutes, and my interest in sports was as limited.

That day, I was so absorbed in a book of photographs I discovered, that I was unaware of the soft music playing in the background. As I glanced through the pages of photos, the lyrics and melody slowly seeped into my awareness. As I began to hum the words, I was suddenly overwhelmed by a feeling of Jamie's presence. The experience left me weak-kneed and stumbling for the exit door, blind to my surroundings until I reached the door to my apartment building.

Days passed, and I began to reason away the significance of the experience until a visit home to meet with a moving company representative. It had been a tense day for all. I convinced my parents to return home while I finished with the details.

Seeking a moment to collect my thoughts before returning to my parents' home, I decided to stop at the town park, which I had been avoiding since Jamie's passing. There's a mermaid fountain and wooden bench a short walk from the parking lot where Jamie and I spent many happy times together planning our future.

Much to my relief, the lot was empty. I parked the car and stepped onto the gravel surface, following the path to the soothing sounds of the splashing fountain.

I settled on the bench and was soon lost in my memories but was jolted back to the present by the unmistakable lyrics of "At Last." I followed the music to discover a convertible parked in the lot with a young couple inside listening to our song, Jamie's and my song!

I was stunned and must have looked a bit crazed, bounding out of the bushes as evidenced by the startled look on their faces. I mumbled a quick "sorry" and scrambled into my car, throwing gravel into the air as I exited the parking lot, only to pull over a few blocks down the street with shaking hands clutching the steering wheel.

"What are you trying to tell me, Jamie?" I wept, but the moment was gone, vanished, leaving only questions lingering in my mind.

Then came the day that left no doubt of the whispers of my angels. I was aimlessly walking along the city streets, trying to pass the hours of a long Sunday afternoon when I chanced upon an antique mall filled with unique shops.

Each shop had a specialty: vintage clothing, antique furniture, and wall hangings of gilt-framed mirrors and paintings.

Entering one and then another, I began to retrace my steps to the street when the name of a tiny shop tucked into a corner stopped me in my tracks. The sign read, "Forget Me Not."

Intrigued, I entered the shop to discover colorful damask-covered tabletops containing collections of delicate teacups and figurines.

I meandered through the narrow aisles of tables; my shoulder bag brushed against a fragile teacup, sending it teetering on its saucer. Startled, I reached to settle the cup.

That was when my gaze fell upon the bride and groom figurine, a perfect match to the one Jamie and I had found, the one that would have set atop our wedding cake, the one that I had broken on the day Jamie died.

My heart leaped. I cradled the figurine in both hands as tears of sorrow and happiness spilled down my cheeks.

It was then that I realized I had closed myself off from allowing his messages of love to be heard. I whispered my understanding. "I love you, my sweet Jamie. I will never forget you."

I carried my treasure, cupped in both hands, to the store clerk who appeared behind the counter. We exchanged no words, but her expression was filled with compassion and understanding as we completed the transaction.

She took great care wrapping the figurine in mounds of tissue paper and placing it in a protective box. She patted my hand with a gentle touch as she returned my treasure to me.

It now rests in a place of honor next to the cookie tin behind the locked door of Grandmater's china cabinet, safe, secure, and visible as a reminder of our forever love.

I realize now that in order to hear the whispers of the angels, there must be no doubt in one's heart of their being. That's what the beautiful lady meant on that day when she whispered the word "believe." It is the belief that opens the door to hearing the whispers. As my belief has grown stronger, so too, have the whispers of my angels.

8

A Visit to HWLC

Blaring horns between two dueling taxis vying for the same customer shakes me from my reverie. I'm surprised to see the Harold Washington Library Center or HWLC as the locals call it, looming before me as I approach the intersection of Van Buren and State.

The building is immense. Not so much in height, rising only ten stories compared to the 110 stories of the nearby Willis Tower, but in pure mass, consuming an entire city block.

Lou informed me that there is much controversy about the building's architecture she described as postmodern style. "You'll either love it or hate it!" she exclaimed. "That seems to be the general consensus, and no, they are not gargoyles as some people say," she snickered on a final cryptic note.

The five-story arched windows that surround the building capture my attention. Arches appear to be a theme as evidenced by its many arched doors.

I gaze skyward above the main entrance on State Street into the deep-set eyes of a great horned owl. It perches with wings spread, its talons clutching a hefty tome, preparing to take flight.

"Ah, a wise old owl, a symbol of knowledge and wisdom and not a gargoyle," I murmur, comprehending Lou's meaning.

"What do you think, Grandmater?" I pause for confirmation. I agree with her urging me to delay my entrance no longer; it's not the exterior but the interior and its contents that are of interest today.

My footsteps echo across the marble floor of the silent grand lobby that fills the massive space. There are few patrons here as most activities take place on the upper floors.

Lou loaned me her library card for today's use. I'll apply for my own at a later date, but for now, I'm too filled with excitement to delay my exploration.

Most of the research could be accomplished using the internet, but my advance search of the library's catalog has revealed a treasure trove of books and periodicals dealing with the era of prohibition in Chicago, Lou's latest endeavor. I cannot wait to hold each book in my hands. That's when the magic begins.

According to the directory, the resources I'm looking for are located on the fifth and sixth floors where the periodicals, microfilm, and historical sources can be found. A visit to the Winter Garden with its exquisite glass roof located on the ninth floor, will be a special treat before I leave for the day.

With a list of previously researched call numbers in hand, I proceed directly to the stacks when I reach the sixth floor. I search with anticipation, looking for the first and most important book on my list, a book of photographs, but, to my disappointment, it's missing.

"Shoot!" I exclaim, casting a guilty look around while continuing to survey the shelf, hoping that the book has been misfiled.

Without success, I settle for the other books on my list and locate a secluded desk tucked away in a corner to begin my journey into the era of the 1920s.

The hours pass quickly as I work my way through the resources located between the sixth and fifth floors. My vibrating cell phone ends my time travel for the day.

Lou's short text, "Starting dinner preparations," is her subtle way of telling me it's time to return to the brownstone. A visit to the Winter Garden will have to wait for another day.

On instinct, I decide to look for the missing book one last time before checking out the books I planned to take home. A wide acknowledging grin fills my face as I spot the book, now shelved in place waiting for my discovery. I respond with a silent thank you to my ever-present muse who has shared this day with me.

The screeching sound of metal upon metal announces the arrival of an approaching train as I exit the library and run to catch the L for a quick ride home.

The rush hour scenes flashing before my eyes remind me of the pages of photographs that fluttered through my fingertips all day. They were moments in time, gone forever if not for these treasured photographs.

A mouthwatering aroma wafts through the brownstone as I enter.

"Perfect timing!" Lou calls from the kitchen. "Grab a chair. There's a glass of wine waiting with your name on it!"

As I take my seat at the table, sipping the much- appreciated glass of wine, Lou bounds into the dining room carrying a steaming plate of savory pepper steak in each hand.

"So, what's the verdict?" She flashes a mischievous grin, setting the tasty plate before me and settling into the chair next to mine.

I furrow my brows. "Verdict?"

"You know." She nudges my shoulder gently with her knuckles. "What do you think of the building?"

"It certainly is massive!" I exclaim recalling my first impression.

"Seven hundred and fifty-six thousand square feet! Did you see the owls?" She quickly changes subjects.

"Owls, as in plural?" I tilt my head in her direction, confused. "I saw one huge owl above the main entrance clutching a book in its talons. There are more?" I hadn't seen any other owls inside the library. I'm surprised to hear there were others.

"Kid, there are five of those owls. The one you saw is the largest, weighs three tons, and is twenty feet tall!" Lou's eyebrows rise in fascination. "There are four more, one on each corner." Lou shakes a hearty dose of soy sauce on her meal and continues without missing a beat. "The building is so big you have to stand at a distance or from atop another building to see all of them."

"I'll do a better job surveying my surroundings next time. I never made it to the ninth floor Winter Garden, either, which I definitely want to visit," I lament.

"That's a must-see for sure, probably my favorite reading spot in the library."

"*But* I was successful finding all the resources on my list. I can't wait to dive into each of them."

"That's the spirit!" Lou smiles broadly. "It's going to be a blast writing this book, especially now with your help. There are so many characters and stories to draw from for inspiration. I'm champing at the bit to get started. But for now, let's enjoy my meal. I'm starving! Bon appetite." Lou waves her fork in the air as I follow her lead scooping a forkful of the tasty dish.

Later that night, I lay in the tiny twin bed, ensconced in a mountain of pillows. I page through the book of photographs I was so eager to locate.

Notorious names of the past flutter in rapid succession as I'm transported to the era of Prohibition. It's the unexpected photos that pique my curiosity like the photo I spot of Al Capone. He's wearing loafers and dressed in a striped robe and silk pajamas, a cigar dangling from his lips as he fished off the deck of his yacht, more often used as his rum-running vessel.

Another photo portrays a ghoulish photograph of the body of John Dillinger in the city morgue. A crowd of curious on-lookers surround the body. Some straight off the beach, still wearing their bathing suits, having heard the news of his killing by federal agents as he left the Biograph Theater in Lincoln Park.

I lean my weary head against the pillows as I study one last photo before surrendering to sleep. It's the unfamiliar nickname that catches my attention. Moonshine Mary Wazeniak. The photographer captured her at the moment she was being arrested for the murder of a man she served lethal moonshine to in her speakeasy home.

She stared blankly into the camera, her face devoid of expression, her posture stiff-necked, seated next to a suited official, perhaps her arresting officer. But the caption does not explain. Is it fear or defiance? I wonder as I recall Grandmater's advice about the stories that are sometimes hidden in these photographs. My challenge will be to discover these stories. I can't wait to get started, but for this late night, sleep wins out.

9

A Partnership Blossoms into Friendship

Time passes quickly with Lou. One year fades into the next, and our relationship matures from a working partnership into true friendship.

We share nearly every dinner together to my demise as evidenced by the extra pounds I've gained dining on Lou's gourmet meals. She scoffs at my comments about gaining weight, declaring that it's time I put some meat on my bones.

It's during these dinners that our friendship blossoms; it's where we share our personal stories with each other. Lou had mentioned earlier that she retired from teaching, but I was surprised to learn that it was from a prestigious Ivy League college as an esteemed Professor of American Studies.

She confessed that her boisterous persona and manner of speech using fragmented sentences were in rebellion to her parents and upbringing surrounded by the hallowed halls of academia. Both of her parents were college professors. I find it interesting that she chose the same career path.

She admitted that she was the bane of her mother's existence. She resisted attempts to turn her into a "girlie girl," and never married to give her mother the grandchildren she yearned.

Although, one evening, after several glasses of wine, Lou confided that she came very close to marrying. "That's a story for another time," she promised with a melancholy smile.

I, on the other hand, choose to remain selective with the information I share about my past, preferring to entertain Lou with stories from my childhood and the Cookie Tin Games, which seem to appease her.

As time passes, Lou's success has flourished, and so too, have my writing and research skills. "Nevy!" she calls out one day. "We've achieved our goal of becoming a well-oiled machine working together. Life is good!"

I realize that Lou is right. I'm content with my life, much to the frustration of my family and friends back home who hoped my Chicago experience would be short-lived. My work and Lou's friendship are all that I need, I tell myself.

Then, on a winter's night as the fire crackles in the fireplace and snowflakes flutter to the ground, Lou keeps her promise to share the story of her lost love.

We are celebrating the completion of her recent novel over a dinner of chateaubriand accompanied by a fine bottle of Cabernet. Soothed by the ambience, we settle into a contented silence until Lou whispers, "My Henry would have loved this meal tonight." She has a faraway look in her eyes. "His favorite. He loved my cooking." Her lips curve upward into a tiny smile.

"Henry?" I repeat hesitantly, taken aback by this revelation.

"My one true love." Lou's eyes twinkle in fond remembrance. "We were so mismatched, star-crossed lovers. He owns an auto repair shop where I would take my car for servicing before I moved back to Chicago."

She pauses, transported in memory, then continues. "First time I met him, we got into an argument about the necessity of regular servicing for the good health of my car." Lou grimaces. "Guess I had neglected a few important things like changing the oil and what all." She taps the side of her head. "Ha! I can still picture him standing there with his hands on his hips, shaking his head at my ignorance." Lou pantomimes the scene, a wicked frown on her face.

Not sure how to respond, I choose to remain silent, a subtle smile creeping across my face. It's enough for Lou to continue.

"He isn't a big guy. All muscle and balding head with tuffs of Brillo-pad hair sprouting from the sides that he hides under an ancient oil-stained baseball cap, permanent grease under his fingernails. Swears like a sailor to his employees, which none of them pay heed. All bark and no bite. Grew up in a mean part of town with a mean family who tossed him out on his own when he was only sixteen. Found a job in the shop he now owns."

I grasp her hand in a tiny squeeze. "How did the two of you end up together?"

Lou obliges, "He tickled the daylights out of me. Called his bluff, loved our sparring matches, and truth be told, so did he. Took him a year to finally get up the nerve to ask me out."

Lou takes a sip of wine and shakes her head. "What a fake. Loving, kind, a real gentleman. He's nothing like the persona he presents to the world. Well read, self-taught, and curious about everything."

She nods as if to affirm her perception and continues. "He always had a project going, whether it was woodworking or painting, even got into the knitting craze one year. Said it calmed his nerves. Gave me a knitted hat and scarf of the most unusual colors for Christmas that my friends all raved about. I think he was a little color blind, but it worked to his advantage. Such a great guy." Her lips tremble into a crooked grin.

Softly, I ask, "Where is he now, Lou?"

Her eyes tear as she looks in my direction. "Oh, still at his shop, I guess. My parents, as you can imagine, never accepted our relationship. Our world of academia was like living in another universe from Henry's way of life. The one time I did bring him home was a disaster!" Lou cradles her head between her hands as memories fill her thoughts, then turns her forlorn face in my direction to explain.

"My parents could not have been more unwelcoming. The grandeur and formality of our home were like nothing Henry had experienced. He was a real gentleman about it, but I could tell he was ill at ease during the visit. I don't know what I was thinking, inviting him here. Head in the clouds, I guess. Our relationship went downhill from there."

"Oh, Lou," I whisper, at a loss for words.

"Meant to be." She shrugs. "Shortly after that, my mother's health took a bad turn, requiring me to return to Chicago more frequently for longer periods of time. Years later, I heard that he had met a lady friend, and they had married. End of story." Lou sighs.

"I am so sorry, my friend."

She turns, looking deeply into my eyes, and in a whisper asks, "Your turn now, Nev. You ever going to tell me the story behind the gold chain and ring you wear hidden from view?"

I place a protective hand over the ring and divert my eyes from Lou's to the delicate spinning wine glass twirling between my fingers.

Gently grasping my hand, Lou states, "I already know most of the story, Nev, from your friends when I checked your references and your parents during their visits here. Mention was made of your tragic losses, one following so closely after the other."

I raise my eyes to Lou's compassion-filled face. I can no longer hold back my sadness. And so, I share the story of my lost love, of the dreams and plans Jamie and I had made for our future together, and my disillusionment with life following Grandmater's passing.

Softly, Lou responds, "You do realize, Nev, that you are turning into an Old Johnny, burying yourself in your work. Do you have any outside interests, girlfriends you hang out with? I have never met—"

"I don't need a bunch of friends!" I snap, jerking my hand from her grasp. "You are my friend, and my work fulfills my needs. I don't need anything else," I blurt. But in my heart, I know Lou is right. I have not honored Jamie and Grandmater's lives. Instead, I've tried to bury the hurt just like Johnny.

And so, it was on that sleepless winter's night that I resolved to turn my life in a new direction.

10

Summer Hill

As part of my recovery, I promised to accompany Lou to the annual spring gala hosted by her dear friends, Contessa and Robert Summer, in celebration of their return from their winter home in Tucson, Arizona. The event will take place at their estate, Summer Hill, located on the exclusive North Shore area overlooking Lake Michigan.

I escaped Lou's pleas in the past to accompany her to this annual party, but she caught me in a weak moment, and reminded me of my promise to reform my ways.

I completely forgot about the looming date on the calendar until dinner one evening when Lou asks, "Have you started shopping for your dress, yet?" A sly expression crept across her face.

"My dress?" I ask, looking blankly in her direction.

"For the party at Summer Hill. You remember it's only a couple of weeks away. I can't wait for you to meet my friends, Contessa and Robert. The party is sure to be a blast filled with people from all walks of life, the arts, business, politics, academia, even some show biz folks."

"Oh, Lou, I..."

"Don't you go oh Louing me, Nevy." Lou pouts like a five-year-old. "I look forward to this event every year," she continues in self-defense. "I will not take no for an answer. I hate walking in there by myself. Besides, you promised," she scolds.

"Are you going to stomp your foot, too?" I chide. She gives me a stern look. "Alright, alright." I raise my hands in surrender. "I'll go, but I am not staying late." Lou grins, satisfied with my ultimatum.

The days pass quickly, and the night of the gala arrives. Lou texts a quick alert. "Limo here, on our way."

I've chosen an emerald-green silk floor-length gown and twisted my unruly curls into a chignon-style held in place by a sequined art deco hair comb, both discovered during a visit to one of my favorite vintage shops on North Broadway.

I stop in front of my foyer mirror; a tiny gasp of horror escapes me.

I had tried on the gown hastily over my camisole days before. To my dismay, I now discover that the bodice is much lower cut than I had realized. Jamie's ring is exposed for all to see.

"Nevy, Nevy, how could you be so blind!" I scold my reflected image.

There's no choice but to remove the chain and ring. To leave it on would bring unwanted scrutiny and comment. I raise the ring to my lips, bestowing a loving kiss, and remove the chain from around my neck. I carry it, cupped protectively in the palm of my hand, to its original velvet box.

I hide the box in the deep recesses of my closet inside the beaded vintage silk purse that Jamie bought for me during one of our antique outings. With tears in my eyes, I watch the chain and ring slide out of sight into the velvet box and place the box back into its secret hiding place.

The limousine is pulling up to the curb as I peek out my apartment window. The cell phone chimes at the same time, alerting me of Lou's incoming text. "I see you," I shout angrily to the air and grab my wrap and purse, swiping the remnants of tears from my face.

The driver stands with the limo door open as I approach the sleek, black limousine. He takes my arm and assists me into the back seat next to Lou who's bedecked in volumes of floral organza.

"Nevy, meet my friend, Bob Tyler; you've heard me mention him on many occasions," Lou beams. It's obvious that she's excited about the night's event. "Best limo driver in the city. I've known Bob now...how long do we go back, Bob?"

Bob turns to face us. "Well, I guess it's going on ten years, Lou. It's a pleasure to meet you, Miss Nevy," he replies in a kind and gentle voice.

"It's nice to meet you as well, Mr. Tyler," I reply.

"Bob owns his own fleet of cars now, but he obliges me by doing the driving whenever I call." Lou's eyes widen as she takes a look at my evening wear. "My, Nev, you look gorgeous! Emerald green is your color, girl. Matches your eyes. I love the way you styled your hair, too. Very chic." She's giddy with excitement.

A sheepish grin crosses my face. "Thank you." I reach to touch my ring for comfort but remember that it's not there. If she notices its absence, she never mentions it.

Lou turns her attention to Bob. "So, tell me, Bob, what's going on with the Tyler gang these days?"

I sink deeply into the soft leather seat and allow their conversation to block out any further thoughts about the black velvet box and its contents. Instead, I focus my view on the show of city lights twinkling alive as the sun sets in the west while the limo glides up Michigan Avenue in the direction of the elite suburb of North Shore.

Our pace begins to slow as the car approaches a pair of stately iron gates standing open in welcome to arriving guests. Bob expertly guides the limousine through the entrance, continuing along a blue spruce-lined driveway.

Distant views of the mansion ablaze with flickering lights dance between the passing trees as we progress up the winding drive.

"This is like entering an enchanted forest," I say, surprised by the excitement I'm feeling.

"And wait until you see the castle, kid," Lou says enthusiastically, squeezing my hand. "Isn't that right, Bob?"

Bob nods his head in agreement. "It's a sight to behold, for sure."

The limousine clears the driveway and enters a brick-paved courtyard. Light shines through a wall of diamond-shaped beveled glass panes like a New Year's Eve crystal ball.

"Oh my," I exclaim as I lean my head back to peer through the sunroof at the majestic stone Tudor mansion to see to the top of its slate-covered roof.

Bob maneuvers the limousine close to the flagstone path leading to the entrance. He exits to assist Lou, no small feat considering the abundance of organza surrounding her. He then comes to my side of the car, offering me his free arm and guides us along the lighted pathway.

"This must be what Cinderella felt like," I say to Lou as she smiles in my direction, pleased by my excitement.

As we approach the ivy-covered arched doorway, the massive door magically opens to an impressive two-story foyer and the sound of distant laughter and music.

"Welcome to Summer Hill, Miss Lou." A man dressed in formal attire, black tailcoat, crisp white wing-collar dress shirt, black bow tie, and striped trousers, greets us as Bob fades into the background.

"Good evening, Edward. I would like you to meet my friend, Nevy." Lou turns to place her arm lightly over my shoulder, sensing my anxiety.

He dips his head in my direction and replies, "A pleasure to meet you, Miss Nevy."

I'm not sure of the protocol, so I smile and nod, with the hope that my response or lack of one is sufficient.

Lou interjects, to my relief. "It sounds like the party is rocking, Edward."

"Yes, it's off to a grand start." The serious fellow cracks a smile amused by Lou's enthusiasm.

"I would expect no less. The city has been abuzz for weeks over this year's Summer Hill gala. It's one of the highlights of the year." Lou's face fills with a wide grin.

"Allow me to escort you to the grand ballroom where the festivities are taking place." Edward directs us with a wave of his white-gloved hand along a richly paneled hallway, toward the rear of the mansion, where the sound of voices and music grow in intensity.

As we follow in his wake, apprehension creeps down my spine as the reality of my situation dawns on me. Silently, I scold myself for acquiescing to Lou's insistence. What was I thinking, joining her to this gala event filled with influential people and hosted by one of the most prominent couples in Chicago?

I have to remind myself to keep my mouth closed as we arrive at the entrance to the opulent ballroom with its gilded-gold ceiling and crystal chandeliers. As I glance around the dance floor, I recognize many familiar faces from the society pages of the newspapers. Women in haute couture gowns of every color, jewels glittering under the twinkling lights of the chandeliers, twirl with their tuxedoed partners to the music of the live orchestra.

"Too bad you can't see the view tonight," Lou whispers. She points to the magnificent floor-to-ceiling windows decorating the back wall. They are partially covered by luxurious golden silk-jacquard drapes. The view overlooks the dark expanse of Lake Michigan.

A lovely voice beckons to Lou. Following the voice, I observe a stunning woman dressed in an off-the-shoulder satin gown. She glides toward us effortlessly as the adoring guests part before her.

Her flawless face is shaped in symmetrical beauty; the golden flecks in her dark brown eyes shimmer in the light of the chandeliers. Cascading waves of raven black hair tumble to her tanned shoulders. Her demeanor is welcoming, but her carriage reveals command of her surroundings. Her name, Contessa, suits her well.

"Welcome, Lou, and this is your friend, Miss Nevy, yes?" It's more of a statement than a question as we are embraced in a gentle group hug, a wisp of luscious fragrance filling the air.

"We are so pleased that you have joined us this year, Nevy. Come, you must meet my Roberto." Contessa enjoins her arms with each of ours and escorts us through the crowd, in the direction of a tall, dignified-looking man with silver gray hair, dressed in formal attire. He is engrossed in conversation, the center of attention, among a group of guests.

"Robert," Contessa calls to him lovingly as we near the group. An endearing look envelops his handsome face at the sound of his wife's voice as he turns in our direction.

"Excuse me, everyone," she says, her voice filling with a charming tease, "while I kidnap my husband for a moment." She skillfully extracts him from the conversation.

"Roberto, my love, look who has come to share the evening with us, our Lou and the lovely Miss Nevy we've heard so much about."

"You are too gracious," I protest, feeling the warmth of a blush creeping across my face. It's easy to fall prey to this most enchanting woman.

He bends his tall frame to grace Lou with a kiss on the cheek, then turns to offer a hand in greeting to me. "We were beginning to think you were a figment of Lou's creative imagination." His eyes dance with delight. "Truly, we are so pleased that you could accompany Lou this year."

In full blush, I reply, "Yes, thank you for the past invitations. I am honored to share this evening with you." In an attempt to change the subject, I hasten to add, "Your home is magnificent!"

"Contessa deserves all the praise." He glows with pride, turning to his wife and placing a loving arm around her waist. "She's done an amazing job renovating. It was like a gloomy dungeon, and I was its prisoner until Contessa rescued me," he proclaims as he looks at his wife adoringly.

"Perhaps Nevy would enjoy a tour of Summer Hill while Lou and I catch up on some news?" Contessa ventures a raised eyebrow in his direction.

"I would love a tour of your home," I blurt out, seizing the opportunity to escape the social responsibilities of mingling with such a distinguished crowd of people.

Robert offers his arm to me. "It would be my great pleasure."

I link my arm with his without hesitation and follow his lead. "I'm sorry, but I'm a bit confused," I confess, looking into his kind face. "But is your name Robert or Roberto?"

He chuckles and offers an explanation. "'Robert' is my given name, but 'Roberto' is Contessa's name of endearment for me. She loves renaming all of us. Did you know that was how Louise became Lou? It can be quite confusing at times, but also quite fun." His eyes twinkle with merriment. "Like being reinvented."

"Ah, I must confess that I am guilty as well. My given name is Geneva. I inherited the habit from my grandmother, my wonderful Alma Mater," I say, enticing him to ask more.

"Alma Mater?" He claps his hands together. "I can't wait to hear the story behind that!"

Joining in his delight, I oblige and launch into my favorite topic of conversation.

As we proceed with the tour, my breath is taken away by the grandeur of the house. Each room sparkles with light from gleaming chandeliers casting reflections against the hand-crafted leaded glass windows.

We pause to peek into the formal dining room containing the longest table I have ever seen.

Robert confesses, "When my sister and I were little, we would sit at each end of the table and bounce the beach ball to each other—when my mother wasn't around, that is!" He feigns an expression of fright. "That's the most fun I ever had at that table until Contessa arrived."

I can feel my anxieties waning in the presence of this lovely man and his natural ability of putting me at ease. I begin to relax and enjoy myself, eager to see where our tour will lead next.

We continue down the hallway, stepping into a grand room designed in classic Tudor style with a wood-beamed ceiling, inlaid hardwood floors, and carved wood paneling. An inviting fire crackles in the massive fireplace that anchors one end of the room. Plush sofas and chairs beckon to be used.

"This room is so warm and inviting." I hide my desire to escape into its interior for the rest of the night.

"You should have seen it before. It was decorated with heavy faded velvet drapes and worn, outdated furniture. Contessa took one look and declared war on this room." He laughs as his arms arch toward the windows. "Down came the drapes, never to be replaced again, exposing these fabulous windows for all to see." I can't help but giggle at his antics.

Pausing for breath, he smooths his hair in place, regains his composure, and launches once again into an account of Contessa's destruction of the room. "Out went all the over-stuffed heavy sofas and chairs—and there were many, oh so many." He turns a forlorn look at me. "With all the tables and dreary dark paintings gone, in came lightness and beauty." Robert lifts his arms, showing what Contessa was able to uncover.

"It's truly all that and more," I reply.

"And now," he says, flashing a mischievous grin, "I'll show you my favorite room."

Filled with curiosity, I follow him, listening as he continues to describe the other rooms in the mansion.

"There are ten bedrooms upstairs, and a media room on the lower level. You must join us some evening. The wine cellar is nearby, making it very convenient on movie night." He stops at a set of richly carved arched wooden doors. "But this," Robert says with a wink, "is my favorite room." He opens the doors and waves me inside.

I gasp at the beauty and elegance of the room as my gaze travels to the paneled wall of bookshelves. The bookshelves continue to a second-floor balcony connected by a spiral staircase.

I step deeper into the room and glance around. A Persian rug patterned in shades of gold and ivory covers the dark wood floor. An ornate tufted velvet sofa sits in front of the stone fireplace. Side tables and softly lit lamps complete the cozy scene.

A pair of distressed maroon-leather wingback chairs and matching ottomans are grouped together, with a tall floor lamp in burnished-gold metal standing between the chairs. A game table and four club chairs are positioned on the opposite side of the room.

A magnificent oil painting of the Grand Canyon covers nearly half of one wall. I move closer as if drawn by a magnetic force. The multicolored layers of cliffs painted in hues of vermillion, sienna-brown, and gold overlap one after the other like a grand staircase leading to the tumbling waters of the Colorado River below.

Robert walks to my side. "It's our favorite place in the whole world. We never miss a visit during our winter sojourn. Have you been there?"

"Never, but it's on my list now," I whisper, in awe of the scene before me.

"It's considered one of the seven natural wonders of the world. Truly unforgettable."

"This room is amazing. I can see why it's your favorite. I could get lost in here," I praise.

"I often do," he murmurs. "This is my inner-sanctum as you can tell by the desk tucked in the corner, my one concession from

Contessa during the renovation. He points to a large ornate desk and chair. "It was a gift from my father when I took over running the company, Prairie Gear and Sportswear.

"You're PG&S!" I am shocked to learn. "My closet is filled with your clothes."

Robert chuckles. "Thank you for the compliment, but the praise belongs to my father who started the company. He was born in Prairie du Chien, Wisconsin; thus, the name for the company.

"The desk belonged to him. It has served me well. Tessa never asked me to remove it, but between you and me, all she would have to do is ask. I can deny her nothing."

"You love her very much," my voice softens as I look into his glistening eyes.

"She saved my life, Nevy. I left the family business after my first wife, Isabel, died. Why? I don't know." He shakes his head in remorse. "I guess I decided it was time to relinquish the reins to my son, Shannon. He was certainly deserving of the opportunity to take over the helm." He sighs. "With Isabel gone and me rattling around alone in this mausoleum, I guess I convinced myself that I was not destined long for this world either. I was becoming a hermit, waiting for my final demise." A regretful frown overtakes his handsome face.

"I understand," I murmur, as his words resonate in my thoughts.

"But then," his voice fills with joy, "my good friend, Nicholas, convinced me to join him on a trip to attend the Kentucky Derby. Thank the Lord he persisted because I nearly backed out of his invitation." He smiles in recollection as he embarks upon his tale. "The day of the race arrives. Nicholas is sponsoring a horse that's running in the Derby, so we know we'll have grand seats for the viewing...or so we thought." Robert arches his right brow and peers at me with a wrinkled forehead.

"That is," he continues, "until Contessa and her entourage arrive to claim their seats directly in front of us."

My hand comes to my lips. "Oh, no." I have a hint of what's coming.

"Oh yes, indeed." Robert shakes his head with a grimace. "You're familiar with the Derby tradition of the ladies and their outlandish hats?" he asks, his twinkling eyes wide with expression.

I grasp his arm gently in delight. "Please don't tell me she—" I begin to giggle as Robert finishes my sentence.

"You guessed it; she chose the seat directly in front of mine. She was wearing the most enormous concoction of chiffon, ribbons, bows, flowers, feathers, you name it, all anchored to the top of that hat!" His arms open wide in exaggerated demonstration of Contessa's hat. He leans against the wall for support, laughing heartily.

I can control myself no longer, erupting into my infamous guffaws.

"Not only that, but she was like a twirling top in perpetual motion with that monstrosity bobbing and dipping in tandem with her every move," he continues, mimicking her actions.

Covering my mouth in a futile attempt to control my laughter, I gasp and ask, "What happened next?"

"I was such a pompous ass back then, Nevy. Excuse my crassness, but it is the absolute truth. Nicholas gave me a warning look, but I couldn't contain my righteous indignation." He stands away from the wall, showing exactly how he approached Contessa. "'Madam,' I say, tapping her none too gently on the shoulder, 'you cannot be serious with that hat.' Well, when she turned in my direction, her beauty took my breath away. I was speechless."

"She is quite stunning," I agree.

Robert's smile is wide as he says, "Inside and out." He continues his story. "Realizing how tongue-tied I was, she replied, 'Isn't it outrageous? How can you see the race?'" He imitates her voice comically. "'Come, your friend and you must join us. I insist.' She took my hand in hers, and Nevy, I swear an electric shock went through me. Contessa teases me that it was Cupid's arrow." A broad smile encompasses his face as we exit the library and retrace our steps to the grand ballroom. "She is absolutely correct about that. Six months later, we were married. That was five years ago, and our love grows stronger and deeper with each new day."

My heart aches for the love they share.

"You are so kind to listen to my antics, Nevy. I've given you no time to tell me about yourself. Perhaps you'll consider another visit soon during the daytime when the view of Lake Michigan is so spectacular. We could include a tour of the gardens."

"You are so gracious, Robert. I've enjoyed your company tonight. I confess, I was suffering a case of the jitters until your kind offer to tour your beautiful home. I would be honored to visit Summer Hill again," I say, realizing that I truly mean it.

As we enter the ballroom, we find Lou and Contessa in conversation. We catch them unaware of our arrival, and I overhear Lou say, "I just hope she agrees. It's the answer to everything." A feeling of apprehension flutters through my thoughts.

Robert quickly interjects himself into the conversation, alerting them of our presence by placing a gentle hand on his wife's shoulder. "Contessa, my love, I've invited Nevy to a return visit and tour of the gardens. Lou, you must join us as well." He turns his head from one to the other.

"Roberto." Contessa turns and places a palm against his face. "What a lovely idea. Lunch in the gazebo overlooking the lake would be fun. I'll call you to make plans, Lou. But now, I am sorry to say..." Her lips form a pout. "We must attend to the rest of our guests. Please enjoy the party." With a peck on our cheeks, Contessa and Robert float into the waves of guests competing for their attention.

Hours later, I cradle my head between my fingertips and apologize to Lou. "I'm sorry, Lou, but I think the champagne has caught up with me." I balance myself against her sturdy body.

It has been a whirlwind night. Lou amazes me with her stamina. She's still going full-throttle but honors my request to leave the festivities and return home.

Lou exchanges a quick text with Bob, and we offer our thanks and appreciation to our hosts with a promise to meet again as planned.

Bob is waiting to assist us into the limousine as we exit the grand house. I sink into the deep leather seat, falling asleep before we exit the iron gates.

11

A Feeling of Foreboding

It's mid-week, and I'm absorbed in doing research on the computer in Lou's office. Lou is writing a draft at her desk located in front of the window overlooking Elm Street when she receives a phone call. Moments later, I look up to see Lou looming over my shoulder.

"Yes?" I inquire, moving my reading glasses to the tip of my nose in order to see her better.

"That was Contessa. She was calling to invite us to lunch and a tour of the gardens this Friday...like we talked about at the gala. It will be just the four of us, a simple lunch by the lakeside. They are excited to share the view with you."

"Hmm, okay." I pause. "But I doubt any part of it will be simple, and what does one wear to a lakeside lunch at Summer Hill? It sounds like a quick trip to the vintage shop is in order. Do I need to buy a straw bonnet too?"

"Ha!" Lou bellows. "You better pick up two then. It's not that formal, but you might want to include a sweater. It can get chilly by the lake this time of the year." Changing subjects, Lou asks, "Say, Nev, do you have any plans for tomorrow night? I have a hunger for Punjabi chicken."

"Whoa. Two invitations in the same day? I don't think my social calendar can handle it. Punjabi chicken, you say?" Lou nods her head vigorously. "You know that's one of my favorite dishes. Count me in."

I'm happy that I accepted when I see the pleased look that fills Lou's face. There's been a change in her mood of late. She seems distracted and not focused on her work like yesterday when I asked where she placed the book I had been using for research. Receiving no answer, I glanced up to see her staring out onto Elm Street with a faraway look.

Perhaps it was my imagination, I reason. We all have day-dreaming moments, but a sense of uneasiness lingers, reminding me of the past moments of premonition I experienced.

Thursday evening arrives, and I enter the house using my own key and give Lou a shout-out as I follow the mouth-watering aroma of simmering Indian spices emanating from her kitchen.

She stands before the massive gas range juggling pots and dials, a captain in full command of her ship.

"It smells heavenly, Lou. We haven't had this meal in a long time."

She continues with her task, not acknowledging my presence. Maybe she didn't hear me enter.

"Hello." I stand on my tiptoes to peek around her broad shoulders. "Can I help?" I ask.

"No, almost ready." Her head bobs furiously at her task. "I'll meet you at the table, Nev. You could pour the wine for us." She dismisses me without a glance.

"Sure." I wander into the dining room, disconcerted by her behavior.

It's not long before she enters with two steaming plates of the savory dish.

I raise my goblet in praise. "A toast to my personal chef." She raises her goblet but avoids eye contact. Silence reigns as we dig into the delicious meal.

"Oh my. I didn't realize how hungry I was." I down the last forkful, leaning back into my chair with a look of contentment. "That was amazing, as always, Lou. I feel guilty not being able to reciprocate, lacking in the culinary arts as I do," I lament.

"Not necessary, kid. The pleasure is all mine. I love that you love my cooking." She stands to remove the plates from the table. Lou fusses, picking up and setting down miscellaneous utensils, and heaves a great sigh. "How about another glass of wine while we coast a bit before dessert?"

Again, uneasiness slithers down my spine. Is she purposely avoiding eye contact with me? Hesitantly, I reply, "A glass of wine would be lovely, Lou."

She refills my wine glass with a generous pour to the brim.

"Whoa," I protest, holding my hands up in surrender as Lou fills her glass, then takes her seat at the table.

"Sorry, I thought this was a favorite wine of yours," she says defensively, her voice quivering.

"Lou, is there something going on that I don't know about?" I ask apprehensively.

She fidgets in her chair, looking everywhere but in my direction.

"Lou?" I force her to look at me.

In a tiny voice uncharacteristic of her, she explains, "Nev, we need to have a talk." Her eyes brim with tears.

Straightening in my chair, I whisper, "Okay..."

"These past few years have been pretty amazing, haven't they, kid?" She attempts a pathetic smile.

A foreboding fills my being. "Yes, they've been awesome, so..."

Lou holds her hand up as she continues. "But I think you realize that this last year has been a struggle for me. The constant trips for book signings and deadlines are beginning to take a toll...and you're having to take on more of the writing responsibilities and getting no credit for it. That's not right."

"I don't want any credit, Lou. I'm so grateful for the opportunities you've given me. I've learned so much from you. That's reward enough." I look at her with pleading eyes wondering where this is heading.

"Nev, I'm tired, dead tired. I need a break." Her eyes are downcast as her mouth forms a sad frown.

Relief floods my thoughts as I attempt to console her. I reach over and gently clasp her wrist with an expression of compassion filling my face. "I understand, Lou. You haven't had a real vacation since I started working for you. All of your trips out of town are business related. What you need is a complete get-away, someplace where you can rest and regenerate." I nod my head vigorously in an attempt to convince her.

Lou pauses. "Well, as a matter of fact, I am thinking of taking a trip back east. You see, a while ago, I received a letter from Henry."

"Your Henry?" I ask in surprise, my eyes and ears alert and wondering how long ago.

"Yes, he wrote to tell me that his wife passed away a year ago of cancer. Sounds like it was pretty bad."

"So..." Lou takes a sip of wine, peering at me from above the rim. Then slowly, she places the goblet on the table. She straightens in her chair. "I called him to extend my condolences, and we've been talking regularly ever since. He's invited me for a visit, and I think I'm going to take him up on it," she says defensively.

"Really?!" I'm at a loss for words, but my shocked look expresses my feelings.

Lou fidgets in her chair. "Yes," she confesses, "our talks have renewed a lot of old feelings between the two of us, made me do some soul-searching. I've come to the conclusion that I'm done with writing. It isn't fun anymore. I've lost the passion. It's become a job. I need my life back or a life period. Reconnecting with Henry makes me realize how much."

Stunned, I blurt out my thoughts. "But where does that leave me, Lou?"

Lou holds her palm up to silence my outrage. "I have a plan, Nev, just hear me out." She nudges me gently.

"You've thought this whole thing out without consulting me? I can't believe this."

A pained expression covers her face. "That's what I'm trying to do now, Nev. Give me a second."

I sit silently, my arms crossed, as Lou continues.

"Contessa approached me about a job offer she would like to make to you."

"A job offer? For me? I can't believe this!"

"Let me explain. I've been sharing my concerns with Contessa, and coincidentally, she's in the midst of a new endeavor, a creation of a travel guide of sorts, and she's in need of a feature writer."

"You're kidding me? A travel guide? I can't work for Contessa. She's nothing like you. Remember how you said we're such a well-oiled machine? You just need some time off."

"Honey." Lou reaches for my hand. "I hate the responsibilities that come with success. All I do is work; there's no play for me or for you."

"But your fans will be devastated," I protest searching for an excuse to change her mind.

Lou shakes her head. "It's time for me to move on; my readers will do the same."

"But what do I know about writing for a travel guide? I haven't been anywhere," I fuss.

"That's the beauty of it. Contessa's dream is to create a guide about undiscovered places as seen through the eyes of someone experiencing them for the first time. Someone who can describe the wonder, beauty, and mystique of a new discovery." Lou pauses. "You didn't know anything about this job when you started, and look how far you've come."

"That was different. You were there to teach me every step of the way." My tears begin to spill over.

"It's time for a change for both of us, Nev. This new job will help you chase away the ghost of Old Johnny." She pats my hand, then says, "Now then, I've arranged for Bob to pick us up at eleven thirty tomorrow morning. Please, do me the favor and listen to Contessa's offer, okay?" She leans her head gently against mine.

"I...I don't know, Lou. I need to think about this. It's very upsetting. My whole world as I know it is coming to an end. I feel secure here. I'm not ready to start over again. I don't want to start over!" My body quivers with worry and fear.

"Nev, you have to take these opportunities when they come available, seize the moment as they say." She shares an encouraging smile. "The world won't wait for you. Think about it, okay?" Lou pleads.

I stumble from my chair, mumbling that I must go home. "I can't talk about this anymore tonight, Lou." I grab my purse from the countertop and make a hasty retreat out the door with a promise to consider Contessa's offer, knowing full well that I have no intention of accepting it.

I walk the familiar route to my apartment with my head bowed. I can't believe how everything has changed in a moment, but then again, yes, I can.

My life is filled with tragic moments. As thoughts swirl through my mind, I realize I have no one I can call to share my sadness and concerns. My best friend is Lou. Mom and Dad will use this as an excuse to encourage me to return home. I have no one else. "Have I truly become another Old Johnny, Grandmater?" I whisper.

I enter my apartment and shut the door, closing off the city sounds. It's illuminated only by the lights from the neighboring condo high-rise. The silence and darkness amplify my scattered thoughts as they bounce in all directions. Unable to come to a resolution, I fall into bed, but sleep is elusive as my thoughts continue to swirl into the night.

12

Sharing Discoveries

The limousine is waiting as I exit my apartment the next morning, absent of a Plan B. I crawl into the backseat, averting my eyes from Lou's.

"Did you get much sleep last night, Nev?" she asks softly.

"No," I whisper.

"Me neither," she whispers back.

It's a quiet ride to Summer Hill.

Today, the massive iron gates leading into the estate are closed. Bob calls on the intercom to alert the staff of our arrival. Shortly, the grand gates slowly inch open, as if they are carrying a heavy burden. How fitting, I think to myself, feeling the same heaviness and reluctance.

The butler, Edward, greets us as the limo arrives. He informs us that Contessa and Robert are waiting for us at the gazebo.

"Allow me to show you the way," he offers and guides our way along the winding flagstone path.

Ahead, Lake Michigan glistens in turquoise splendor. Tiny sailboats bob on the waves as miniature people scamper about the sandy beaches below. The panoramic view from this high point is spectacular, but it brings no joy to my heart today.

Contessa and Robert's shared laughter can be heard as we approach the gazebo. We've caught them unaware of our arrival and observe them sharing a wicker loveseat together, holding hands, engrossed in conversation.

The dogs, matching Great Danes lazing in the sun beside Contessa and Robert, are the first to notice our presence. They jump up, springing to alert and stopping us in our tracks.

Robert jumps to his feet, issuing a command, "Deacon, Lady, stay, my beauties." They turn adoring eyes to their master and obey, settling into their original spots. Contessa joins Robert at his side.

"We've ordered a perfect day for your visit." He smiles as he waves his arm broadly before the lake, like a maestro introducing his orchestra.

They're dressed in casual attire. Robert wears a polo shirt that matches the cyan-blue color of the lake, a pair of khaki pants, and leather deck shoes. The soft lake breeze ruffles his silver hair, creating a handsome, roguish look unlike the distinguished tuxedoed gentleman I met the night of the gala.

Contessa wears her hair free, held away from her face by a silk floral headband tied and knotted at the nape. Her simple but chic dress matches the monarch butterfly gold color in the scarf, accentuating her tan. No wonder Robert was smitten at first sight.

Deacon and Lady have been moved to a distant location during our welcome. Lou and I settle into the deep sun-warmed cushions of the wicker chairs as they return to the loveseat.

The tinkle of silverware and china and the quiet chatter of the staff preparing our lunch fills the background.

"How I have missed Summer Hill." Contessa flashes a loving smile in Robert's direction.

"Yes." He takes her hand bringing it to his lips for a quick kiss. "It's good to be home."

"The desert has its own kind of beauty. We love our winter retreat there, but nothing compares to the amazing view before us, don't you agree, Roberto?"

"Not since your arrival, my Tessa."

Robert turns to us and continues. "I used to take all this for granted until Contessa opened my eyes to its beauty once again.

"This is my family home, as I shared earlier with you, Nevy. As a kid, I loved the lake and water activities it offered. But when my father retired, and I became head of the company, I became consumed with the business end of things. I hope to keep Shannon from following in my footsteps."

"I don't think you need to worry about Shan. He's a lover of life, a natural. We had to teach you," Contessa teases.

A staff member interrupts to advise that lunch is ready.

"Ladies..." Robert leads the way to the table sparkling with china and crystal. A magnificent floral arrangement serves as a centerpiece.

"The bouquet is exquisite," I compliment.

"Cut this morning from our garden," Robert beams proudly.

Taking his place at the head of the table, he raises a flute of champagne and offers a toast. "Welcome to Summer Hill, Lou and Nevy. We are so honored that you could join us on this glorious afternoon."

The sip of champagne tickles my throat as I glance around the table at the welcoming faces of our hosts and Lou. Their warm reception softens my uneasiness.

"I don't think we'll be getting much work done today, Lou," I offer.

"I think we've earned a Friday afternoon off." She tips her flute in my direction with a sympathetic expression, reflecting her concern for me.

A gourmet lunch of grilled salmon follows, with Lou providing the entertainment with a description of her latest and perhaps final novel.

I'm beginning to wonder if a job offer is on the day's agenda. Perhaps Lou is confused about Contessa's intent, I reason, gazing into the hypnotizing beauty of Lake Michigan glistening in the distance. But Contessa's words draw me back into the conversation.

"It was one of our favorite pastimes when we were in Tucson. And now, wherever we travel, we try finding undiscovered places, little treasures that often go unnoticed. That's how we arrived at the idea of a travel guide where we can share our discoveries with others and theirs with us." Contessa glances in Robert's direction for confirmation. He continues where she leaves off.

"Each issue will include a feature article describing a location and its distinction, the special attraction that will intrigue others to visit."

Contessa turns to me and smiles. "We would like to offer the position of feature writer to you, Nevy. Lou has shared samples of your writing with us. You are a very creative writer, and your research skills are an added bonus. I know that Lou has shared our dream with you, yes?"

All eyes turn to me. Contessa's directness has taken me by surprise. "Uhm, y-yes, just last night. It has been a bit of a shock," I confess.

"Of course, I understand," Robert interjects. "In less than twenty-four hours, we've changed the direction of your life. You must take time to make the right decision for yourself."

"True." Contessa nods her head in confirmation, a serious look on her face. "However, we are excited to begin this project. It depends on finding the perfect feature writer. We chose you, Nevy. I hope you won't keep us waiting long."

Contessa's smile is warm and assuring, but her message is clear and direct. I reflect on the night of the gala, watching her glide through the crowd of guests, stopping to chat with one and then another while keeping a keen eye out for new arrivals, making introductions, and alerting staff to her guests' needs—cordial, but always in command. She is a true force of nature, unlike the Mother Earth persona of my Lou. Our working relationship will be very different from the one I share with Lou.

She continues, not waiting for my reply. "We already have a location in mind for our first publication."

Once again, Robert interjects. "You see, Nevy, last year during our visit to Durango, Colorado, we became intrigued by the history of the gold mining towns."

"Then," Contessa glances around the table, her eyes wide with excitement, "when we returned home to Summer Hill, we spotted an article in the *Tribune* featuring the gold mining history of Colorado. It included a photograph of a log cabin located in the town of Prophecy, Colorado, now an abandoned ghost town. Can you believe it? It's meant to be!" Contessa's face fills with elation.

Robert chuckles. "There's no holding Contessa back once she puts her mind to something."

Contessa asks, "Have you been to Colorado, Nevy?"

"Me? I've never been anywhere." I glance away, feeling embarrassed having to admit this before these world travelers.

Lou comes to my defense. "She's been too busy holding down the fort for me while I traveled around the country for book signings."

"But that's perfect, don't you see? Just what we're looking for—someone who can describe the wonder of discovering these hidden treasures firsthand," Contessa assures. "I hope you'll accept our offer, Nevy. Our heart is set on you. You come highly recommended." She glances in Lou's direction.

I'm relieved when Robert suggests a break. "I think we've given Nevy enough to think about for today. Let's enjoy a walk through the gardens," he offers, sharing a loving smile with his wife, who graciously relinquishes control of the conversation.

With great relief, I accept Robert's arm as he leads the way. Contessa and Lou follow.

As we stroll through the fragrant rows of flowers, Robert bends his head to my ear, "I'm afraid we've turned your world upside down."

Looking into his compassionate eyes, I confess, "I'm so honored that you and Contessa would make this offer to me. In all honesty,

I knew this day would come. I sensed a change in Lou's mood. She seems unusually quiet and melancholy. I've seen how exhausted she is when she returns from a book signing, and how the joy for her work diminished over time."

"Change can be very good, Nevy. I think about it all the time. What if I hadn't accepted Nicholas' invitation to the Derby? I would still be rattling around in my gloomy dungeon...or worse." He frowns. "Maybe, it's time to liberate Lou. She is very dedicated to you but eager to visit her friend back east. This could be her last chance for true love."

I pause to consider his words while reaching for the place where Jamie's ring hangs in memory. Silently, I admonish myself for how selfish I've been, wallowing in my own self-pity at the expense of Lou's chance at happiness. I've been so blind to Lou's needs.

To my relief, we're nearing the end of the garden tour. I'm exhausted and ready to return to the isolation of my apartment, where I can sort through my feelings.

Contessa calls to her husband, "Roberto, Lou says she would love to see the renovations to the carriage house."

Her eyes twinkle as I turn in her direction with an artificial smile covering my face.

Robert directs us along the path while Contessa entertains us with the story of her renovation of the 1890s carriage house.

Shadows from the towering blue spruce trees offer a refreshing break from the bright sunlight we've been walking in during our garden stroll.

The carriage house emerges in peaceful solitude in a clearing among the spruce trees. Like the mansion, it is striking in appearance. Tudor in style, its most prominent feature is the pair of cross-beamed wooden doors.

"We decided to keep the original doors that were used for the carriages to enter through. Aren't they grand?" Contessa gushes as she grasps an iron door handle, revealing the house's interior.

The large room beyond is empty of furnishings, displaying a stunning view of Lake Michigan from floor-to-ceiling windows built into the east-facing wall.

"It was Robert's idea to remove the matching exit doors and replace them with the windows," Contessa explains. She crosses the room, her footsteps echoing across the wide plank oak floors as we follow to observe the view of the lake below.

Contessa turns to advise, "Remind me to show you the before and after photos, so you can see the transformation."

"Yes, I would love to see them sometime," I say, hoping she doesn't mean today.

"It was a big empty barn with dirt floors and a century of neglect. As you can see, the renovation has been quite extensive," Robert joins in.

"It's amazing," I offer at a loss for words.

"Come, let me show you the patio." Contessa is eager to continue the tour. We follow her lead, exiting through a set of French doors to a secluded patio. The ground is covered with steppingstones with Irish moss planted in the crevices between. It contains a small wrought-iron table and two chairs.

"The exposure provides a view of the sunrise over the lake each morning—a peaceful place to sip morning coffee," Contessa advises, her eyes filling with delight. Her enthusiasm is overwhelming as fatigue begins to take its toll, and I wonder how much longer this tour will last.

"But my favorite room," she teases as we enter the carriage house again, "is the master suite." Contessa disappears as we follow the sound of her retreating footsteps up the staircase at the front of the house.

"Wow! I see why this is your favorite room, Contessa. It's as big as all of the downstairs," Lou praises, out of breath from the trip up the stairs.

Contessa is lost in her excitement. Her eyes rove adoringly over the renovated space. "I have one more treasure to share with you, I promise." She exits the room to enter the master bath. "Look at this fabulous antique tub we found!" We all follow to see a huge claw-foot tub that takes center stage in the room.

"You could put a whole family in that." Lou laughs.

When we return to the master suite, Contessa turns to her audience. "This renovation has been such fun, but now it's finished, just in time for our new venture, *Sharing Discoveries*, our travel guide." Her voice fills with anticipation.

After a few seconds, I realize the room has suddenly become silent. All eyes are on me, and I rush to fill the void. "It's amazing, like a fairy tale cottage. Will you be using it for guests?"

Contessa shares a conspiratorial look with Robert and Lou. "What would you think of living here, Nevy?"

Am I hearing her correctly? "Of me living here?" I falter.

"You may not like the quiet," Robert warns. "It would be different from living in the city."

Contessa places her hand lightly on his arm. "Let Nevy decide, Robert." He nods his understanding.

I'm overwhelmed by the possibility of living in this enchanting place. "Are you serious?" I ask wide-eyed.

Thoughts swirl through my mind. In my heart, I know it's time to release Lou from her commitment to me, to allow her to fulfill her dream of happiness.

I hear Grandmater's whisper reminding me that it's time to break the chains of the ghost of Old Johnny that bind me from moving forward.

"It comes with the job, Nevy. It'll be much easier to collaborate together, don't you agree? I can help you furnish it," Contessa offers.

"Oh, I have furniture!" Visions of the carriage house filled with my treasures shrouded at Grandmater's Victorian fill my thoughts.

"Is that a yes to our offer?" Contessa arches an eye in my direction, a smile forming on her lips in anticipation of my answer.

"Yes, I accept your offer!" I shout with laughter.

Robert beams. "I think this calls for another glass of champagne."

Suddenly, my fatigue vanishes, replaced by happiness and certainty filling my heart.

13

The Move

There is no reason to delay my move. Contessa is excited to get started with the project, and Lou is as excited to proceed with her plans for the visit with Henry.

A few weeks later, I awake before sunrise to the luxury of sleeping in the antique queen bed delivered yesterday with the rest of my belongings. The furniture is in place, but many treasures have yet to be unpacked.

I reach for the chain pull to light the Tiffany lamp that sits on the bedside table. Light fills the room while happiness fills my heart at the sight of all that is familiar and loved.

The hand-carved wooden bookcase looks handsome against the reclaimed antique brick wall, just as I envisioned. I can't wait to unpack the collection of daguerreotype photos and photography books to place on its shelves.

I'm pleased that Dad's desk fits perfectly into the notch created by the dormer window that overlooks the lake. In the adjacent corner stands the hall tree, soon to be decorated with my collection of vintage silk purses. As in the Victorian, the hope chest sits at the foot of my bed filled with notebooks, old and new, for easy access.

Each piece of furnishing once belonged to someone else—a loving family member, a cherished friend, or a treasure chanced upon along life's pathway. They all connect a memory to a person or a place close to my heart.

A cool breeze floats through the open window, a remnant of winter's breath. The song of the cardinal atop the blue spruce serenades my first day.

It's tempting to snuggle deeper into the cocoon of quilts, but the music box chimes of the Country French grandfather clock—bequeathed to me by Great Aunt Geneva—beckons from the first floor. It stands sentry in the entrance hall before the carriage doors as a welcome first sight to visitors to my home. I smile at the significance of those words. My home.

The rich aroma of coffee brewing in the automatic coffee maker entices me from the cozy nest. I'm grateful this cool morning for the polar fleece robe I discovered in the last box I unpacked the night before.

The rhythmic ticking of the clock leads my path down the darkened stairway. I follow the glow of light cast by the globe lamp left on last night. It sits on the side table next to Grandmater's rocking chair.

The rocking chair has claimed its rightful spot on the braided rug placed in front of the large east-facing windows. I pause to admire the beauty that my treasures have created in the room.

The braided rug has brought warmth to the cool wooden floors. The china cabinet has found a perfect home next to the fireplace, a warm and cozy spot for my bride and groom, which I transported myself from the studio apartment along with the cookie tin and carnival glass bowl. The brocade step stool sits at the cabinet's side, a faithful companion.

Memories flood my thoughts as I resume my trek, weaving around the stacked boxes and into the kitchen to fill the ceramic spider-webbed coffee mug—Grandmater's favorite—with the rich brown liquid, reserving room to add a splash of cream. "Just like you taught me, Grandmater," I whisper.

Retracing my steps into the great room, I place the mug on the side table and retrieve the heirloom quilt that graces the arm of the rocker. I wrap myself in its warmth and memory. With a sigh of contentment, I settle into the worn leather seat to watch the show before me. The horizon begins its slow dance with the sunrise, the sky shimmers awake in golden grandeur.

As the sun rises higher into the sky, I trade the coffee mug for the new pen and notebook, gifts from Lou, to inspire my return to daily journal writing. Resting the notebook on the wide armrest as I have watched Grandmater do all those years writing her column, I write the first word that pops into my thoughts. "Home."

14

Colorado

Two weeks later, armed with a backpack full of Colorado data I researched, I climb into the back seat of the limousine heading for O'Hare. Bob maneuvers the early morning traffic, and, in no time, signs to the airport emerge as do the butterflies I've been feeling all morning. The reality of my Colorado adventure draws near.

After checking in and boarding, I gratefully nestle into my assigned window seat and avert my gaze from the last of the boarding passengers, amazed that I escaped a seat mate. I can't believe my good fortune of snaring two-plus hours of uninterrupted silence.

I reach for my backpack stowed under the seat and narrowly escape collision with a projectile flying through the air in my direction. It falls with a thud into the center seat on top of my new linen jacket. The missile, upon closer inspection, is an over-stuffed faded canvas backpack.

I stare into the bespectacled face of a young boy who plops into the aisle seat as I pull my crumpled jacket from underneath his backpack.

"Hi. My name's Jess. Looks like you're stuck with me!" he chirps in a munchkin-kind of voice, looking at me through a pair of eyeglasses much too large for his tiny face.

Amused, I reply, "Hi, Jess. My name is Nevy."

"That your real name?" He cocks his head to one side giving me a questioning look.

I chuckle, charmed by this precocious fellow, and begin to explain when he cuts me off.

"You know, like my name is short for Jessica!" He reaches to remove the cowboy hat from his head, releasing a cascade of golden curls that fall to his shoulders. I can clearly see now that my initial impression of Jess was wrong.

"Gotcha." She giggles.

"You sure did." I grin and make a second attempt to explain. "My name is Geneva, but—"

"Oh yeah, I get it." She peers over the top of her eyeglasses, which are slowly descending on her nose. She rummages through the backpack, yanking a smartphone from its deep recesses.

A passing flight attendant pauses to wag her finger at Jess.

"I know," Jess protests with a frown. "I promise not to use it until you give the okay."

"You will need to stow that backpack under the seat in front of you as well, young lady," the flight attendant instructs in a no-nonsense manner before she continues down the aisle.

"Yes, ma'am," Jess obediently replies, tugging at the heavy backpack.

She turns her attention to me and asks, "This your first visit to Colorado?" catching me off-guard.

"How did you know?" I ask as I attempt to help her by grabbing hold of one of the backpack's shoulder straps.

She points to my lap full of Colorado material. The backpack tumbles from my grip with a thump to the floor.

Jess shrugs and grasps the back of the passenger seat in front of her with both hands. Using her feet and a charming little wiggle for leverage, she manages to wedge the backpack under the seat to the annoyance of its occupant.

I watch the disgruntled passenger peer menacingly through the opening between the seats. The effect is wasted on Jess, whose attention is now directed toward the passenger information packet in the seat pocket in front of her.

"How about you, Jess? Are you visiting Colorado too?"

"Nope, been visiting my Nana and Papa, who live in Chicago. I'm on my way back home now." She turns to share an infectious grin with me.

"Do you live in Denver?"

"No way! I live in Golden, you know, the town where they make all the beer," she whispers. "I'm a Colorado native, born and bred," she states proudly.

Jess pulls the pre-flight brochure from the seat pocket and wriggles into her seat, her denim legs and western boots dangling midair as she fastens her seatbelt. She smiles sweetly and flashes the brochure at the flight attendant as she begins her instructions for takeoff.

Time passes quickly, consumed by the activities designed by the airline and those contained in Jess's backpack. Snacks and accompanying soft drinks, a *Go Fish* card game, a collaborated coloring book activity and trips to the bathroom requiring my help unloading her tray-top have taken a toll. I surrender, lulled to sleep by the sudden absence of activity due to a merciful set of earphones attached to her smartphone.

Prodded into consciousness, I peer down with half-open eyes to discover a stubby finger jabbing repeatedly into my rib cage.

"We're starting to land!" she screeches, her voice a decibel higher than I thought possible. A grin stretches from ear to ear.

"I think somebody's pretty excited about arriving home," I tease. She signals a thumbs-up in my direction as she strains to look out my window. A quick exchange of seats solves her dilemma, and we share the view below.

In a practiced voice the flight attendant begins the arrival announcements, alerting passengers to their expected behavior. Trays are fastened, and seat backs are brought to an upright position with a final appeal to obey the illuminated overhead seatbelt signs.

I've gleaned little information about Colorado from the research material now stuffed into the seat pocket in front of me. It's a fair trade for the time I have shared with Jess.

As the plane begins its slow descent, I scan the empty expanse of prairie, anticipating my first view of the snow-capped mountains. Shortly, I spot the glistening white peaks rising like a mirage out of the prairie sands in the far distance. But something is not quite right.

"That's the airport," Jess informs, following my gaze.

I realize, then, that it's the Teflon coated peaks of the airport terminal building that I read about and not the snow-covered peaks of the Rocky Mountains. It materializes like a grand white wedding tent erected by a prairie baron for his princess bride.

"But where are the real mountains?" I ask, bewildered.

"Ya see those clouds way back there?" Jess points a crayon-stained finger at the window as I look over her shoulder. "They're covering up the mountains today. That happens sometimes."

"You mean the mountains are that far away?" I look into her upturned face. "Shoot, I thought they were at Denver's doorstep. That's what the brochures say." I pout.

Jess gives a delighted chuckle. "No, silly."

"How far away are they?" I lament naively, forgetting the literal thinker at my side.

"Way, way far away," she advises, shaking her head up and down, her golden curls dancing on her shoulders. "First, you have to go through a long, long tunnel. Daddy always blows the horn for me. Then," she pauses to gather her thoughts and replies, "you're in the mountains," she ends with a triumphant smile.

"Hmm..." I contemplate this information, rummaging in my backpack for the Colorado map tucked inside. I've been so consumed with the move to the carriage house and gathering data about the gold mining era that I failed to consider researching actual mileage distances. Lesson number one, Nevy, I reprimand myself.

"Wait 'til you see the airport. It's really neat," Jess interrupts my thoughts. "First, you get to take a train to get your luggage. There are lots of restaurants and shops. Sometimes we stop for lunch, but that's usually before we get on the plane, not when we come home. The best things are the fossils on the floor that they found when they were digging up the earth to build the airport."

Her enthusiasm is infectious. "I can't wait to see it all!" I clap my hands together as a broad smile covers my face.

The flight attendant arrives at our aisle. "Jessica, we are going to be landing soon. I want you to remain in your seat until I return to accompany you off the plane, okay?"

Jess looks in my direction. "My friend, Nevy, can take me off the plane." She flutters her long eyelashes while flashing a charming smile.

The flight attendant raises an eyebrow in my direction and replies, "I'm sorry, Jessica, but the rules say I am responsible for your care. You will need to wait for me, okay?"

Jess looks crestfallen as she answers a meek, "Yes, ma'am."

Ah, what the heck, I think to myself. I have no set schedule. "Jess, would you like me to wait and walk with you?" I offer.

Like magic, the disappointment vanishes as she signals a high-five in my direction.

We're the last to deplane as the flight attendant ushers us from the aircraft. Jess drags the backpack as it bumps and bounces down the aisle. I follow, trying to avoid tripping over the cumbersome bag, and nearly collide with Jess when she abruptly stops to bid goodbye to the pilots.

As we exit and enter the gate area, it's easy to spot Jess's parents. A handsome blond-haired man of medium height dressed in jeans, a western shirt, and boots stands next to a petite, pretty woman dressed in similar fashion, waving wildly, their faces filled with matching grins.

Jess gives a great whoop, drops the backpack at my feet, and gallops into the loving arms of her parents.

The flight attendant shrugs her shoulders and shares a smile with me. I scoop up Jess's backpack and wait at a distance as the flight attendant fulfills her responsibilities of checking ID and obtaining signatures on the release form.

Jess motions for me to join the family reunion. "Mommy and Daddy, this is my new friend, Geneva, but most everybody calls her Nevy. This is her first time ever in Colorado!"

They smile in unison as their eyes turn to me. Her mother is the first to speak, holding her hand out in greeting. "Welcome, Nevy. My name is Jody. I hope our Jess didn't wear you out. She can be," she pauses for the right word, glancing at her husband, who looks at Jess with a grimace, "quite active and a practical jokester."

I reach to shake her hand. "You're right about that. She got me good." I chuckle in good humor.

"Oh no, Jess, what have you been up to?" Her father tickles her sides, sending her into giggles as he offers his hand in greeting. "Tom Sheely. Welcome to Colorado, Nevy. I hope her joking was all in good fun."

"It absolutely was," I attest. "It was my pleasure to share the flight with Jessica and Jess as well."

"The old cowboy hat trick, huh?" He peers lovingly into his daughter's eyes.

"So, this is your first trip to Colorado? Business or pleasure?" he asks.

"Business and pleasure. I'm here on a new endeavor. It's my employer's dream to create a travel guide of sorts to introduce folks to little known sites, undiscovered gems. I'm eager to explore your beautiful state and learn more about it to encourage others to do the same," I reply.

"I may be a little biased," Tom says, looking at his wife, who rolls her eyes as he continues, "being a native and all. If we can be of any help, please don't hesitate to call." He reaches into his back pocket for his billfold and withdraws a card embossed with the words, "Jefferson County, Colorado."

I slip the card into my pocket. "That is so generous of you. Beware, I may follow up on your kind offer."

It would be our pleasure, Nevy." Jody nods her head in agreement.

"But right now," I say, surveying the happy family, "I think I had better catch up with my luggage and let you continue your family reunion." I stoop to give Jess a hug and receive a hearty one in return.

With a wave goodbye, I turn to join the throng of travelers on the moving walkway, my eyes glued to the overhead signs directing me to the underground transit system.

I'm relieved to see all of my luggage circling the conveyor belt as I reach the baggage area. Bags in hand, I follow the signs to the car rental and shuttle service.

The ride to the rental car agency is a distance from the terminal, but my mind is a million miles away as I search for the material I downloaded earlier. To my dismay, the butterflies have returned.

Arriving at the rental car parking lot, I approach the sales agent at the counter. "Hi," I chirp, my voice at an abnormal pitch. "My name is Geneva Ellis. You should be holding a reservation for me." I pull the tattered copy of my reservation from my backpack.

He looks up from his computer. "Got it right here, Miss Ellis. Hmm, two-door compact? That right?" He shares a questioning look.

"Yes, that's me. Is there a problem...Ty?" I ask while reading his name tag.

"No, ma'am, we have your reservation. May I ask if you're planning any mountain driving during your visit?"

"Yes, that's my destination. I'm heading for the town of Blue Eagle. This is my first visit to Colorado."

"Hmm..." With raised eyebrows, he asks, "Have you considered renting a four-wheel drive or perhaps something with a little more horsepower? The compact will get you up the mountains, but it'll be slow going, for sure. I'm not trying to do a sales pitch to a more expensive vehicle, I promise." He holds his hands up in defense.

"Really? I guess I didn't think about that," I confess.

"Oh, yeah, these compacts roll out of the mountains like roller skates, but it'll feel like you're driving a cement truck uphill. And forget about doing any off-road driving in it."

"I suppose this is going to cost a lot more?" I frown at the thought of adding more costs to my expense account at this early stage of my assignment.

"We've got a four-wheel-drive SUV we're running through the wash. I could give you a deal on it being so early in the summer season. It'll handle mountain driving, no problem. Shouldn't take more than ten minutes longer." He waits for my reply.

The last thing I need is car trouble, I reason as I accept his offer. Paperwork complete, I drag my baggage to a corner, and catch sight of a rack displaying a variety of Colorado brochures that I can check out while I wait.

I've booked my first night's stay at a hotel in Breckenridge until I get my bearings, disappointed that I was unable to find a listing for accommodations in the town of Blue Eagle. Serendipity makes her appearance when I spot a brochure advertising fishing cabins located on Meadow View Lake in Blue Eagle. Perfect. I'll keep the reservation in Breckenridge as a backup but check out the fishing cabins first.

Ty informs me the rental is ready and parked in space A-2. I wheel my luggage across the parking lot. There is no missing the fire engine red SUV sparkling in the sunshine. So much for anonymity, Nevy.

I pop the hatch and stow my luggage, tossing the crumpled linen jacket on top—another reminder of how unprepared I am for this trip. A linen jacket for the mountains of Colorado. What was I thinking?

I settle myself behind the steering wheel and make the necessary adjustments for comfort, sight, and safety, ending with programming the GPS for Blue Eagle. With all excuses exhausted, I give the dash a final pat and whisper the words, "Ready or not." I heave a great sigh and exit the parking lot onto Peña Boulevard, guided by the comforting voice on the GPS.

As I near the city limits, I see the cloud cover begins to part over the mountains beyond to reveal a glimpse of the snow-covered peaks of the Rockies, but I'm too focused following the road signs and traffic on I-70 to allow more than a peek at their grandeur.

The city of Denver fades into the background. I spot a billboard advertising the Coors Brewery in Golden reminding me of Jess and her upturned cherub face as she whispered the word "beer." I realize how much I missed spending time with my little ones as memories of my teacher-filled days flitter through my thoughts.

I-70 continues to climb ever higher into the foothills. Evergreen trees, their shadows blanketed by patches of snow, cling to the slanting hillsides.

As I crest the hilltop near the town of Genesee Park, the mountain range surfaces like a majestic breaching whale. "Whoa!" I screech, not believing the beauty of the scene before me. I scan the highway for the first opportunity to pull over. The next road sign sends me into a fit of giggles.

Buffalo Herd Overlook. The skyscrapers of Chicago seem like a distant galaxy away.

A glance in my rearview mirror reveals no nearby traffic behind me as I signal a right onto Exit 254 and continue to follow the signs to the overlook. The parking lot is nearly empty when I arrive.

I hop out of the car and shiver. The temperature has dropped at least fifteen degrees since my arrival at the rental car terminal. Shading my eyes from the brilliant blue sky and sunshine, I'm not sure which direction to turn first. West, toward the view of the spectacular mountain range or immediately toward the gentle giants grazing on the golden grasses on the nearby hillside?

A male voice breaks the silence, sending me teetering on my heels. "Sorry, didn't mean to scare ya. I was saying how lucky we are to see the bison herd so nearby this morning. They aren't always visible like this."

I turn to observe a young man dressed in hiking boots, jeans, a polar fleece jacket, and a backpack standing behind me.

"Beginner's luck, I guess. This is my first trip to Colorado. I'm visiting from Chicago."

"Well now, welcome to Colorado." A grin lights up his youthful face. "I'm a transplant myself. A corporate move brought our family here, then when Dad got his next promotion, I opted to remain here to finish college. Pretty sure this is where I'm going to hang my hat permanently. Can't get enough of this beauty."

"I can understand why. Did I understand you correctly when you called them bison and not buffalo?"

"Pretty much interchangeable these days, but bison is the correct term for these critters. Buffalo are indigenous to South Asia and Africa like the water buffalo."

"Thanks. I love tidbits of knowledge like that to impress my friends back home. Looks like you're doing some hiking today?"

"Yeah, waiting for my buddy. Just doing some trails in Genesee today. Here he comes now." He points to a motorcycle coasting to a stop in the parking lot. "Enjoy your stay in Colorado." He tips the brim of his cap in farewell.

"Thanks and enjoy your hike!" I shout to his retreating figure.

The shaggy giants munching upon the spring grasses capture my attention, and I wander to their fenced enclosure. A curious calf meanders to the wire fence, allowing me to reach through to pet his wet nose before he kicks up his heels and gallops off. I follow his path, bringing the Rockies into view.

With renewed spirit and excitement coursing through my veins, I breathe in a gulp of fresh mountain air and return to Red, my name for my new steed, to continue our adventure westward.

15

Blue Eagle

Ty warned me that the turnoff to Blue Eagle is easily missed. I catch sight of the fading road sign at the last moment, taking a sharp right exit onto the gravel-strewn road and creating a cloud of dust in my wake. A quick glance in the rearview mirror reveals no traffic close by, to my relief.

The road meanders in a northwest direction. After several miles of uninhabited tree-dotted hillsides, I begin to wonder if I read the road sign correctly and contemplate turning around.

As I round the next curve, I spot a building in a clearing ahead. The word "ARI'S" is painted in bold black letters above the door. It appears to be a local convenience store offering gas and groceries. I decide to stop, not knowing where or when the next opportunity might be.

While I wait for the tank to fill, I wrap my arms around my body to ward off the chill and survey my surroundings.

The one-story building is constructed of barn siding with a tin roof, giving it a rustic look, complete with a hitching post for horses.

Further up the road, I spot several buildings tucked into the hillside as the road dips and curves, continuing in its northwestern direction.

As I enter the store, the cowbell above the door creates a great clunking sound, striking a discordant note with the soothing sound of Pachelbel's Canon playing softly in the background.

"Stay, Athena." A gentle male voice commands a glossy black-haired Chow peering around the counter in my direction. A distinguished older man with snow-white hair and matching mustache approaches from a back room. He looks nothing like the western cowboy I was expecting to see.

He wears a crisp white button-down oxford shirt with sleeves rolled to the elbow, khaki pants, and polished brown loafers. His stylish metal frame glasses complement the blue-gray color of his eyes. His smile is warm and welcoming.

"Good day, Miss. Aristotle Tagos at your service." He extends his hand in greeting and adds, "But most folks call me, Ari."

The incongruity of the scene sends me into a fit of giggles. "I am so sorry," I apologize, blushing as I attempt to explain. "I think I'm feeling a bit giddy from jet lag and the effects of the mountain air."

With a widened grin, he informs me, "You are not the first visitor to be smitten with a bit of high-altitude giggles. Welcome to Blue Eagle, Miss..."

"Nevy Ellis." I grasp his hand in mine and continue. "Greenhorn from Chicago. I owe you for gas, and I was hoping you might help me with directions to the fishing camp featured in this brochure," I say as I pull the crumpled brochure from my pocket.

He adjusts his glasses and dips his head for closer inspection. Straightening, he combs his fingers through his thick hair, failing to hide the sadness creeping across his face.

"I'm sorry to inform you that the fishing camp is no longer in operation. It closed when my dear friend, Jacob McLean, passed away."

"I am so sorry," I say, unable to hide my disappointment. "I was hoping to rent one of the cabins during my stay. It would be perfect for my needs."

"I doubt that will be possible. The whole place is undergoing renovation. Jacob's granddaughter, Leigh, inherited the property. She's remaking it into a year-round lodge."

"What happened to the fishing cabins?" I ask, hope flittering through my thoughts.

"Still there, but the cabins will be getting some updating as well, pretty quickly, I would imagine, as the renovation to the lodge is nearly finished."

"But none of it is open for business?" My hope fades.

"Not to my knowledge," Aristotle confirms.

"I wonder, would you know of any other accommodations nearby where I might rent a room with extra living space? I plan to be here for a while."

"Hmm..." He leans in a casual manner against the counter, arms crossed, considering my request. "Your best bet will be the ski resorts up the road. Meadow View has always been our only source of accommodation for overnight visitors. What brings you to Blue Eagle, if you don't mind my asking?" he inquires with a sympathetic smile.

I remove the backpack from my shoulder and retrieve the newspaper article Tessa gave me that included the accompanying color photo of a weathered log cabin perched on the mountainside. I spread it open on the countertop for him to see. "Are you familiar with this cabin?"

He straightens with a look of surprise on his face. "I know that cabin well. It's the old McLean cabin. May I ask where you found this article?" A troubled look covers his face.

Treading lightly, I respond, "I, uh, my boss chanced upon it in the Sunday travel section of the Chicago Tribune. The article is the inspiration for her new venture, a travel guide highlighting less traveled locations, little undiscovered places folks might not be familiar with..." My words fade to a murmur under his scrutiny.

He doesn't respond. The change in his demeanor is disconcerting. Stumbling on, I offer, "The article mentions the gold mining town of Prophecy and a brief description of how these towns are vanishing from sight and history. We're intrigued to learn more. She hired me to write the feature article." I pause, considering whether to proceed. "I'm wondering if there is anyone living in the cabin who might be able to help me with information for the article."

An uncomfortable silence ensues as he considers my explanation. He answers slowly, "I hate to spoil your plans. There is someone living in the cabin, an old recluse by the name of Ruby. Other than an occasional trip to my store to stock up on supplies, Ruby keeps to herself. She guards her privacy, literally, if you know what I mean," he answers seriously.

"You mean literally like with a gun?" I ask wide-eyed.

"Locked and loaded. I would suggest you stay clear of Ruby and select a new location." He nods his head to confirm his warning. "There are several old mining towns in this area."

"Hmm," I pause and consider a new direction for my questioning. "What if I just want to take a look at the town of Prophecy? Would that be okay?"

"Private property. The road leading there, Miners' Alley, is public use primarily as a fire trail. He places his hands on his hips. "Keep in mind that you would have to drive past Ruby's. I would give her a wide berth if I were you."

Realizing my conversation has gone sideways, I make an attempt at amends. "I sure don't want to start off on bad footing, but, you see, I've come all this way...I don't know how I'm going to break this news to my boss, this being my very first assignment and all." I don't have to fake my disappointment.

His demeanor softens as he replies, "Not much to see of the town anymore. Most everything has collapsed in on itself, but the boardinghouse and a few other buildings are still standing. That and the old cemetery are all that's left. The hills are dotted with hidden mine shafts, so I would be very careful in your explorations."

"Is the town visible from the road?" I ask, distraught at this news.

"There's an overlook at the top of the ridge you can pull onto for a panoramic view of the old town."

The cowbell clunks, accompanied by a cloud of smoke that floats through the open doorway.

"Howdy do, Professor? Thought I'd stop by to see if I can talk you into an extended lunch hour or two? The fish are hopping and it's a beauty of a day."

I turn to observe a wiry old fellow dressed in bib overalls. His faded sweatshirt is worn and frayed at the collar and cuffs, and he's wearing wader boots on his feet. A tackle bedecked fishing hat completes the outfit. Smoke erupts Vesuvius-style from the strong-smelling pipe he holds between his teeth.

"Benjamin, my friend, you are a corrupter of good intentions. I was planning to tackle that pile of receipts I've been avoiding," Ari says to the new arrival.

"'Tackle' is the keyword, my friend, but I like my use of the word better." The newcomer chuckles at his joke. "Fish are jumping. Those receipts can wait."

Ari turns to me. "Pardon my poor manners. Ben, I'd like you to meet Miss Nevy Ellis, who's journeyed from Chicago to visit our town. Miss Ellis, this is Ben who oversees our library—when the fish aren't jumping that is." He smiles in his friend's direction.

Ben snorts at Ari's comment and nods his head in agreement. He approaches the counter and shifts the fishing pole and pipe to one hand to offer his other hand in greeting. "Nice to make your acquaintance, Miss Ellis. What brings you all the way from Chicago to our outpost?"

I reach for his hand as Ari intercepts to explain. "She's contemplating the prospect of writing an article about Prophecy and hopes that Ruby will be of some help to her." He shares a doubtful look with Ben.

"Whoa." Ben drops my hand, his smile crumpling into a frown.

"I've forewarned her of the dangers of such a deed," Ari adds.

"Best to listen to the professor, ma'am. Ruby is an ornery cuss and don't like nobody snooping around her cabin. Keeps a double barrel twelve gauge loaded with rock salt standing by her cabin door." He pulls at the whiskers protruding from his chin.

They've piqued my curiosity. "I appreciate the warning. I wouldn't want to do anything to upset her."

As silence ensues, I use Ben's entrance as an excuse for my exit. "So nice to meet you both. I won't delay you any longer from your fishing plans. Enjoy your day." I smile and walk to the door, setting the cowbell in motion, but I am still able to overhear their conversation.

"Reckon she'll heed our advice?" Ben asks.

"Not likely, my friend," Ari replies.

I climb into Red and check for traffic before exiting. My thoughts are in turmoil as I contemplate a Plan B. I'm coasting along Main Street when a diverse assortment of structures outside diverts my attention from my concerns.

The building beyond Ari's is constructed in an A-frame style and painted in a shade of pistachio green. A mix of brightly painted picnic tables and benches decorate the attached wooden deck. The sign above the door reads, "Liddy's Ice Cream and Sandwich Shop."

Across the street from Liddy's is the Blue Eagle Interfaith Church. A wall constructed of the same rock as the church encircles its gravel parking lot.

Farther up the street, I spot the Ore House Rock Shop and Museum tucked into the hillside. I'm curious and pull over to park at the curb. The entrance door is locked so I peer into the dusty display window with my nose against the glass, using my hands to frame my eyes as a shield against the bright sunlight. The view reveals an assortment of rocks and relics from Blue Eagle's gold mining past, stored on dust-coated shelves and countertops. Rusted lanterns, tarnished metal miners' hats, and a collection of gold mining pans hang from long hooks on the ceiling. Old pickaxes fill an oak barrel that sits in a corner. I'm clueless to the purpose of many of the items on display but intrigued to learn more.

I return to Red and continue up Main Street, the only vehicle on the street. As I near the end of the commercial section of town, I glimpse down a side street and spot a small log cabin. According to the signpost, this is the library Ari mentioned that Ben oversees.

The commercial district fades into open space as I scan the road, watching for its intersection with Miners' Alley, but it's difficult to keep my eyes on the road. The valley floor explodes like a fireworks display put on by Mother Nature. A flower-filled meadow appears before me, canopied under a flawless blue sky with towering snow-capped mountain peaks forming the backdrop. It's breathtaking.

I force my focus back to the roadway and notice a dirt road branching off to my right leading into the mountains. This has to be it, I reason. There's no road sign to direct me. As I approach the turnoff, the lodge comes into view. It's an impressive two-story log and rock structure nestled among a grove of aspen trees. Beyond the lodge, the lake glistens in sky blue reflection.

The fishing cabins are strung along the lakeshore in a horseshoe design, offering each a view of the lake and towering mountains.

Midway between the lodge and lake, there's a boy and a frisky white puppy in a tug of war over a stick. It appears that the puppy is winning.

I coast to a stop at the turnoff and shift Red into four-wheel drive, according to Ty's instructions. I take a deep breath and give my full attention to the narrowing uphill road.

My knuckles turn white as bone as I clutch the steering wheel in a stranglehold. It's slow going up the road. There are no guardrails to provide a semblance of security for this novice mountain driver.

Rounding the first switchback, I slow to a crawl as Ruby's cabin comes into view. It would've been at this spot, I figure, where the photographer captured the photo printed in the Tribune. There is no comparison between the photo and the scene before me.

Sheer cliffs of purple and gray are capped with peaks of shimmering silver-white snow. They create a dramatic backdrop for the weathered log cabin perched precariously on the mountainside, facing the verdant valley below.

I strain to catch a glimpse of Ruby, but the only movement I observe is a lone rocking chair on the porch, swaying in the Rocky Mountain breeze.

As I inch around the second switchback, the pathway becomes narrower. Large rocks and small boulders are scattered along the roadside. Puddles of snowmelt dot the sunny side of the road, while remnants of unmelted snow blanket the shadowed areas.

I'm thankful for the aspen and evergreen trees that line this part of the roadway providing a barrier from the edge of the road and what looks like oblivion far below. To my relief, I see a sign for the scenic overlook ahead. This must be the spot Ari referred to for a view of the town.

The overlook teeters on the crest of the ridge, providing one graded parking space, which I gratefully claim and come to a complete stop. I turn off the engine and apply the emergency brake as an extra precaution, resting my head on the steering wheel for a few seconds.

I slowly raise my head and unclench my hands. The mining town materializes like a mirage before me. "Hello, Prophecy," I whisper, not wanting to disturb the ghost town slumbering in solitude in the valley below.

Silence reigns as I exit Red, and cling to her side as I edge my way forward to a panoramic valley view. A fast-flowing stream, swollen with spring runoff, cuts a silver path down the mountainside and across the valley floor. Along the stream and dotting the hillside are the remains of log cabins scattered in haphazard fashion like an upended box of Lincoln logs abandoned in child's play. There are other buildings on the opposing ridge, but they are too far to define. The majestic mountains rise in the background like an impenetrable wall.

I itch with curiosity about the stories waiting to be discovered, but yielding to Ari's warnings about abandoned mine shafts dotting the landscape, I decide to save my explorations for another day, accompanied by a local guide familiar with the terrain.

My eyes are glued to the road as I head down the mountainside, rarely using peripheral vision as I bless my surefooted steed. Cautiously, we rock our way down, maneuvering the twists and turns, the rocks and boulders, risking a quick glance as we pass Ruby's silent cabin.

16

Meadow View

The view of the lodge and its surroundings grows larger as I descend. I signal for a left turn onto Main Street and glance in the rearview mirror causing me to burst into a fit of nervous giggles when I realize that I'm probably the only vehicle that has come down this mountain road in a long time.

Another quick left, and I'm driving under the impressive wooden sign marking the lodge entrance. It hangs on hinges drilled into a large log beam supported on each side by matching rock pillars. The words "Welcome to Meadow View Lodge" have been burned into the wood.

The tires crunch on the gravel drive as I slow to a stop under the covered entryway.

The use of rock has been incorporated throughout the log construction. Rock slab steps lead to a spacious porch. The wooden entry doors are intricately carved with a floral motif and accented with heavy iron door handles, copying the floral pattern.

Midway into a full stretch after exiting Red, I'm body slammed with a direct hit to the back of my knees. "Whoa!" I yelp in surprise, struggling to retain my balance.

A high-pitched voice screeches from behind. "Down, Mogul! Bad boy!"

I turn to observe a battle between the boy I saw earlier and his puppy, who lurches from his master's grip, engulfing me in a frontal attack of paws and slurps.

"Hey, buddy." I bend to one knee in an attempt to calm the frisky pup. After many ignored commands, the boy is able to attach a leash to his collar.

"Sorry about that." He tugs at the struggling puppy. "He's not totally trained yet." He grimaces as he twirls in a circle with the wild pup. "Hi," he gasps, gaining momentary control of the spinning dog. "My name is Jake, and this is Mogul." He offers a broad-faced grin in exchange for a handshake, fearful of releasing his two-handed grip on the leash.

I am charmed by his welcoming smile and chuckle at the antics before me as I observe this handsome fellow with wind-tousled, golden brown hair and teddy-bear brown eyes. Like Jess, he's dressed in a denim jacket, jeans, and western boots.

"Nice to meet you, Jake, and you, too, Mogul," I say, sending the dog into another spasm of woofs and jumps at the mention of his name.

"My name is Nevy. I'm visiting from Chicago and looking for a place to stay during my visit to Blue Eagle. I'm wondering if any of the cabins by the lake might be for rent?"

"You looking to do some fishing?" He raises a grimy hand to shade his eyes from the sun as he squints in my direction.

"No, not much of a fisher lady. I need a place with a little extra space to work. I'm a writer."

A look of consternation replaces the grin as Jake ponders my question. "Used to rent them when Papa was here, to the fishermen, but we don't anymore," his voice quivers. "Someday soon we will, though. We're doing some fixing up first." He smiles, eager to please, but his attention is suddenly diverted.

I follow his gaze to observe a grown-up version of Jake exiting the entrance doors of the lodge. She carries a paint brush in her hand and is dressed in a pair of paint splattered bibs. Her chestnut brown hair is highlighted with golden strands woven into one thick braid that adorns her right shoulder with escaping tendrils framing her face. Her face is devoid of makeup, but there is no need. She is a natural beauty.

"Uh-oh. Hi, Mom," he replies, wide-eyed.

Her lovely brown eyes match those of her son's, but at the moment they're partially hidden under her furrowed brow. She remains standing with her hands on her hips, looking down on her son and his pup. "Jakie, get that wild thing into the backyard where he's supposed to be," she commands in a firm but gentle manner.

"Sorry, I was trying to be helpful and welcoming to our guests like you told me." His solemn face peers into his mother's, begging for forgiveness.

"Oh, you." She proceeds down the steps to stand before Jake, her fingers lovingly combing through his tousled hair, unable to hide the grin on her face. "Scram, you two."

Jake's frown converts into a broad smile, and he gives the leash a tug. "See you later, Nevy!" he shouts as he and Mogul disappear in a gallop around the house and out of sight.

The woman shakes her head at the retreating figures and turns her attention to me. "I'm so sorry about Mogul. He's a work in progress, as you can see. My name is Leigh McLean," she says and extends her hand.

"Nevy Ellis, and it's absolutely okay." I reach to accept her handshake. "My parents are both vets. I grew up in the country surrounded by all kinds of critters. Rambunctious puppies are of little worry to me."

"Thank goodness," she responds, but concern replaces her relief. "Jake mentioned something about a guest at the lodge? I hope there hasn't been some misunderstanding. The lodge is currently closed for renovation."

"No, no," I quickly reply to put her at ease, "I don't have a reservation. I'm visiting from Chicago...this is my first trip to Colorado. I'm planning to do research here for an article I'm writing to be published in a travel guide, a new venture we're trying out. I was hoping to find lodging that will provide a little extra workspace.

I spotted this brochure in Denver at the car rental agency." I pull the brochure from my pocket. The gentleman at the convenience store told me about the renovations, but I thought, maybe... there might be a cabin available? I don't mind rustic," I end with a hopeful smile.

Surprise covers Leigh's face. "Oh, my gosh! I forgot about those old things," she says, her voice softening as she takes the brochure from my hand.

The sound of an electric saw chewing through a piece of lumber pierces the air and makes further conversation impossible. Leigh grasps her ears and nods for me to follow as she leads the way up the steps and through the entry doors.

The heavy doors silence the noise. "That's my foreman, Charlie. He's helping to renovate the lodge, making the structural changes, and as you can see..." She pirouettes in front of me displaying the paint brush. "I'm the interior decorator. I wish you had come later in the season. We're converting the fishing camp into a full-fledged lodge with many other amenities and accommodations."

"Edna—Charlie's wife and our chef—will be dishing up some local fare. She's an amazing cook. They've been with Meadow View since Papa Jake ran the fishing lodge. I don't know what I would do without them." She pauses and shakes her head. "Excuse my rambling, the paint fumes must be getting to me."

I can't hide my disappointment. "So, none of the cabins are available for rent?"

"Afraid not." She sighs. "We saved the cabins for last. Each one of them is in a state of renovation. Walls are knocked out and new plumbing is being installed. In hindsight, we should've started with the cabins, but we started with the lodge, which was easiest because of the many renovations it's gone through over the years. We're nearly finished with it except for a few touch-ups. Opening day is looming, and we're in a bit of a panic."

"So then, you do have rooms available in the lodge?" Hope stirs in my heart.

Caught off-guard, she pauses to consider my request. "I guess you could say they are ready, but we're not! I mean, I don't even know where the registration book is at this point." She frowns at a pile of boxes stacked in a corner. "I'm afraid I wouldn't be much of a host. All of our energy is being consumed by the renovation process," she says, giving a futile shrug.

Don't let this get away, Nevy, I think to myself. "Sure, I understand, but I'm an easy guest. I promise I would be no trouble. I spotted a restaurant as I drove through town where I can get my meals. It would make things so much easier for me if I could stay locally in Blue Eagle."

I can see the hesitation on her face as I offer one more suggestion. "Consider me your guinea pig. It would be an honor to be the first official guest at your new lodge."

"You are not easily dissuaded, are you?" A grin spreads across her face.

She takes a moment. "Hmm, as long as you understand what you're getting yourself into. I may have to include a caveat emptor clause in your official registration...once I find it. Just be forewarned that there are sure to be some glitches. But we can guarantee some awesome home-cooked meals, so no need worrying about depending on meals from Liddy's Ice Cream and Sandwich Shop."

"Deal!" I exclaim, holding my hand out to complete the transaction.

"Deal." She grasps my hand with both of hers, and pride spreads across her face. "How about a tour of the lodge? You'll have your choice of rooms."

As we begin the tour down the long hallway, Leigh starts to narrate the history of the lodge. "The lodge is built on the site of the home my great-great-grandfather Isaiah built for his bride, Rose

René. Sadly, she died giving birth to my great-grandpa, R.J. The original structure burned to the ground in the early nineteen hundreds."

"Oh, no." I gasp. "How tragic."

"Yes, there's much mystery surrounding her death and the fire, but no one seems to know the whole story. Papa Jake—R.J's son and my grandpa—told me it was a forbidden subject among family members when he was growing up. "Anyway, the little I know is that Isaiah, Isa is what most folks called him, and his son, R.J., lived in the mountain cabin while they built the ranch house on the original site. When they finished, they turned the property into a cattle ranch. The cattle used to graze in the meadow and water at the edge of the lake."

"So, your family goes back," I stop to count, "six generations counting your son, Jake. That's an impressive lineage. What happened to the cattle ranch, if you don't mind me asking?"

"No, not at all," she answers, and pauses at the end of the hallway before a set of double doors. "The McLeans continued cattle ranching but started taking in boarders during the depression to supplement their income. When Papa Jake inherited the ranch, Nana and he turned it into a full-fledged fishing lodge. The trout fishing here is amazing! It became so successful, they got out of the ranching business completely. The lodge has grown considerably in size from the original." She smiles broadly while opening the doors to reveal the room beyond. "This is the great room, where our guests can relax and plan their adventures." She turns a beaming face toward me, stepping inside and motioning for me to follow.

Sunlight filters through floor-to-ceiling windows built on each side of a towering rock fireplace that reaches to the vaulted ceiling at the far end of the room. A view of the shimmering lake, meadow, and snowy mountains is visible from each window. Sofas and armchairs have been placed within view of the windows and within reach of the warmth from the fireplace.

Leigh points to the fireplace. "Isa and R.J. carried each of those rocks from the river to construct the fireplace. This room was a lifelong dream of Isa's. He drew up the plans, but never got beyond gathering the rocks. When Papa Jake inherited the lodge, the first thing he did was create this room in memory of Isa and R.J."

My eyes are drawn to the magnificent antler chandelier hanging from the center of the ceiling.

Leigh's gaze follows mine. "Papa Jake helped Isa gather the antlers for the chandelier. He commissioned a local artist to create the light fixture. Even the Douglas-fir was milled here in Colorado at a family-owned lumber yard. Papa Jake was adamant about following Isa's plans "to a T" using native building materials and artisans."

I lower my eyes to Leigh's. "The whole room is spectacular," I praise.

"Quite a legacy Jake and I have inherited, don't you think?" She smiles humbly with pride.

"Yes, I agree. I'm sure they would be very proud of Jake and you for carrying on their legacy."

"I sure hope so. They're some pretty big shoes to fill." Leigh smiles in a melancholy way, lost in memory. She swipes away a tear, wiping away her reverie. "I'm sorry. Memories of my Papa Jake haunt my days. I still can't believe he's gone."

Instinctively, I raise my hand to her shoulder and give it a gentle squeeze. "I understand. I still haven't gotten over the passing of my grandmother. I don't think I ever will."

She pats my hand. "Oh gosh." She sighs. "Let's go see what magic Edna is creating in her kitchen today." Leigh points the way. We enter the kitchen through a set of doors off the great room. A heavenly smell of baking bread wafts through the air. Leigh turns to me.

"Something tells me Edna has been busy." Her eyes twinkle. "Come meet our chef."

We catch Edna removing a loaf of homemade bread from the oven.

"Edna," Leigh calls out a notch above a whisper, not wanting to startle her. "We have a guest I want you to meet."

As Edna turns our way, a warm smile spreads across her plump, round face, capped by a head of springy silver curls with a round body to match. "Oh my goodness, just one second while I set this pan on the counter with the rest of them," she says.

My eyes follow the loaf of mouthwatering bread as Edna hurries across the room to place it on the cooling rack in a row with half a dozen others. She tosses the potholders on the counter and attempts a futile pat down to the resistant curls bobbing from her head. I cross the room to meet her.

"Edna, it's a pleasure to meet you. I'm Nevy Ellis." I extend my hand and add, "Your reputation precedes you. That is the most divine aroma I have ever smelled."

Her hazel eyes crinkle in delight at my praise. "Nevy, welcome." Her hands, warm from the oven, enclose my body in a gentle hug. She faces Leigh. "Did I hear you say 'guest'?"

"That's right. Nevy is a very persuasive lady. She says she's willing to be our guinea pig as our first guest to the new Meadow View Lodge," Leigh replies with a grin.

"How wonderful." Edna claps her hands. "Let's give you a taste of Meadow View hospitality, then. Come, both of you. Sit yourselves down and have a sample of homemade bread while it's still warm." Edna clucks and guides us like baby chicks to the table.

"Are you a coffee drinker, Miss Nevy?" Edna calls out. I turn to watch her bustle about the kitchen, pulling cups, plates, and silverware from the cupboards and drawers in expert fashion. It's obvious this is her domain.

"Absolutely. It's one vice I refuse to give up."

"Me too." Edna nods.

Half an hour later and sated from several pieces of thick sour dough bread slathered with butter and homemade blackberry jam, I push away from the table when Leigh invites me to join her outside on the deck. I follow, but not before acknowledging the chef. "Edna, you are a baking wizard. That was amazing!"

Edna replies with a rose blush covering her face. "You are too kind, Miss Nevy."

I follow Leigh through doors off the great room leading to a large wooden deck outside. The absence of man-made noise punctuates the silence, magnifying the natural sounds outdoors. A gentle breeze whispers through the tall evergreens, and the distant sound of the stream flowing through the meadow greets us like a lullaby created by Mother Nature.

Bracing my hands on the log railing, I inhale a deep breath of intoxicating mountain air. I shield my eyes from the intense sun as I observe the scene I glimpsed from the roadside on my way up the mountain.

The lake shimmers in the sunshine, a mirror image of the unblemished blue sky. The log fishing cabins and tall spruce trees hug its perimeter facing the towering majestic mountains in the background. To the right, the meadow spreads out like a spilled painter's box, flowers covering the valley floor.

"Heaven." I sigh.

"Yes, it is," Leigh concurs. "One of these days, I hope to have more time to appreciate it." She shares a hopeful smile.

My gaze follows Miners' Alley. I stand on tiptoes and spot the rooftop of Ruby's cabin before the road disappears around the switchback. I decide to leave the subject of Ruby for another day.

Leigh motions for me to follow her down a rock-lined pathway that leads to a cleared area where hand-hewn logs have been carved into benches, circling an open fire pit.

She walks straight-backed with head erect and at a fast pace. It's a challenge to keep up with her. The pathway continues from the campfire area to the lake and cabins beyond.

"This is where we plan to have our cookouts under the star-filled skies—a view you will never forget. We plan to offer a variety of meal styles, western barbecues and fish fries here, and more traditional meals in the lodge. Edna will be in charge of those decisions, thank goodness. But you're welcome to join us at the family table for your meals during your stay, Nevy."

I hesitate, thinking it would be so easy to fall back into my old habit of isolating myself. "That was the old Nevy," a whisper reminds me.

I look into her kind face and reply, "That is very gracious of you, Leigh. It would be my pleasure to join you."

She nods and continues with her story. "We'll be hiring additional staff in the future. This first year will be a balancing act, generating funds to keep the operation going. It makes my head spin thinking about it." She turns to me and frowns. "Gosh, Nevy, you look done in. Come, let's take a quick tour of the rooms so you can make your selection and take a rest. I'm so sorry. Sometimes I get carried away sharing my love of Meadow View," she apologizes profusely.

I've enjoyed every moment of it. But I agree, the combination of the high altitude, plane trip, and feasting on Edna's heavenly homemade bread is beginning to take a toll. A nap sounds like a good idea.

Leigh leads our way indoors, where she continues her description of the lodge and its offerings. "There are two suites on the east wing and three guest rooms on the west. Our living quarters are on the second floor."

Leigh chuckles to herself. "We did have our light-hearted moments during our planning, like when we were trying to think of a theme for each room. We tossed around a lot of ideas like a wildlife theme to go along with the fishing history. That was a disaster!"

"How so?" I ask.

"Well, we started off in a serious vein like the Rainbow Trout Room, Elk Room, Eagle's Nest. But then Jakie and Charlie got silly. Jakie suggested the Munk Bunk to represent the chipmunks, and Charlie piped in with Skunk Bunk. It was downhill from there." Leigh laughs.

I join in her laughter. "Have you come up with any ideas yet?"

"It was so obvious, Nevy, but it took the innocence of a child to see what was right in front of us." A loving expression covers her face.

"One gorgeous morning Jakie and I were snuggled together on the swing, under one of Edna's homemade quilts, when he whispered to me, 'Mom, aren't the flowers in the meadow so beautiful? We should call our rooms flower names.' It was the perfect solution. It also gave us our color themes like the cabin we named Shooting Star for its magenta-colored flower and Miners' Candle which is a sweet little white flower with a yellow center."

"I can't wait to see them all."

Leigh holds a hand up. "I'm afraid not yet. I haven't begun to decorate the cabins. We have so much work to complete on them. Today, I'm going to show you the two suites, so I don't wear you out completely. I would love to give you a full tour sometime."

"I would be honored, Leigh," I say. We exit the great room and enter the hallway pausing at the first door on the left.

Leigh opens the door and ushers me inside. "This room is named the 'Blue Columbine' after the Colorado state flower." She follows me inside the room.

My eyes fill with delight. The king-size brass bed is covered with a buttermilk-yellow quilt. The quilt is centered with an exquisite hand-stitched replica of the blue columbine flower. Sliding wooden doors separate the bedroom from a private sitting area with a rock fireplace. An easy chair and ottoman sit in front of the fireplace. A blue columbine-colored throw blanket graces the arm of the chair. A reading lamp and side table are positioned beside the chair.

"I think I've made my choice," I gush, eyeing the comfy bed, begging for a tryout.

Leigh turns to me with a mischievous grin. "Don't be too hasty; we have one more room to see." We return to the hallway. I follow Leigh, wondering how the next room could top the one we just saw. The plaque on the door reads "The Wild Rose."

Leigh opens the door and steps aside for me to enter.

"How beautiful," I gasp. Leigh has succeeded in transforming the rustic log cabin feel of the lodge into a room filled with elegance and charm. The centerpiece is an antique four-poster bed clothed in an ivory downy-soft quilt dotted with embroidered clusters of dusty pink roses. The bed is piled high with an assortment of luscious stuffed pillows in varying degrees of rose colors.

Positioned in the far corner of the large suite is a rock fireplace, a miniature to the one in the great room. But what captures my attention is the leather upholstered rocker with wide wooden armrests, a near copy of Grandmater's. An ornate, hand carved wooden armoire and desk complete the suite.

A grin creeps across my lips as I whisper, "It's perfect."

Leigh crosses the room toward a set of French doors. "We're not finished yet." She beckons for me to follow. "Come and see the sitting area outside."

She leads me across the porch and down three steps into a private garden, complete with a cushioned glider where the sounds of the stream can be heard gurgling beyond. A lattice-style divider provides privacy from the wraparound porch.

Leigh beams. "Have you made your decision about which room you'll choose?"

"Is there any doubt? I love the Blue Columbine, but this exceeds my expectations." I can't contain the smile spreading from ear to ear.

Leigh confesses, "Sometimes I sneak off to sit in its quiet beauty and peace, my private sanctuary. But right now, let's get you settled." She motions for me to return to the suite.

We re-enter the room. I pause to admire the framed portrait of the stunning woman that hangs above the four-poster bed. The words "Love is like the wild rose" with credit given to Emily Brontë are handwritten below the portrait.

"That is my great-great-grandmother Rose René." Leigh stands beside me. "We named this room after her and the wild roses that grow in the meadow."

"The woman who died in childbirth?" I murmur.

"Yes," Leigh whispers softly and adds, "I would love to learn more about her. I have a suspicion that we named the room quite fittingly from the bits and pieces of information I've gleaned over the years. Wasn't she beautiful?"

"Striking. You bear a close resemblance, you know?" I say, glancing from the portrait to Leigh.

She gently grasps my arm. "I wish. I do see some of Jakie's features, though, especially her eyes. Only hers have a bit of intrigue in them, like she's hiding a secret. How the portrait escaped the fire is a true mystery." She studies the portrait. "Anyway," she says, changing the subject, "I'll let you settle in. You're welcome to join us for appetizers on the deck before dinner, say around four p.m?" She tilts her head in my direction.

I look forward to it," I respond, unable to divert my gaze from the mesmerizing portrait.

"You can exit through the French doors and follow the porch around to the deck where we were earlier. Enjoy your rest." Leigh retreats, closing the door softly behind her.

Silence reigns and, with it, a feeling of exhaustion as I collapse into the bed's heavenly comfort.

17

Appetizers and a Ghost Story

The sounds of galloping feet on the porch outside my room and Mogul's yip awaken me from my nap.

The bedside clock reveals half-past three. I roll from bed and exit the French doors in a run, following the porch to the front of the lodge.

A coating of dust gathered on the trip up Miners' Alley has settled over Red, still parked under the covered entranceway. "I promise a proper cleaning soon, my faithful steed." I pat her flank and settle behind the wheel for the short drive to the guest parking lot. I retrieve my travel bags and hurry back to my room.

"Hmm." I pause before the open suitcase and realize I've underestimated my wardrobe for this mountain visit. I settle on a pair of jeans and a sweatshirt while contemplating a shopping trip in the near future.

I shove the rest of my items into the suitcase and stow it in the armoire, stopping before the wall mirror in a futile attempt to tame my unruly curls, then exit to the porch and follow Leigh's directions to the deck.

Leigh and Jake are in deep conversation, their heads bent close together at the large log table. I overhear Leigh say, "I'm sorry, Jakie, but that's the way it's got to be until Mogul is trained better." A sad, corralled puppy dog wail breaks the silence in the distance.

"Hi, guys," I call out to them. "I can't believe I overslept. This view takes my breath away every time I see it!" I throw my arms out and spin in a twirl to encompass the totality of the scene in an attempt to lighten the mood. "Whoa!" I yelp as I wobble for the chair that Leigh offers. It's worth the theatrics to see the effect on both of them as they erupt into laughter.

"I think Nevy has the high-altitude sillies." Jake giggles.

Leigh replies, "He could be right. It takes time to acclimate. We are at eighty-six hundred feet elevation here. Let me help you, Nevy." She runs to guide my direction.

"I guess I won't be doing any mountain climbing anytime soon." I gratefully plop into the waiting chair.

"Edna and Charlie promised to join us. She shushed us out of the kitchen while she prepared the appetizers, and Charlie, well..." Leigh turns to Jake.

Jake obliges by finishing her sentence. "Charlie says he's fixin' to quit in a minute, which usually means a whole lot more minutes later." He peers into his mother's face as they share a chuckle.

"So," Leigh continues with furrowed brow, "we're never sure when Charlie will make his appearance. Oh, I didn't mean to make that sound so harsh," Leigh explains. "We love them both to pieces, like family, don't we, Jakie?"

His head bobs in affirmation.

"Papa Jake hired them years ago to help Nana and him run the fishing lodge. They're originally from Grand Junction."

"So, they're native Coloradans too? I guess that's more common than I thought."

"More so with western slope folks, it seems. I wish we could claim the same. Both Jakie and I were born in Florida. When my dad, Andrew, graduated from college with a degree in hotel management, he was offered a job with a hotel chain in New York City. Papa Jake and Nana were so disappointed when he didn't return home. Then, that job led to an offer to manage a golf resort in Florida."

"Did you find it a big adjustment moving from sea level to the Rockies?"

"Not at all. I spent all my summers here with my grandparents, where my true heart has always been. Jakie and I moved here when Papa Jake offered a place for R and R after my divorce. One month led to another, and we decided to make this our home permanently, didn't we?" Leigh turns to her son and ruffles his mop of hair.

"Mom," he scolds lightheartedly, smoothing his hair with his hand. "But then," his voice cracks, "Papa Jake died."

"Yes," Leigh whispers. "But we had some wonderful years with him. Those are the times we remember, right?" She caresses the side of his face as he playfully swats her hand away.

The door to the lodge opens, and Edna appears, carrying a large charcuterie board laden with cheeses, meats, vegetables, fruit and other tasty-looking finger food. "Appetizers, anyone?" she announces in a sing-song voice. Her joyful demeanor lightens the somber mood, as we scramble from our chairs to help.

"Edna, Edna, let us help you!" Leigh chides, attempting to take the board while Jake rushes to hold the door. I pull a chair from the table to clear a pathway.

"I've got this handled." She swooshes past and places the board on the table with little difficulty.

"Better believe it," warns a gravelly male voice behind. "Hi, loves."

I turn and see a real-life cowboy following in Edna's wake, carrying a tray with a pitcher of lemonade and glassware. He's dressed in a pair of faded, worn denim jeans and a western chambray shirt with sleeves rolled to his elbows, exposing muscular, tanned arms. His western boots are covered in sawdust.

After placing the tray on the table, he reaches to remove his straw cowboy hat, revealing a head of thinning salt and pepper hair that matches a neatly trimmed beard. A shower of sawdust floats through the air from his hat.

"Charlie Lambert, don't you go getting sawdust all over my appetizers now," Edna admonishes as she busies herself by filling the glasses with lemonade.

He growls teasingly, stepping away from the table with an ornery grin directed at his wife.

"Okay, you two," Leigh teases. "Charlie, come and meet our guest, Nevy."

"Guest?" He looks from Leigh to me.

"I know." Leigh holds up a hand to ward off a reply from Charlie when he raises a questioning eyebrow in her direction. "Nevy has been forewarned of our work in progress."

"She's going to be our official gopher," Jake adds.

"Say what?" Charlie turns to Jake with a confused look as Leigh, Edna, and I erupt into chuckles. Jake turns a bewildered look at all of us.

"Guinea pig, silly," Leigh corrects.

Jake erupts into giggles. "Oh, yeah, guinea pig. Sorry, Nevy."

"I am honored to be your guinea pig and gopher, helping wherever I'm needed. I'm so thankful for your hospitality." I extend my hand to Charlie. "Nevy Ellis, greenhorn from Chicago and first-time visitor to your beautiful state."

His large, calloused hand engulfs my own in a hearty handshake as he shares a quick glance with his wife. "A pleasure to meet you, Miss Nevy." His slow western drawl stretches the sentence into twice its length.

"Everyone, settle yourselves down at the table," Edna instructs while she fills the plates with appetizers.

"Whoa there, girl, we won't have room for your fried chicken dinner," Charlie teases.

As we savor Edna's appetizers, Charlie turns in my direction and asks, "Miss Nevy, mind if I ask, what brings you to Blue Eagle? It's not the usual tourist stop for most folks."

"But we hope to change that soon, don't we Jakie?" Leigh chimes in.

Jake nods his head in agreement, a loving smile filling his face. "Maybe Nevy can write about Meadow View in her article," he replies while reaching for a second helping of pizza rolls.

"It would be my pleasure to give Meadow View Lodge some advertisement," I respond. Turning to Charlie, I explain, "This is my first assignment for a new endeavor my boss, Contessa, has undertaken, a travel guide focusing on little known sites around the country." I realize all eyes have turned in my direction, so I continue. "Contessa has chosen Colorado, and specifically, the mining town of Prophecy as the site for our first edition. She hired me to write the feature article." My smile fades as I observe the look of concern on his face.

"I don't know about that idea," he advises bluntly. "Lots of other old towns you might want to consider instead," he says in a tone and manner similar to Ari's at the mention of Prophecy.

I continue cautiously, "Um, you see, Contessa stumbled across a photograph in our Chicago newspaper of the cabin I passed on my way up Miners' Alley. The caption mentioned the name of the ghost town as Prophecy. She personally took it as a kind of omen that this should be the featured location for her first edition."

"Not much left to Prophecy no more. Probably not worth your trouble. Lots more interesting places to investigate, I would imagine. Colorado's full of 'em," he replies.

I decide to change to a different subject. "I understand that someone still lives in the cabin?"

"Yes, an elderly lady by the name of Ruby," Leigh replies. "Papa Jake befriended her years ago when she came to town and had no place to live."

Jake pipes in, "She moved into our cabin just like it was her own!"

"Hush, Jakie." He ducks his head at his mother's uncommon admonishment. Leigh continues, her voice softening, "Papa didn't have the heart to evict her." She peers lovingly at her son. "Then, when Papa passed, Ari, his best friend, took over the responsibility for Ruby. Each month, he drives Ruby to his store to stock up on supplies. Otherwise, she pretty much keeps to herself. She's known to guard her privacy."

"Ah." I nod. "Yes, that's what Ari cautioned me about."

"She has a mean old goat, too," Jake adds in youthful innocence, unaware of the comparison he's made to Ruby. Charlie tries to contain a chuckle under the scolding eyes of Edna.

Jake looks in Charlie's direction, shrugs, and continues. "And a burro. Those are her only friends." His sad expression melts my heart.

"It does sound awfully lonely, I agree, Jake."

"Maybe to us." Charlie leans back, balancing on two chair legs, his muscular arms spread eagle along the deck railing. "There's all kinds of folks in this world. Some, like Ruby, are loners. We've learned to respect her privacy." He pointedly looks in my direction.

I fidget in my chair under his scrutiny and hasten to reassure them. "I promise to respect her privacy, too. It's not my intention to cause any worries.

"I'm most interested in learning about the history of Prophecy. I wonder what you might care to share?" I glance around the table.

Leigh turns to Charlie. "You probably know the history of Prophecy better than any of us, Charlie."

"Some, I reckon, but Ari is the true historian." Settling the chair on four legs, Charlie rests his forearms on the table and clasps his hands together in prelude to telling his story.

He stares into the distance, following Miners' Alley as it wends its way into the mountains. A far-off look graces his face, perhaps seeking inspiration from the past. Then, turning his attention to us, Charlie clears his throat and begins. "The story of Prophecy begins with two fellers: Isaiah McLean and his partner and best friend, Jonah LaPierre."

Jake puts his hand on Charlie's arm and asks, "What does 'prophecy' mean Charlie?"

Looking into Jake's eyes, Charlie places his hand on top of Jake's in a show of affection and considers his question. "I guess I'd say prophecy means a prediction about something that's going to happen in the future. You see, Isaiah and Jonah predicted that one day, they was gonna strike it rich." Charlie chuckles. "Like all the gold seekers before and after 'em. But in their case, their prophecy came true."

"They found gold!" Jake's eyes widen in wonder.

"Sure did, enough to make 'em rich men. So, when they was thinking of a name for their mine, Prophecy seemed the obvious choice for a couple of reasons. First, because their prediction came true. Second, 'cause back in Cripple Creek where they first teamed up, they was known as 'The Prophets' bearing the names of two of the prophets in the Bible, Isaiah and Jonah. So it was only fitting that they would choose the name of Prophecy."

"Oh, yeah, I learned the story about Jonah and the whale in Bible School, but I never heard of the other guy." Jake sits straighter in his chair proud of his contribution, while Leigh stifles a reply to the "other guy" comment.

"So, you really was listening during them studies," Charlie chides, and Jake responds with a good-natured punch to Charlie's arm.

Curious, I ask, "What is Cripple Creek?"

Charlie shakes his head and turns a slow look of astonishment in my direction. "Why, the Cripple Creek Mining District, nearby Colorado Springs. If you're gonna write about the Colorado mining days, you better know about that!"

"Charlie," Edna cautions, sending a subtle warning glance his way.

"Hello, Charlie, greenhorn from Chicago," I remind him, laughing at myself.

Charlie explains, "The Cripple Creek discoveries are some of the biggest in the history of Colorado, set off a national gold rush. Thousands of folks crossed the plains in search of gold. That's the area you should focus on for your article," he suggests.

"My boss is pretty set on Prophecy, Charlie," I remind him. "And besides, how could I leave now after having met all of you and the beauty of Meadow View?"

Undefeated, Charlie offers, "You might consider the French Gulch area over near Breckenridge then. You could still use Meadow View as your home base. There was tons of claims along the Blue River and gulches, a real bonanza! Did every sort of mining, placer, lode, hydraulic, drifting, dredging…still have an old dredge boat, the Reliance, sitting in a pond over there you can take a look at. There's also a tour of the Country Boy Mine that would give you a lot of insight for your article."

"I don't think—"

Charlie interrupts, "The history of French Gulch is loaded with colorful characters you could write about. Prospectors, miners, investors, merchants, gamblers, swindlers of every kind, and shady ladies, too, if you know what I mean."

Jake gives Charlie a confused look, but before he can ask, Charlie pats him on the arm and advises, "Never you mind, Jakie Boy."

In an attempt to calm the waters, I respond, "Those are great suggestions, Charlie. I'll be sure to add a visit to Breckenridge to my plans. But I'm curious. How did Isaiah and Jonah end up here in Blue Eagle?"

"Yeah, Charlie, tell us the rest of the story," Jake pleads excitedly.

It's obvious Charlie's aware of my attempt to sidestep our choice of Prophecy for the article, but, yielding to Jake's interest, he agrees to finish the original tale. "Reckon I need to back up a stretch to tell that story." Charlie clears his throat. "It was during the boom days in The District, at the turn of the century—that would be nineteen hundred, Jake,—when Isaiah and Jonah first met. They was workin' for one of them big mining companies and struck up a friendship, decided to go into partnership on their own claim. That way, one could work a shift at the mining company while the other one worked their claim and protected it from the claim jumpers."

"Claim jumpers? Who were they?" Jake asks wide-eyed.

His mother explains, "They were bad people who would steal another man's claim if it was left unprotected."

"That's right, Jake. They was all kinds of disreputable folks trying to take advantage of others," Charlie adds. "But it didn't matter because Isaiah and Jonah wasn't having much luck with their claim anyway. On top of that, there was big labor disputes going on between the miners and the owners of the mining companies; mostly over the poor wages the miners were being paid and the long hours they was required to work."

"What happened next, Charlie?" Jake's animated face encourages him to continue.

"Well, now, Isaiah and Jonah decided they didn't want no part of them problems, so they decided to strike out on their own for Blue Eagle, where Isaiah's father and uncles had mined during the first big Colorado gold rush."

"What?!" Leigh blurts out. "That would have been my great-great-great-grandfather. I never heard this part of the story before. How do you know all of this, Charlie?"

"Mostly from Ari. My guess is he learned it from your Papa Jake. You know how close them two was."

"Yes, but I wish Papa Jake would have shared some of it with me. Family history has always been a taboo subject. My dad sure doesn't know any of this." She pauses and adds, "And probably doesn't care. What else can you tell us?" She's intrigued like the rest of us.

Charlie strokes his beard in thought. "As I understand it, Isaiah's father and brothers journeyed from Missouri during the gold rush of eighteen fifty-nine, mining along the streams near what would become Blue Eagle. But it wasn't long before their money and provisions ran out, and they had to join the 'go-backers.' That's the name they gave folks returning home empty-handed. There was more hard times than good times back then."

"That must have been so disappointing and demoralizing as well, coming all the way here filled with hopes and dreams only to return home with nothing to show for it," I utter my thoughts aloud.

"Yes, ma'am." Charlie sighs. "Isaiah grew up listening to the stories his dad and uncles told about how they was sure there was a mother lode of gold still waiting to be found in the hills above Blue Eagle. Them stories planted the idea in Isaiah's mind to find that hidden treasure."

"I wonder what Isaiah's dad and uncles thought about him pursuing their dream?" I ask.

"Don't know, but when he turned eighteen, he did exactly that. 'Cept, he headed for The District first, most likely to earn a grubstake to pursue his dad's dream. I reckon he didn't want to become one of them go backers hisself.

"But when trouble hit The District, them two decided it was time to follow the stories shared by Isaiah's dad and uncles. That would be my guess."

"Tell them about the old prospector, Charlie," Edna chimes in, excitement in her voice.

"I'm getting there, Missy," Charlie teases.

"What prospector?" Jake has changed his position from sitting to balancing on his knees in the chair, unable to still his curiosity.

"As the story goes," Charlie continues, "while Isaiah and Jonah was panning for gold up near current day Prophecy, they met an old prospector by the name of Pappy Young coming out of the high country."

"Old Pappy Young, the ghost!" Jake shrieks interrupting Charlie.

"Oh, Jakie." Leigh chuckles. "You don't believe that old ghost story, do you?"

Jake turns to his mother with a solemn look on his face. "The guys swear they've seen him wandering around with his lantern at night up in Prophecy and in the cemetery, too."

Leigh places a comforting hand on her son's arm. "Those are ghost stories the older kids tell to scare you younger guys."

Jake shakes his head, unconvinced.

Charlie shifts in his chair and resumes his story telling, "Anyway, as I was saying, Old Pappy Young was a prospector who had been hunting gold in the high country as long as anyone could remember. He was searching for the mother lode, the main vein of gold. It's where the gold that's washed down and deposited in the stream beds and rivers, what we call placer gold, comes from."

"Placer gold, that's the kind of gold the miners panned the rivers and creeks for, right, Charlie?"

"Got that right, Jake, and still do to this day. But placer gold can be found in other places, high above the rivers and streams." Charlie pauses for effect and studies my puzzled expression.

"But how?" I ask.

"Here's a little lesson for you, Miss Nevy. You see, there's two kinds of gold deposits. There's lode deposits that are embedded in veins of ore, and then there's placer deposits, which have eroded with other minerals from these veins and carried down into the streams and rivers."

"So how did the placer gold end up in these spots, away from rivers and streams?" I'm confused by his explanation.

"For that, you have to go back millions of years to the locations where ancient rivers flowed. Over all them millions of years, the river channels changed course due to the mountains rising and the land shifting. That caused these ancient riverbeds to be left high and dry."

"This is so interesting; I never knew this."

Pleased by my praise, he continues. "So Old Pappy tells the boys about a spot he had come upon as he was coming out of the high country that had all the indicators of an ancient riverbed."

"What kind of clues?" I blurt, unable to contain my curiosity.

"Yeah, Charlie, tell us." Jake's enthusiasm matches my own.

Charlie rests his back against the chair with a smirk, enjoying the effect his storytelling is having. Looking from one eager face to the other, he teases, "I reckon there's a bit of gold fever in the air."

"Charlie, stop the torment and finish your story," Edna admonishes.

He emits a low growl but obeys his wife's command. "Things like trees and plants growing in a dry gravelly spot where they normally wouldn't grow indicating a source of water somewhere nearby, rounded rocks and boulders smoothed by flowing water at one time rather than the normal sharp-edged rocks found on dry land, things like that, but it takes an experienced eye to spot 'em."

"But they found it, right?" Jake clutches the older man's arm.

"Sure did, Jake. Them two tracked the location Old Pappy described to them, dug themselves a coyote hole in the side of the hill, and—"

Jake's eyebrows come together in question. "Wait, did you say coyote hole?"

Charlie's face fills with a grin. "Yes, sir. Them miners would dig themselves a hole in the side of the hill, sometimes real deep. And when they heard any kind of disturbance, they would pop out of them holes like the coyotes pop out from their dens, so those holes they dug got called coyote holes. Anyway," Charlie continues his story, "by some kind of miracle or *prophecy,* they found that gold!" He slaps the tabletop, sending us teetering on the edge of our chairs.

"Unbelievable," I murmur. "But what would make Pappy tell these two strangers rather than making a claim himself?"

"You see, Miss Nevy, Old Pappy was one of the true old-time prospectors in search of the mother lode to beat all mother lodes, where legend tells there's veins as big as a man's arm to be found. For Pappy, it wasn't about the riches as much as it was about the hunt. He couldn't be bothered chasing after placer gold like them other prospectors." Charlie shakes his head. "Like the Bible says, 'a chasing after the wind.' Isaiah and Jonah took good care of Old Pappy later, when they struck it rich a second time."

"A second time?!" we exclaim in unison.

"Sure enough. You see, that first claim played out over time, but it provided the grubstake they needed to invest in their true dream."

"What dream?" Jake asks what we're all wondering.

"Why, Isaiah's father's dream, to find a mother lode themselves. During their time in The District, they had learned a lot about hard rock mining—lode mining, that is—and they put that knowledge to work, opening their own mine, the Prophecy. Them fellers have to be two of the luckiest miners ever 'cause they found one of them rich veins that led them to more discoveries, and the rest, as they say, is history. That's where the Prophecy Mine sits to this day, all boarded up now, in the hills above the boardinghouse."

"When the discovery got out," Edna continues where Charlie left off, "it set off a big stampede of miners to Blue Eagle. They say the hills above Prophecy were busy as ant hills, with miners crawling all over them. You can still see the piles of waste rock peppering the hills above Prophecy."

"So, in conclusion to this tale," Charlie exhales, "them discoveries is what put Prophecy on the map and turned Blue Eagle into a boom town, supplying materials and services for the miners and everyone else it brought to Prophecy."

"But that can't be all?" I ask, sorry to hear the story ending. What happened to Prophecy that it became a ghost town?"

"Like most booms, Miss Nevy, it was followed by a bust when the Prophecy Mine played out. Lucky for Isaiah, he had invested in real estate turning the property we're sitting on into a prosperous cattle ranch. I guess you could say he discovered his mother lode after all. End of story."

"What a story, Charlie!" I applaud while thinking, this can't be the end of the story, but more like the beginning.

Edna gets up from her chair. "My darlins', if we're going to have that fried chicken dinner I promised you, I best get busy." She shuffles about, cleaning the table.

Leigh glances at her watch and scrambles from the table. "And I need to make a phone call." She looks at Charlie, who nods his head in her direction.

On cue, Mogul chooses that moment to resume his mournful wailing. Jake turns a sorrowful look in the puppy's direction.

Taking pity on Jake and his pup, I suggest that we take Mogul for a walk around the lake path with the legitimate excuse of building up my lowlander lungs.

"Can we, Mom?" Jake turns to his mother with a grin from ear to ear as Leigh shares an appreciative smile my way.

"Yes, please go rescue that ornery pup."

Charlie excuses himself to return working on the renovation with a promise to finish in time for supper as Edna shares a doubting look in his direction.

"Race you to the barn, Nevy!" Jake is off in a flash as his mother shouts instructions to take the leash. She shakes her head throwing her arms into the air.

"Don't worry, I'll watch them—if I can catch them," I promise, before running to catch up with Jake's retreating figure.

Mogul's whine is replaced by a loud puppy dog bark and acrobatics as he catches sight of Jake heading toward him, leaving me in a cloud of dust.

When I reach the barn, I collapse with arms flailing across the wooden rails of the fence as Jake exits the gate, battling a reluctantly leashed Mogul, who has a mind of his own as to the direction they're going to take.

"You okay, Nevy?' His face fills with concern.

"I am now. It takes me a second or two to catch my breath." I gulp in a mouthful of mountain air.

"It'll get easier. It just takes time," he consoles while patting my back.

Jake releases the retractable leash to give the dancing dog more distance as we begin our trek on the path circling the lake.

The high-altitude air and low humidity create a clarity in my senses as I breathe in the scent of the wildflowers covering the meadow and evergreen that line the path.

The lake is so calm this late afternoon that it's taken on a glass-like appearance. A silvery-pink fish leaps from the water, creating a great splash upon reentry, stopping Mogul in his tracks.

"Did you see that?!" I screech, taking advantage of the still pup to catch up with Jake.

"Yeah, the lake is loaded with rainbow trout." Jake reigns Mogul into a steady pace so that we can walk side by side.

"Are you a fisherman, Jake?"

"Papa Jake, Ari, and me used to fish together all the time. They taught me lots about fishing. Ari and Papa were best friends. They called us the 'Three Amigos.'" He tips his head to look at me, his eyes watery with tears.

"I'm so sorry, Jake. I know how much it hurts to lose a loved one, especially someone as close as your papa. I lost my grandmother a few years ago. She was my best friend," I share in an attempt to reveal my understanding.

"Yeah," he replies in a sorrowful voice.

"What about Charlie? Does he fish?"

Jake giggles and shakes his head. "Naw, he can't sit still long enough to catch a fish. He's a terrible fisherman! Charlie couldn't catch a fish if his life depended on it. At least that's what Ari and Ben say." He glances a guilty look back, assuring that our conversation isn't overheard.

"Sometimes Ari fishes with me, but mostly on Sundays when Ben can watch the store for him."

I place my hand on his shoulder and offer, "Maybe you could teach me sometime."

"Maybe, are you afraid of worms? 'Cause my mom is. I always have to bait her hook while she turns her head away."

"I have to admit that I am a little squeamish, too, but I'm willing to give it a try if you are."

"Girls!" Jake teases. "Deal, and I'll even bait your hook."

"Deal. That's an offer I can't refuse."

As we approach the end of our trek around the lake, I pause for a final look back. The fishing cabins sit silent, almost mournful in their vacancy. I try to imagine what it must have been like in its heyday with fishing boats dotting the lake and fishermen relaxing on the decks together in the cool summer evenings, each vying to top the other's fish story.

Mogul has again reached the limits of the retractable leash, and Jake reels in the rambunctious pup. "I better get Mogul back to his pen." He tugs at the resistant dog, turning in the direction of the barn and waving a silent goodbye.

I turn and follow the path to the lodge.

18

A Visit from Edna

That evening Edna and I cuddle on the cushioned glider in my private garden. We sit under the warmth of a hand-knitted blanket she carried tucked under her arm while balancing a tray of hot tea and a warm loaf of banana bread.

The star-studded sky provides a ceiling of indescribable beauty, as Leigh promised. But for all the warmth and goodwill tucked into Edna's gesture, I sense a purpose for her visit. Something is troubling her.

Intuition tells me it has something to do with the heated argument I observed between Charlie and Leigh when I returned from the lake.

I overheard Leigh explaining to Charlie that he needed to speed up the work on the cabins. He replied that he was working as fast as he could, but he needed more help. It was one of those awkward moments where momentary paralysis is replaced by an inadequate apology as I stumbled around the corner returning to my room.

At dinnertime, Charlie was missing from the table. The conversation was limited to small talk until Jake asked about Charlie's absence. Edna fidgeted in her chair and explained that she fixed Charlie a tray so he could eat his dinner in front of the TV to watch a baseball game. In an effort to change the subject, Edna offered Jake a second helping of fried chicken. His eyes lit up like he had hit the lotto. He wasted no time snagging a second fat drumstick before his mother could object.

Leigh began to clear the table and reached for Jake's plate. He grabbed for the drumstick knocking the plate from his mother's hand. It landed with a crash spilling the contents across the table.

Following the clean-up, Edna interceded over our protests with orders to "skedaddle!" I declined Leigh's invitation to join Jake and her on the deck, sensing her need to be alone with her son, using the pretense of returning to my room to do research for the article.

Edna's troubled fingers work the knotted tassels of the blanket. "I want to explain the argument you witnessed between Charlie and Leigh today, Miss Nevy." She heaves a sigh. "Sometimes Charlie and Leigh butt heads. We work, live, and play together twenty-four/ seven and..."

I reach to give her hand a comforting squeeze to put her at ease. "My previous boss and I were a lot like that, Edna. I understand."

"Thank you, Nevy. You see, my Charlie," she says shaking her head, a crooked smile appearing on her face, "is a perfectionist when it comes to his work. He is a true craftsman. But Leigh is under a tight schedule to finish the remodeling so we can start earning income. That can cause conflict, especially after Leigh spent the afternoon going over the books and seeing all the money going out and nothing coming in. So, every once in a while, they get their feelings hurt when they disagree over things. They'll make up; they always do."

"But then you're caught in the middle of the two, aren't you?"

"Oh, I don't mind," Edna's voice wavers. "I wish I could help more. Since Grandpa Jake passed, all the responsibility has fallen upon Leigh. It must feel like the weight of the world to her with no family here to help share her worries. Charlie and I love Leigh and Jake like family, but there is only so much we can do."

"Do you have family nearby, Edna?"

"Not nearby, I'm afraid. Our son, Nathan—our only child—is career military, a graduate of the Air Force Academy." Her expression reflects her pride. "He's currently stationed at Ramstein Air Base in Germany. He married a local girl there, Elsa. They have two children, Lilly, who's three, and Max who's six. We only get to see them twice a year; Christmas, when we travel to Germany, and in the summer when they visit us here." Edna swats away a tear.

"That must be heartbreaking being separated by so many miles."

She heaves a sigh. "Yes, thank goodness for our weekly visits on Skype, but it's not the same as those hugs and kisses." Edna pauses in thought and continues. "In fact, Nathan is the reason we moved to Blue Eagle."

"How so?"

"When we received the news that Nathan had been assigned to Bagram Air Base in Afghanistan, we were beside ourselves with worry!"

"Oh, Edna, I can't imagine!"

"Worried us to death! Then, during a conversation with a rancher friend, we learned about Grandpa Jake needing a couple to manage the fishing camp so he could devote more time to his ailing wife. We didn't have any responsibilities holding us in Grand Junction, so we figured it might be the answer to keeping us too busy to dwell on our worries about Nathan. Best decision we ever made."

"How fortunate for Jacob to find you."

"No, we were the lucky ones. Miss Elizabeth and I bonded immediately, which was a great relief to Jacob. After a time, he graced me with the privilege of caring for her while he helped Charlie with the fishing camp.

"We spent many treasured moments together, Miss Elizabeth and me. I think it brought her comfort to share her concerns with another woman, much as she revered her Jacob."

"She was blessed to have you, Edna."

"No, Miss Nevy, I was the one blessed. Never once did I hear her complain about her condition." Edna shares a sad look. "Cancer, and believe me, that sweet lady suffered. The only worries she expressed were centered around her Jacob and Leigh and what would happen to them when she was gone. She was such a tiny thing, but she was the pillar of the family, an amazing woman." Edna smiles in fond remembrance. "But there were joyful moments, too. Elizabeth loved to share her stories about Leigh's visits to the fishing camp when she was a kid. She was quite a wild child. Each year, her parents would ship her out to Elizabeth and Jacob to spend the summer."

"Wild child, really? She seems so composed and in control."

"She carries a heavy load these days, Nevy, with the responsibility of the lodge and raising Jake as a single mom." A grin creeps across Edna's face. "Oh, how Elizabeth would laugh, telling me about Leigh's visits. She said Leigh was underfoot all the time either knee-deep shoveling cow manure in the barn with her Papa Jake or elbow-deep in pie dough in the kitchen with her Nana. Leigh soaked up their attention like a dry sponge."

Edna pauses in memory as we sway to the glider's motion. "Elizabeth liked to say that Leigh could wrap Papa Jake around her little finger like no one else, and often teased him about the 'other woman' in his life. What a joy she brought to them."

"She was a lucky little girl to have been surrounded by so much love, Edna."

"Yes, I think they tried extra-hard to fill her life with love. You would think being an only child, Leigh would be spoiled rotten, but she was all sweetness, according to her Nana, a miracle considering how she was raised." Edna shifts in the glider, pulling the blanket about her shoulders as the evening's coolness settles around us.

I reach to tuck the blanket about her, asking, "Not a good home life?"

"Well, you see, her daddy, Andrew—or Drew is what everyone calls him—could not wait to move away from Blue Eagle after college. He chose hotel management as his major, giving his parents the assumption that he would return home to help them fulfill their dream of turning the fishing camp into a full-fledged lodge. Broke his parents' hearts when he took the job in New York City. They kept hoping he would change his mind, but the move to Florida convinced them he was never coming back."

"Leigh mentioned that both Jake and she were born in Florida. That's a long way from Colorado."

"A world away. He hated the job in New York City, but then he met Mr. Richardson, the owner of a golf resort in Florida, while attending a conference. Mr. Richardson apparently took a liking to Drew and, a year or so later, offered him the position of reservations manager at his resort. Drew jumped at the opportunity to leave New York. A few years after that, the general manager retired, and Mr. Richardson offered the position to Drew."

Edna shifts in the glider to face me. "That Drew. He was pretty full of himself when he got the promotion, but he met his match when Charlene, Leigh's mama, set her sights on him." Edna chuckles.

"This sounds intriguing." I encourage Edna to continue.

"Drew might be a smart businessman, Nevy, but he sure is short on common sense when it comes to women. Charlene is a real looker and oozes southern charm when it's to her advantage. She was the hostess in the resort's restaurant when Drew was hired."

I give Edna a teasing nudge. "Not your favorite person, I take it?"

Edna frowns. "Shame on me. I shouldn't be talking about her, but she has a way of getting under a person's skin like no other person I have ever met. I've tried to be kind to her, knowing her background and all, but she's a true test of one's patience."

My curiosity piques. "Her background?"

"Charlene grew up barefoot poor in rural Florida, a real embarrassment for her. So she's created a much more favorable made-up version of herself." Edna's voice trails off as she reaches for her cup to take a sip of tea. "There are some people in this world, Nevy, who are so...self-centered, if you know what I mean." Edna shares a sideways look.

"I've met a few." I nod in confirmation.

The swaying glider creaks to-and-fro filling the silence. "Long story short, it wasn't long before Drew and Charlene were engaged and married. Word is she lorded over the resort like the Queen Bee! She never did take much interest in Leigh who was raised by a variety of housekeepers and resort staff rather than her own parents. Her father was too consumed with running the resort, and Charlene was too busy with her social agenda. Leigh's visits with her grandparents were the highlight of her year where she could bask in their attention and adoration."

Edna leans her shoulder next to mine and bends her head to ask, "Are you sure you want to hear this, honey? I don't mean to be bothersome, but it's a great comfort being able to share these concerns with you."

Memories of Grandmater's wise words flutter through my thoughts. I turn to reassure her. "I love visiting with you, Edna, and I want you to know that anything you tell me will be held in utmost confidence. That's one of the most important lessons my beloved grandmother taught me."

She shares a grateful smile and continues her story. "Years passed, and it was time for Leigh to go to college. She chose to major in hotel management like her daddy. But between Leigh and her grandparents, the real plan was always to move to Colorado to help her grandparents realize their dream of converting the fishing camp into a full-fledged lodge, but then everything changed." Edna's voice quivers.

"Changed how?" I whisper.

"Miss Elizabeth was diagnosed with breast cancer during Leigh's last year of college, but...Elizabeth and Jacob decided to keep the news from Leigh. Their intent was to shield her from worry."

"Oh no. Just when they needed her the most."

"Yes, Leigh was devastated at graduation when they suggested she get some experience at her daddy's resort before moving to

Colorado. She took it as a rejection from the two most cherished people in her life. With no other prospects in sight, she had no alternative but to take a job at the resort."

"I take it things didn't go well?"

Edna arches her eyebrow in my direction. "Depends on who you ask. You see, Miss Charlene got it into her head to do some matchmaking between Leigh and Bryce, the grandson of Mr. Richardson. The Richardsons are old money, Nevy, the royalty of the town. Uniting these two in marriage would give Charlene membership to the social elite of the town, something she could never accomplish on her own."

"And she succeeded." I sigh.

"Beyond her wildest dreams. Leigh was no match between the two of them, Charlene and Bryce. According to her Nana, Leigh was unaware of the beautiful woman she had become. Her focus had always been graduating and moving to Colorado. She had dated a little in college, but never anyone like Bryce, a smooth operator, if you know what I mean. He's a charmer like Charlene, two peas in a pod, and he was smitten with Leigh."

I nod my head in understanding. "I take it they achieved their separate goals?"

"She sure did. Nana and Papa Jake were shocked when they opened the mail to find an invitation to Leigh's wedding. You see...Leigh was pregnant. Charlene couldn't have been happier, but the Richardsons, not so much." Edna's shoulders sag in resignation.

"All their dreams shattered," I murmur.

"Poor child. Then on her wedding day, Leigh happened to overhear her mother sharing the news about Mrs. McLean's illness while explaining their absence at the wedding with the new in-laws."

"How devastating."

"Leigh was heartbroken to learn of her Nana's illness and filled with guilt for blaming them for breaking their promise to her."

"This is so sad, Edna."

"Yes, and Bryce couldn't have been less understanding." Edna twists the blanket tassels between her clenched hands. "Little by little, he stripped away Leigh's self-confidence and free spirit. We could see it during her visits here with her Nana, but we were powerless to do anything and too overcome with grief over Elizabeth to take action."

"It must have been heart-wrenching for all of you."

"It was, and the bad news kept coming." Edna winces. "Jake was born prematurely and required a lot of medical attention. You can tell that he's small for his age, nine years old. Bryce couldn't accept a son who was anything but perfect, him being a macho sports guy and all. He teased that little boy relentlessly under the guise that he was trying to toughen him up."

"That's just evil."

"Isn't it? But one day," Edna grits her teeth, "Bryce went too far. Leigh had left Jake home with him to run errands. When she returned, she found Jake cowering in a corner of the room with Bryce looming over him, screaming nasty words about Jake ruining a football game recording."

"What a..."

"Yes, indeed. A real horse's you know what!" Edna exclaims. "But something snapped in Leigh that night; a flicker of her old self set her in motion. She called Papa Jake, packed a bag, and that night, she and Jake were on a plane headed to Colorado."

"That couldn't have gone over too well with her mother."

"Lordy, no! Her mother was enraged. She blamed Leigh for destroying their lives, and Drew let Charlene rant, never once coming to Leigh's defense."

"Not even for Jake?"

Edna shakes her head in silence. "It was Papa Jake who helped Leigh with the divorce and custody of Jake. Bryce was elated, especially when Leigh agreed to no child support or support of any kind. Bryce had convinced his family that Jake was not his son, with Jake looking so much like Leigh and not Bryce. He told them she tricked him into marrying her. They never approved of the marriage to begin with, so this was an easy out for the family. It wasn't too long before Drew was asked to seek employment elsewhere. He found a job running a small hotel in upstate New York. I bet Miss Charlene is freezing her southern hiney off!"

I giggle at the vision Edna's description creates as she, unable to hold in her frustrations, erupts into chuckles as well.

"Oh my, that felt good." Edna casts a guilty look in my direction and continues. "Even though the years were heartbreaking with the passing of Miss Elizabeth and, later on, Jacob, there was lots of joy. Jake brought so much light, love, and laughter to us. He has been a godsend."

"I know what you mean. Children can be the magic elixir to shake the blues away."

Edna exhales. "I didn't mean to take up your evening, Miss Nevy. Thank you for listening to an old woman's concerns. I hope you'll understand some of the tension you observed. Leigh has lost the two most important people in her life and inherited the full responsibility of making their lifelong dream come true. Failure is not a consideration for her."

Placing my hand over Edna's folded ones, I confide, "I have personal experience of losing loved ones like that. I've found that in time, if you are open to it, the heavens put special people in your world who help you find your way again. You are one of those special people, Edna." I lean my head against her soft curls.

"Bless you, sugar. I think you're one of them, too. Now, time for the two of us to call it a night." Edna folds the blanket as I take a last glimpse at the star-studded heavens and whisper a silent thanks to Grandmater for her wisdom and the lessons she shared with me.

Following Edna's lead, I climb the steps into the suite and wish her a good night.

19

Return to Prophecy

Silence blankets the lodge as I awaken before sunrise, filled with anticipation about a return visit to Prophecy. The room has grown chilly during the night. I scramble into my fleece robe and tiptoe across the room to light the globe lamp and gas fireplace and settle into the oak rocking chair.

Warmth and light fill the room as I take up the journal and pen that await my attention, returning to the morning ritual of free-writing to stoke my thoughts for the article.

Balancing the journal on the rocker's wide wooden arm, I begin with the first thoughts that come to mind. *A new day dawns, Grandmater, full of promise and discovery, perhaps even a meeting with the reclusive Ruby..."*

Consumed with writing, I lose track of time until I hear the sounds of the household coming to life. The hardwood floor outside my room creaks with the sound of passing footsteps.

Yearning for a cup of Edna's coffee, I shower and change into jeans and a flannel shirt. I'm thankful for the hiking boots I thought to bring and retrieve the down-filled vest, jacket, and knit hat Leigh loaned me. I exit the room and follow the rich aroma of brewing coffee.

"Good morning!" I chirp when I enter the cozy kitchen.

Charlie, seated at the family table, peeks above the morning paper. "How do, Miss Nevy."

Edna turns from the griddle of sizzling bacon and skillet of sunny-side-up eggs. "Good morning, sunshine." She flashes an infectious grin.

Jake sits at the table, slipping a piece of bacon to Mogul, who sits in rapt attention at his side. He places a finger to his mouth, causing me to giggle at the conspiracy taking place.

"Grab a plate from the table, Nevy. Breakfast is ready."

"My tummy is doing flip-flops over that heavenly smell, Edna." I say, following her directions. "I see we have an additional guest at the table this morning," I tease.

A door closes upstairs, and footsteps advance down the steps, sending the trio of conspirators into action. Jake latches onto Mogul's collar, and Charlie springs to lead Jake and Mogul outside as Edna commandeers the door as lookout. All three resume their posts just before Leigh enters the room, oblivious to the silence that reigns except for Mogul's pathetic whine.

"Shame on you guys for letting me sleep. You know I wanted to get an early start to Denver." She places a gentle hand on Charlie's shoulder, who responds with a loving pat on her hand.

Edna glances in their direction, affection covering her face, her mending of hurt feelings achieved.

Charlie folds the paper and lays it on the table. "I reckon it's going to be a long day for you, Leigh, talking to them banker fellers so we figured an extra half-hour of sleep would do more good than fighting rush hour traffic into the city."

Leigh grimaces. "Either the traffic is getting worse, or I'm getting spoiled the longer I'm out of it." Switching subjects, she asks, "Charlie, you do plan to give that fellow...what's his name?"

"Chris, Chris Mitchell," Charlie replies.

"Yes, you plan to give Mr. Mitchell a call today, right?"

"Number one priority on my list." Charlie nods.

"Remember," Leigh warns, "no commitments until I get the okay from the folks at the bank, right?"

"Yes, ma'am. I sure hope he's available. There's some other guys I could hire, but Chris is the best, a real craftsman. Not too many of them left."

"Oh, Lordy." Leigh sighs with a wry smirk. "Not another one."

"Darlin', you'll thank me in the end. The way these guys are putting up some of this construction these days, slapping things together—"

"Okay, you two." Edna waves the spatula in their direction.

Both chuckle and answer contritely at the same time. "Yes, Miss Edna."

"Leigh, you tell 'em we've already got folks knocking down our doors wanting to stay at the lodge." He turns to me with a wink. "The sooner we can hire Chris and his crew, the faster we can open."

"I hate this part of the business." Leigh winces. She turns to her son and instructs, "Jake, you need to stick around Edna today." She peers at him with a wrinkled brow, anticipating a reply.

The frown on his face reveals his displeasure. "Mom," he protests, "that means I have to stay inside 'cause Edna spends all day doing house stuff." His shoulders sag in defeat. But then his eyes twinkle with inspiration. "Nevy, what are you doing today?"

"Oh, no." Leigh waves her finger at her son. "No fair involving Nevy in this."

"In all sincerity, I would love for him to join me on my hike to Prophecy today, if it's okay with you, Leigh?"

Jake nods in excitement, his mop of hair flying in all directions. "Me and mom—"

"Mom and I," his mother corrects.

"Yeah, we, um, Mom and I..." He peers at his mother, who nods her approval. "We hike up to Prophecy sometimes. I know the way real good." Jake flashes Edna a flirtatious grin. "Maybe Edna could pack a picnic for us...and we could take Mogul too." He teeters on his tiptoes and awaits his mother's response.

Leigh asks, "Nevy, are you sure about this?"

"Absolutely!"

"Yes!" He fist pumps in triumph.

"Jacob, listen to me." Leigh's stern address settles her rambunctious son. "Take Mogul's leash with you, and before you reach Miss Ruby's, I want you to attach that leash and keep it on until you return home. I don't want to worry about that wild thing bothering her or running off on you up there. Do not," she pauses for emphasis, "go beyond the town. Remember what Charlie told you about those abandoned mines?"

Jake looks in Charlie's direction, who confirms Leigh's orders with a solemn nod.

"Yes, ma'am, I promise." He inches two steps closer toward the door.

Leigh crosses the kitchen and stoops to lock eyes with her son, continuing in a serious tone. "And where do you think you are going without giving me my morning hug?" She breaks into a wide grin while grabbing her son in a bear hug. "Gotcha!" She tousles his thick head of hair.

"Mom!" Jake protests. "I told you I'm too old for that stuff." He combs his fingers through his hair and turns toward the door.

"Hold on there, partner." Charlie reaches for his Stetson. "I'll help you get the leash down from the hook. See ya, loves." Charlie waves as they exit the kitchen.

"What a whirlwind. I'll give him strict orders before I leave, Nevy. He'll be a good guide. He knows the trails as well as any of us. I have a suspicion that he knows a lot more about Prophecy than I want to admit. Just stick to the trails and town. Whatever you do, do not go beyond the boardinghouse. The hills above are loaded with old mines and caved in shafts."

"Please don't worry. I take your warnings very seriously," I reassure her.

"I wish I could join you. It is going to be a beautiful day."

My heart aches at her forlorn expression.

Jake and Mogul create a cloud of dust as they scamper together at the beginning of Miners' Alley.

"Jake, are you sure you can control that wild critter on the walk?"

"He'll settle down once we start walking. He hates standing still like I do," Jake replies, hopping from foot to foot.

"Well then, let's head 'em out." I flash a smile in his direction.

Jake bends to unleash Mogul. He races up the gravel and dirt road, stopping on occasion to check that we're following.

"I know a shortcut we can take that'll save a lot of time." Jake points in a diagonal direction.

"Hmm, probably better stick with the plan we made with your mom. Did she talk to you about that?"

Jake hangs his head. "Yes, ma'am. I take orders from you, not give them," he murmurs, talking more to himself than to me.

"It's tough being the youngest one all the time, isn't it?" I look down at his bent head. "That's how it was when I was growing up, too. I get it."

"Yeah, it's okay." He raises his head, smiling. "At least I got to come."

What a sweet fellow, I think to myself, recalling Edna's description of the love and light that he brings to their lives. "That's the spirit, Jake."

"Hey, let me help you with that backpack." I reach to take the heavy bag from his shoulder. "Oh my gosh, did Edna pack the kitchen sink, too?" I frown, exaggerating the weight of the bag.

Giggling, he replies, "I think she put the stove and refrigerator in there too! We can take turns carrying it," he offers.

"Deal." We high-five and continue up the road. The grade becomes steeper and rock-strewn; my low-lander lungs begin to feel the effect of the change in altitude and thinning air.

Our path is interspersed with alternating sunshine and shadow created by the towering pine trees that dot the trail. Clusters of roadside pink alpine daisies, their bright yellow faces pointing in our direction, watch our progress.

In the quiet of the morning, each noise is punctuated; chipmunks skittering across the needle carpet, a chorus of songbirds hidden in the pine trees, the crunch of gravel beneath our feet, my labored breathing.

The lodge and out-buildings grow smaller, reduced to a collection of umber-colored rectangles and squares; the flower-filled meadow fades into a Monet painting, gracing the valley floor.

The beauty that towers before us is breathtaking. The unblemished sky provides a brilliant backdrop for the glistening snow-capped peaks of the high country beyond.

I stop to catch my breath. "Wow, Jake, look at that sky. I don't see a cloud in it."

Jake squints as his gaze follows my pointed finger. "I like it better when there are puffy white clouds in the sky. So you can play the cloud guessing game, taking turns guessing what each cloud looks like. Me and mom er... Mom and I do that on our walks."

"You two are pretty close, aren't you?"

His voice fills with compassion. "We're best buddies. I have other friends, too, but Mom, she doesn't have anybody 'cept Edna and Charlie...I mean anybody her age."

"I know what you mean. No offense to Edna and Charlie, but sometimes it's nice to have a friend your own age.

His look melts my heart. "Maybe you could be Mom's friend."

"I would be honored to be your mom's friend, Jake, but that's something that comes naturally, so we'll let your mom decide, okay?"

His cowboy hat bobs in agreement.

"So, trail guide, how much farther until we reach Ruby's cabin?" I scan the road ahead.

Jake points. "Do you see that curve up ahead? That's the first switchback, so not much farther."

"Already? I think you better leash Mogul. Where did he go?" My voice grows with concern as I search the road for the missing pup.

Jake places two fingers to his lips and gives an ear-piercing whistle. "Mogul, come here boy!" Mogul bounds down the road, creating a cloud of dust and screeches to a halt in front of Jake, who quickly fastens the leash to Mogul's collar.

"Impressive, Jake. Do you think you could teach me to whistle like that?" I reach to scratch the pup's head.

"I could try." Jake shares a dubious look, making me laugh.

"I wonder how far we've walked?" I turn to glance behind us at the winding road we've been following.

"I know it's half-a-mile to Ruby's cabin. Mom and I checked it the day we drove up when Ari told us Ruby was sick. Edna fixed a basket of food for her, but she wasn't home. So we left the basket by her door."

"That was a nice thing for you to do. Did she thank you for it?"

"Naw, Ruby doesn't talk much to anybody but Ari. But the next day, I hiked up to see if the basket was still there and guess what?"

"What?"

Ruby was sitting on the porch in her rocker, looking through the magazine and eating one of Edna's cookies we put in the basket."

"What's she like?"

Jake tilts his head in thought.

She's really old, 'cause her face is all wrinkly like." He scrunches his face in imitation as I stifle a chuckle. "And she wears her hair in a long white braid. She likes different colored clothes and funny hats. The day I saw her, she was wearing a winter hat, the kind with the furry ear flaps like hanging bunny ears." Jake mimes the ears. "But she didn't look scary or mean like the kids say."

"Did you try talking to her?"

"No, just watched. She has a pretty smile like she was happy just sitting there looking through Mom's magazine."

"I wanted to tell Mom, but I knew she would be angry that I came up here by myself. She's always worrying that I'm going to fall into a mine shaft, even though they have all told me a hundred million times to be careful!" Jake gives an exasperated sigh. "I wish she would trust me."

"You can't take the worry out of a mom, Jake. My mom still does the same thing to me, and I'm all grown up. Better get used to it."

"Yeah, I guess. Anyway, I think Ruby saw me because she glanced over to where I was hiding, but I'm not sure because then she looked back at her magazine and kept rocking."

"Maybe we'll be lucky, and she'll be home today. Let's go see."

As we round the switchback, Ruby's cabin comes into view, but as before, there's no sign of her. Respecting her privacy, we continue our journey, but with eyes and ears alert to any sighting of the elusive old woman.

We round the second switchback. "How about a water break and a short rest, Jake? I am tuckered out."

"It's the altitude," he explains. "You have to take it easy your first time up. It gets easier, I promise."

Gratefully, I plop onto the white-washed skeleton of a fallen Bristlecone pine. "Come join me, Jake." I pat the spot next to me and offer a bottle of water. Mogul settles beside him, his head on Jake's leg.

"What can you tell me about the town of Prophecy, Jake?"

He considers my question, and in an unassuming manner replies, "Not much more than Charlie told you, but there's a book in the library with old pictures of what Prophecy used to look like." He offers Mogul the last of his water.

"Is that right? That's just what I need. I'll be sure to look for it when I visit the library this week."

Jake chuckles. "Our library isn't like a regular library, Nevy. We go to Georgetown for that. It's more like a homemade library. You'll see what I mean when you go."

"Hmm, you've piqued my curiosity. I can't wait to visit. But right now…" I jump to my feet. "Let's go check out the old town for ourselves!"

Jake and Mogul wait patiently at the crest of the ridge as I trudge behind. I pause when I reach them with my hands on my hips for a breath of air, scanning the vista before me. The scene is surreal, like looking at a set of an old western movie.

I realize that my first impression of the size of the town was misguided. From this viewpoint, I can see more accurately the multi-levels of terrain that the town was built on.

The two-story boardinghouse, along with several single-story buildings, sit high on the second ridge, looking down upon the original crumbling log structures built at the base of the bowl clustered near the stream. Additional remains, with an occasional intact building of log construction, are scattered haphazardly, clinging to the hillside below the boardinghouse, each level of construction representing a new phase as the town grew.

Jake points to the slopes above the boardinghouse. "See those yellow-colored waste rock piles up beyond the boardinghouse, Nevy? Those are the abandoned mines and shafts Charlie warned us about."

"There sure are a lot of them."

"Yeah, and those are the ones you can see. The hills are full of them. That's why they're off-limits." We share a silent nod, wide-eyed at the lurking danger.

A worn path leads from the ridge into the bowl. "Best to stick to the path, Jake. Mogul and you can lead since you know the way."

The roar of the tumbling stream becomes louder as we near the base of the bowl. We continue to follow the path as it winds its way toward the opposing ridge where the boardinghouse sits, stopping to peer into a log cabin. "Not much to see," Jake pipes.

"Maybe not with your eyes, but what does your imagination see?" I grin.

"Hmm," he ponders, the wheels turning at my challenge.

"Maybe... this is where Old Pappy Young used to live when he moved to Prophecy, and he hid his map under the floors somewhere...and that's what the ghost of Pappy Young is looking for at night when people see the light of his lantern moving around Prophecy."

"Much better description, but it gives me the chills. So, who told you these ghost stories, Jake?"

"My best friend, Ethan, for one. He saw Old Pappy with his own eyes!" He stares at me wide-eyed.

"What did he see?"

Jake gives me a wary look. I place my hand over my heart. "I promise not to tell anyone. Honest." I share a solemn expression.

"So...one day, Ethan and his older brother, Ryan, walked up to the boardinghouse to join some of Ryan's friends. It's where the older guys go to smoke cigarettes."

I nod, encouraging him to continue.

"Ryan was supposed to be watching over Ethan while their parents were in Denver at a wedding. Ryan really wanted to join his buddies, so Ethan swore he wouldn't tell if he could go along. Ryan didn't have much of a choice, so he let Ethan go. But, when they got to the boardinghouse, the older guys made Ethan sit across the room by the window as lookout for them."

"Hmm, not such a good deal after all."

"No, Ethan said it was pretty boring sitting there watching the older guys laughing and having fun. It was starting to get dusk out, and Ethan was worried about getting home before his parents." Jake's voice becomes ominous. "That's when he spotted a flicker of light outside the window."

I grab Jake's arm. "What did he do?"

"First, he tried to get the guys' attention, but they were talking and laughing so hard they couldn't hear him. So, he slowly raised his head and peeked out the window. He said he almost fainted, because there was Old Pappy walking down the porch!"

"I think I would have fainted, for sure. Did he say what Pappy looked like?"

"He said he only saw the back of him at a distance and that Pappy was walking all hunched over like old people walk. He was wearing a western hat, red shirt, and pants with suspenders. He had a shotgun in one hand and a lantern in the other, and a backpack on his back with miner's tools, shovel, pickaxe, and other stuff sticking out.

"Did any of the other guys see him?"

Jake sighs. "No, by the time Ethan got their attention, Pappy had disappeared. They ran outside and checked around the buildings, but he was gone."

"That's quite a story. Do you believe him?"

"Yeah. Like I said, he's my best friend. His face was real serious when he was telling me, and he acted kinda scared, too."

"If these old walls could talk, right, Jake?" I glance around the four walls and up at the blue sky. "Hey, what happened to the roof of this cabin?"

"Charlie says that a lot of these first cabins had canvas roofs made out of the tents the miners brought to live in first. There weren't any motels around when they first arrived, Nevy." He chuckles at my expense as the mood changes to light-hearted.

"Very funny." I join in his laughter. "Let's go check out the town for ourselves."

We've reached the final climb to the boardinghouse. Jake turns with a look of concern on his face. "Do you think you can make it up the ridge, Nevy?"

"You betcha." My affirmation belies my doubt.

"See you at the top, then!" Jake shouts as he and Mogul turn to lead the way.

"Stick to the trail!"

His head bobs in agreement.

They wait for me on the boardinghouse porch. I plop down on its weathered steps, which give a great, mournful creak, mimicking my physical state at the moment. "Whew, I made it! What a view. I feel like we just landed in a time machine back to the nineteenth century.

"Yeah, pretty awesome. Thanks for letting me come today, Nevy. Mom doesn't like going this far. We usually turn back at the first ridge."

"I enjoy your company, Jake. I'm so glad Mogul and you could join me today." Mogul thumps his tail on the wooden porch at the mention of his name. "This looks like a perfect spot for our picnic, and I'm starving. Let's see what surprises Edna packed for us."

He joins me on the step as we spread the red and white checkered tablecloth on the porch and empty the backpack of its contents: country-fried chicken, brown-sugar baked beans, homemade biscuits, and Edna's famous blue-ribbon apple pie. Edna thought of everything, including the paper plates and plastic utensils.

Without delay, we dive into Edna's feast sharing pieces of our bounty with Mogul.

"Oh my." I lean against the porch support. "I can't eat another bite. Should we save the dessert for later?"

"Yeah, I'm stuffed too." He pats his stomach. "Let's do some exploring."

We quickly stow the remains of our lunch into the backpack.

"Follow us, Nevy." Jake motions. "We can start with the buildings at the end and work our way back."

The first structure is built using vertical frame construction that's precariously tilting horizontally. The wooden roof is intact but curling severely at the edges. We peer into the window opening and look at the darkened interior. It's empty, except for the decaying remains of what was once a bar now caved at one end, appearing more like a slippery slide rather than its original purpose.

"This must have been the saloon, Jake."

"Saloon?" he repeats with a questioning look.

"Sorry, that's probably not a word in your vocabulary. It was like a tavern or a pub where the miners would go for a drink after work, a beer or maybe a whiskey."

"You mean a bar where they serve beer, a beer joint, Charlie calls them."

"Yes, that's exactly what I mean. Let's move on to the next building. It looks a little safer." I cast a wary eye at the support posts bracing the aging structure.

The next building is much smaller and built of logs with a pitched shingle roof. There's one window and door opening in the front and a tiny window opening in the rear as we circle around. "Any idea what they might have used this building for, Jake? It's very small."

He shakes his head. "No clue."

"Let's save the boardinghouse for last," I suggest, passing it by to reach the final building in the line of structures, our footsteps echoing on the wooden porch. Mogul nudges his way between us as we poke our heads through the large window opening. Like the others, it's empty of contents except for rows of lopsided wooden shelving built into the back wall. A century of suspended dust moats caught by a ray of sunshine float through the air.

"I bet this was the general store with those shelves used for canned goods and other items for sale," I guess.

He nods in confirmation, losing interest.

"We saved the best for last. Let's check out the boardinghouse." He backtracks across the wooden porch, Mogul at his side, halting suddenly to exclaim, "Nevy, if you look between the buildings, you can see the old cemetery on the hill."

I catch up with them and stop to observe a steep path winding up the slope to the fenced entrance of the cemetery.

"You see the big monument at the top?" Jake points with enthusiasm. In a ghostly voice, he says, "That's the grave of Old Pappy Young."

Playfully punching his shoulder I reply, "Very funny and creepy." Chills tingle down my spine, not of fright but of the thought of the untold stories hidden in the graves of these original residents of Prophecy waiting to be discovered.

Remembering Leigh's warnings not to go beyond the boardinghouse, I advise, "I think I'll save the cemetery for another day, Jake. After we take a look at the boardinghouse, I think we should head back to the lodge."

"Race you to the boardinghouse, Nevy!"

The ancient plank boards rumble beneath Jake and Mogul's footsteps as I take a more cautious route, meeting up at the boardinghouse doorway.

Jake and Mogul enter first, and I follow. We pause to take a look at the scene before us. It's much larger than the other buildings. A rickety wooden staircase encased in cobwebs climbs to the second floor leading to a long hallway, no doubt, containing the bedrooms of the boarders. Cigarette butts litter the floor, but the dark interior is much the same as the other buildings, devoid of anything but memories.

"Not much to see." Jake sighs in resignation.

"Time to head home anyway, Jake."

We stop to gather the backpack and begin the journey home, turning at the ridge to bid farewell to Prophecy.

"I feel sad to leave the old town all alone, Jake."

"Yeah," he whispers. Cupping his hands to his mouth he shouts, "We'll be back, Prophecy! We promise!" His words echo across the silence of long ago.

20

Edna's Blue-Ribbon Apple Pie

The return down Miners' Alley seems much quicker, and in no time, we spot the rooftop of Ruby's cabin peeking through the trees below.

Mogul screeches to a halt, ears alert. He whimpers a high-pitched whine, turns to look at Jake, then takes off in a run, yanking the leash from Jake's grip. We follow in pursuit, arriving to observe a standoff in progress between Mogul and a prancing, menacing billy goat with his head down, horns bared. Mogul sits on his haunches, emitting pathetic puppy dog howls.

The cabin door crashes open and a flash of color bounds down the porch steps. "Dad-blast you, Sass, escaped from your pen again, didn't you?" The old woman shakes a warning finger at the escapee.

"Ruby," Jake whispers, turning to share a shocked look with me.

In one swift movement, she collars the billy goat with a worn leather belt, gives an authoritative pull, and guides the stubborn goat to his pen. Slinking in shame, Mogul finds refuge cowering between Jake's legs.

Ruby can be heard scolding the billy goat. "Crawled under the fence again, didn't ya? Got dirt all over your nose to prove it, don't go telling me no different." The billy goat utters a clipped "baa" in response. "And don't give me none of your sass! In you go." The gate bangs closed, and Ruby reappears from around the corner of the cabin.

Jake's description of Ruby's fondness for color is no exaggeration. She wears a stocking cap knitted in the colors of the rainbow, a maize-yellow, long sleeve blouse, a chili pepper-red skirt, hunter's gray socks, and buckskin moccasins.

She stares in our direction, hands on her hips, diminutive with the exception of her large hands. I'm reminded of the muscular hands of the dairy farmers' wives grown large from a lifetime of milking. Her face is a map of wrinkles scrunched into an expression of agitation that I surmise has nothing to do with the billy goat.

"Don't need no guard dog with Sass around, but Dolly there is sweet as pie, ain't ya, girl?" Ruby nods in the direction of the pen. The small burro raises her head at the mention of her name and peers shyly in our direction.

I hurry to introduce Jake and myself and make amends. "My name is Nevy, and these are my friends Jake and Mogul. I'm so sorry for the commotion. We know now to keep Mogul on a tighter leash."

"Hmpf," Ruby snorts. "Seen ya yesterday in that red car, looked like you, anyway, with that mop of red hair bouncing up the road towards the ridge."

I stifle a chuckle and confess, "Yes, that was me. Jake volunteered to be my guide today for a closer look at Prophecy. I'm a guest at his lodge, Meadow View."

Ruby points a gnarled finger toward Jake, who moves closer to my side. "Tell your mama thanks for the basket. Mighty fine food." She flashes a crooked grin at Jake.

An idea pops into my head. "I wonder... would you care to join us for another taste of Edna's home cooking to repay for the disruption we've caused you? We saved our dessert from lunch. We have plenty and would be honored to share it with you."

It's Edna's blue-ribbon apple pie," Jake blurts.

"Is that so?" Ruby turns her attention to Jake.

His shyness disappears. "It's the best in the county. You have to try it."

She hesitates, her lips quivering into a tiny smile smitten by the boy's charm.

"Reckon I could try a piece, being that you're so set on me having a taste. Come on up to the porch then while I grab another chair."

We follow Ruby's lead and climb the weathered steps to the porch. Mogul follows in a subdued fashion while Jake and I exchange a surprised look at this turn of events.

"Be right back," she informs, and disappears into the dark cabin.

"We have plates!" I offer to her retreating figure.

Jake shares a shrug in my direction, nearly falling from the porch as the door bangs open at Ruby's practiced kick. She hobbles out, dragging a wooden chair behind her in one hand and a handful of forks in the other.

I spring to hold the door open and use the opportunity to peek inside the cabin. A quick glance reveals a sparsely furnished room with a single bed against one wall and a wooden table with chairs. On the table are a kerosene lamp and a large Bible. A wood-burning stove and stack of wood fill one corner of the room.

Ruby barks a warning. "Let that door be and have a seat." I skitter across the porch, obeying her command.

Ruby slides a footstool with a quick shove with her foot in Jake's direction and settles into her rocking chair.

Jake drags the footstool next to my chair, with Mogul following close behind. Under Ruby's scrutiny, I retrieve the plates and pie from the backpack and divvy up a piece for each of us. Silence reigns as we eat.

Ruby is the first to finish. She licks both sides of her fork and shares her approval. "Yep, I 'kin see why she won first place with this apple pie. Used to make 'em myself a long time ago. Had to make 'em for a living. This here is almost as good as mine." Ruby smacks her lips savoring the last taste of pie.

I can read Jake's thoughts, wondering what Edna would think of Ruby's comparison of pies.

"So, what's your interest in Prophecy?" she snaps, turning to me and catching me off guard.

I tread lightly. "Curiosity, mostly. I read an article in our Sunday newspaper about the beauty of Colorado, and a photo of your cabin was featured."

Ruby's posture stiffens at my words. Her face scrunches as if she is in pain. In a sarcastic voice, she replies, "My, my, so that's what those two yahoos was doing nosing around up here with their cameras. Scared 'em off with my double barrel twelve-gauge. Didn't hurt 'em, but I bet that rock salt stung like the devil. And what are you so curious about?"

"Nevy's writing an article about Prophecy and maybe our lodge too." Jake grins innocently at me.

Ruby's demeanor changes at this news. She leans forward in her rocker with a menacing look and spits out, "Writer? Why, that's worse than a photographer!"

Jake ducks, caught by surprise at Ruby's anger.

I hold my hands up in an attempt to diffuse the situation and try to explain. "I promise to respect your privacy, Ruby. It's the history of Prophecy that I'm interested in."

"Wouldn't go snooping around there, ain't safe. We don't need no tourists traipsing around, disturbing things. Just leave Prophecy be."

"I'm just getting ideas at this stage," I say evasively.

"And leave my property out of it."

"Your property?" Jake turns a questioning look at me. "That's my papa's—"

I squeeze Jake's knee to silence any further comments and hasten to advise, "I think it's time to head back to the lodge, don't you think, Jake? Before they start worrying about us."

Jake takes my lead and jumps from the stool. He is down the steps in a flash. Mogul and I follow with Ruby at our heels.

I turn to offer my hand in goodbye. She hesitates until Jake raises his hand as well.

"Bye, Miss Ruby," he says with a genuine smile.

Her face softens, and she accepts his handshake. "Be sure and tell your mama and Edna thanks for the basket."

I drop my hand and abandon the handshake. "I hope we can visit again, Ruby," I offer.

She responds with a clipped, "Maybe."

With a final wave, we return to Miners' Alley. It's a quiet walk back with each of us lost in our own thoughts about the day's events. As we near Meadow View, Jake stoops to unleash Mogul. We can see Charlie engrossed in a conversation with another man. He gestures with his hands in an animated fashion.

The visitor rests with his back against the side of the cabin, arms folded at the chest, legs crossed at the ankle, western hat cocked below his eyebrows, nodding in response to Charlie.

Mogul hurtles toward the newcomer, who stoops to calm the pup with soothing words and a scratch behind the ears.

"Lordy, Lordy!" Charlie exclaims, catching sight of us. "I was hopin' we wasn't gonna have to call out the search posse for you two. Where you been all this time?" He flashes an ornery smirk in our direction.

Jake has taken refuge behind me, the first sign of shyness I've seen him exhibit.

Ignoring Jake's silence, Charlie continues. "Miss Nevy and Jake, this here is Chris Mitchell. He's going to help us get the lodge up and running. Chris, this is Miss Nevy, our guest at Meadow View visiting from Chicago." Charlie pauses. "And the feller belonging to them arms and legs behind Miss Nevy is Jake, Miss Leigh's son."

He removes his hat and extends his hand in greeting. "A pleasure to meet you, Miss Nevy." His hand encompasses mine with a solid but gentle grip. My eyes travel up the muscular arm to his handsome face, his lips curving into an easy smile. His sun-blond hair has a charming way of falling over his eyes that are the color of the

Colorado sky. In a quick, habitual manner, he combs his fingers through the escaping strands of hair while placing his hat on his head.

He wears business meeting attire: a crisp long-sleeved white western shirt with pearl snap buttons, a pair of deep blue denim pressed jeans, and onyx leather boots that add another two inches to his already tall height. His slim waist is wrapped in a matching leather belt clasped with a large silver and gold eagle-engraved buckle that glints in the daylight sun.

Charlie, unaware of my momentary loss for words while meeting this handsome cowboy, comes to my rescue. "Chris has agreed to accept our offer to help finish the renovations. Miss Leigh called from Denver to give us the okay to get started."

Then, peeking around my shoulder, Charlie growls, "Jake, come on around here and meet Chris yourself."

"Hi there, Jake." Chris extends his hand and stoops to the boy's level.

Jake steps from behind my back and timidly offers his hand in greeting with a whispered hello.

To avert the growing silence, I suggest to Jake that we return to the lodge to share our news with Edna.

Curious, Charlie asks, "What news is that?"

Jake's shyness disappears at Charlie's question. "We met Old Ruby! I'll tell you all about it later."

"Well, I'll be," Charlie blurts in surprise.

I turn to say goodbye. "Chris, so nice to meet you. I'll see you at dinner, Charlie." I turn to follow Jake and Mogul, wondering about Jake's unusual display of shyness. Could it have anything to do with the story Edna shared about Jake's relationship with his father?

21

A Visit to the Library

The next day dawns as beautiful as the previous day. "Paradise." I rejoice, reveling in the scene outside my window.

The lodge is busy with activity. Chris has arrived with his crew, and Charlie has joined them at the cabins. Leigh and Edna are preparing for a day of grocery shopping with a stop at Edna's favorite meat market in Idaho Springs. Jake is joining their ride as far as Ari's, where he'll spend the day.

It's perfect timing for my visit to the library. I can't wait to get my hands on the book of photographs Jake described.

The warped wooden door of the log cabin requires a hardy shove to enter. The historic plaque fastened to the wall outside indicates that the building is over 150 years old. "Take your time, old girl, you've earned the right," I murmur and give the door a gentle nudge this time.

Sunlight floods the dark interior as I enter. An earthy, aged wood smell permeates the structure. A handwritten sign that reads "Honor System" is placed in the center of the checkout desk. My greeting goes unanswered, revealing that I am the only occupant.

"Shoot," I grumble as I survey the surroundings and wonder where to begin my search.

Pathways meander in precarious routes among the rickety metal bookcases and battered cardboard boxes filled with donated books waiting to be shelved.

"Oh my," I whisper at the sight of hand-printed signs directing patrons to the fiction and non-fiction sides of the room. Forget computers; there is no hint of the Dewey Decimal System in use, either. The fiction side has been organized alphabetically by author's name, but the challenge will be in the non-fiction section, where I'm interested.

Where, oh where, to begin, I wonder. It becomes apparent by the wide diversity of topics that the collection has been created primarily from the contribution of local benefactors involved in a myriad of interests ranging from a beginner's book on yoga to a college chemistry book.

This may take longer than I planned, I sigh. Starting with "P" for Prophecy, moving to "B" for Blue Eagle, and "G" for gold, I discover a plethora of books in this category, but not the one I'm searching for.

"Come out, come out wherever you are," I sing to the unresponsive stacks as I meander the narrow aisles. I pause to seek inspiration, and my eyes travel to the top of the shelf where I have stopped. An over-sized book lying on its side juts out beyond the shelf. I stand on tiptoes with my arms and fingers stretched, but the book is out-of-reach.

The door to the cabin lurches open with a great thud. Ben enters like an apparition, highlighted by the rays of sunshine pouring in from outside. In his hand, he holds an aromatic bag from Miss Liddy's Ice Cream and Sandwich Shop.

"Yikes!" I screech, sending Ben tottering on his heels at the sound of my yelp.

"Didn't 'spect no one to be here," he snaps. "Just been gone a couple of minutes. Can't leave this place for a second without someone barging in," he mutters.

Is this not the public library? I think to myself.

Observing his discomfort at being caught derelict of duty, I shift into charm mode. "Ben, I'm so glad you're here. I could use your help." I flash a hopeful look.

Ben's demeanor changes as he assumes the role of librarian. He sets the bag on the desk and walks to my side, perching a pair of wire rim reading glasses on the end of his nose. "How can I be of service to you?" He peers down at me.

"I'm looking for a book that Jake described to me, but I'm not having much luck. It's a book of photographs that contain old pictures of Prophecy in it."

Ben reaches his arm over my head and removes the large book I had spotted on the shelf above. He wipes the dust from its cover with the sleeve of his flannel shirt, and hands it to me. "This what ya' lookin' for?"

I grasp the book with both hands and read the title, "A Look Back at Bygone Days in the Colorado Gold Fields."

Ben explains, "It's a collection of photographs gathered by different folks over the years, then bound together in one collection. Prophecy was the last big strike of its era even though some folks still swear by Old Pappy Young's legend about his discovery of the mother lode."

"Yes, I've heard about Pappy Young."

"Spent his life looking for the mother lode. Legend says he found it but went to his grave with the secret of its location. Lots of legends floating around about lost gold mines. Guess them miners wasn't no different than us fishermen with their tall tales about the one that got away!" He chuckles to himself.

"Thank you for your help, Ben. I was afraid I was going to have to drive to the library in Georgetown to do my research. Your library saves me a lot of time."

His voice softens. "This here is my pride and joy. Spend a lot of time reading these books. Bet you never would've thought so, poor old farm boy and all, but I do. Been doing this now for over ten years. Was my idea...well, along with the professor's to open a library here in Blue Eagle. Volunteered to get it off the ground and been at it ever since." He straightens to his full height."

"Ben, that is so admirable." I attempt to redeem myself in his eyes. "You'll be a valuable resource for me."

He studies me for a moment, then deciding in my favor, replies, "I would be honored to be of assistance."

I glance around the room and spot a table and chair against a wall next to a small window. "That table looks perfect." I point in its direction.

"Yes, ma'am, it is available for your use."

"Thank you. You go ahead and eat your breakfast before it gets cold."

"Don't mind if I do. First food I've had today. You need anything else..." He pauses and gives an ornery grin. "Just give a whistle," and makes a hasty retreat in the direction of his breakfast.

I drop my backpack on the marred wooden table and remove the supplies I've brought: pen, a writing tablet, and my most valuable tool for studying old photographs, a magnifying glass. I place them on the table and settle into the chair.

Silence blankets my surroundings as I begin the journey to the bygone days in the Colorado gold fields. The thrill of anticipation fills my heart. My love for old photographs is rekindled as I cradle the treasured book in my hands. Let's see what secrets we can uncover, Grandmater. I issue a silent plea to my ever-present muse.

With great care, I turn the aged pages and begin scanning the contents. The names of towns, some familiar, most not, flutter by; Animas Forks, Black Hawk, Boreas, Breckenridge. I pause to survey a photograph of girls dancing to the music of the hurdy-gurdy in a dance hall in Breckenridge, circa 1861. I peer closer, using the magnifying glass to study each face, wondering what each story might reveal. This one photograph could fill a month of research.

Realizing I skipped the page for Blue Eagle, I flip to the lone photo dedicated to it, circa 1860, of a group of miners scattered along Clear Creek near the future site of Blue Eagle according to the caption. My excitement builds at the thought that one or more of these men could be the ancestor of Isaiah McLean.

Some of the men stand mid-stream, and others stoop at the water's edge, while several sit on small boulders that line the side of the creek, all busy at the task of panning for gold. Dotting the hillside are a number of small tents pitched in a haphazard fashion.

The men wear their pants tucked into knee-high boots and their shirt sleeves rolled to their elbows. Each wears a brimmed hat of diverse styles, western hats, top hats, anything to protect against the bright Colorado sunshine. All sport long hair and beards, absent access to a local barber shop, Jake would remind me. It's a hodgepodge of styles as diverse as the men who wear them.

I resume my search, pausing to look at several photos devoted to the Cripple Creek Mining District, circa 1900. The photos reveal a bustling metropolis of multi-story brick buildings and clog-filled streets with every conveyance imaginable. A team of horses pulls a stagecoach going in one direction while a trolley car goes in the opposite direction. It's no wonder why Jonah and Isaiah were drawn to this epicenter of the gold mining industry.

A second photograph intrigues me. It reveals a group of miners holding strike signs in front of the Miner's Union Hall in Victor, Colorado, circa 1903.

Charlie was right. This would have been about the time of the boys' quick departure for Blue Eagle.

Unable to contain my curiosity, I fan the remaining pages to locate Prophecy. My heart skips a beat. The photos exceed my expectations.

The first photograph is a panoramic shot of Prophecy. It's like looking at the completed puzzle of the scattered pieces Jake and I witnessed yesterday.

The three levels of Prophecy's development are distinct, revealing a thriving mining town. Fully constructed buildings replace the roofless cabins and crumbled remains. A spider's web of miners' trails laces the steep hillside behind the boardinghouse dotted with tiny human figures and animals.

I utter a muffled, "Wow," when I turn to the next photo, leaning closer for a better look at the boardinghouse and adjacent buildings.

"What's that?" Ben cackles.

"Nothing!" I reply, hoping to keep him in his seat.

"Just give me a yell if ya need anything!"

"Thanks, I'm good for now," I reply, never taking my eyes away from the photograph.

Using the magnifying glass, I'm able to read the signs on the buildings. I chuckle at the discovery of the purpose of the small building squished between Jonah's Tales and Ales and the McLean Boardinghouse. The sign clearly reads "Calaboose," Prophecy's jailhouse conveniently constructed next to the saloon. Good town planning, I think to myself.

The final photograph wins the prize for discovery as I come face-to-face with Isaiah McLean and Jonah LaPierre. The photographer has centered Isaiah and Jonah among a group of men dressed in varying degrees of Sunday suits and top hats. The sign above their heads reveals that they are standing before the new shaft house of the Prophecy Mine.

The numerals "1" and "2" have been handwritten in ink above the figures of Isaiah and Jonah. In the margin of the book is each of their names with the corresponding numerals and the words, "The Prophets."

Isaiah, a tall and slender man, stands ramrod straight, looking uncomfortable in his ill-fitting suit. The sleeves and pant legs expose his bare wrists and ankles, and his expression is filled with a frown.

Jonah stands with his arm casually around Isaiah's shoulder, grinning from ear to ear. His handsome face beams with pride. His top hat sits rakishly pushed to the side of his head, a lock of dark curly hair falling over one eye. He is much shorter than Isaiah, but evenly proportioned and appears very much at ease.

"Jonah LaPierre, I bet you were a charmer," I whisper.

Lost in observation, I'm startled when Ben reaches his lanky frame over my shoulder and points to the photograph. "That there is Isaiah McLean and Jonah LaPierre, owners of the Prophecy Mine. Put Prophecy on the map."

I turn and come nose to nose with Ben, who takes a hop backwards. Giggling, I ask, "What else can you tell me about them?"

"Don't know nothing about that feller, Jonah, 'cept that he and Isaiah met up in Cripple Creek first, then moved to Blue Eagle, where they struck it rich with the Prophecy Mine. When the mine played out, Isaiah started his cattle ranch in Blue Eagle. Don't know what happened to Jonah. Likely moved on like the rest of 'em did when a mine closed." He tugs at his whiskers, scratches an ear, and nods to himself in agreement with his conclusion.

"Ben, would it be possible for me to check this book out for a short time?"

"Check it out? Don't know about that. That there is considered a reference book, limited edition as it is, and not allowed off the premises." His voice fills with righteous authority.

"I don't suppose you have a photocopier?"

He clucks, "Not on our budget!"

You cantankerous stinker, I think to myself as I debate a new strategy. "Would you consider making an exception? I would like to share it with Ari when I have coffee with him in the morning." I had called Ari after Jake's and my visit with Ruby, hoping to learn more about the history of Isaiah McLean and the Prophecy Mine.

Ben ponders his dilemma. "You say you're having coffee with the professor?"

"Yes, tomorrow morning. I'd love to share this treasure you found for me. I think he'll be very impressed."

He chews his lip, pauses in thought, and relents. "Reckon I could make an exception this one time, one day only, twenty-four hours, period, dot!"

"Thanks, Ben." I stand on my tiptoes and give his grizzled cheek a peck.

He backs away, turns, and hurries to his desk, pulling a watch from his bib pocket as I follow behind. He scribbles the words "Due back at 11:37 AM!" on a 3x5 index card and inserts it into the middle of the book.

Baffled, I ask, "Do I need to sign a check-out card?"

"I know where to find ya," he snorts.

Before he has a chance to renege, I slip the book into my backpack. "I'll be sure to tell Ari how much help you've given me today, Ben," and quickly cross the room giving the stubborn door a powerful shove to aid my fast exit.

The bright sunlight is welcome but nearly blinds me as I feel my way back to Red. I promised her a bath, and I could use a few more pieces of clothing suitable for my surroundings. With everyone involved in their own activities, it's a good day to check out the town of Breckenridge.

I make a quick return to the lodge to drop off the precious book for safe keeping, and scribble a note to Edna advising my destination and plans to find a restaurant in Breckenridge for dinner.

I settle into the SUV and program the GPS for Breckenridge. The route looks straightforward, much to my relief. West on I-70, exit 203/Frisco onto CO-95, and follow to Main Street in Breckenridge, about a fifty-five-minute drive.

Traffic is light, and I'm enjoying the view until I spot the sign alerting drivers to the approaching entrance of the Eisenhower Tunnel traversing the Continental Divide. My first tunnel ever. I'm swallowed whole into a world of artificial lighting and tile walls, with only the sound of tires on the pavement to keep me company. The tunnel seems endless.

A glimmer of natural light flickers ahead. "We picked the mother of all tunnels, Red!" I exclaim with relief until I realize we'll need to repeat this route heading east on our return to the lodge.

Lake Dillon, the reservoir for the city of Denver, glistens in blue beauty framed by snow-capped peaks in the distance. It's not easy to keep my eyes on the road into Breckenridge, surrounded by this breathtaking scenery. I spot a drive-through car wash as I approach the town limits and emerge minutes later with Red gleaming in crimson splendor.

There is no comparison between Main Street in Breckenridge and Blue Eagle's Main Street. I marvel at the shops and restaurants waiting to be explored. Breckenridge is a metropolis compared to Blue Eagle.

After several hours of shopping and an early dinner of elk medallions, a local favorite, I take refuge on one of the sun-warmed boulders that line the swiftly flowing Blue River that meanders through the town.

As I sip on a cup of espresso for renewed energy for the drive back to Meadow View, I reflect on the day's events. It's been a good day, a necessary day, to clear my thoughts and rethink the purpose of my article. My phone call to Contessa earlier in the day confirmed my thoughts, call it intuition, to spotlight the McLean history and Prophecy linking it to Leigh's plans to reopen Meadow View as a full-fledged lodge with the intent of generating future customers for her.

Contessa was elated when I shared the information I've learned to date. I'm happy because I'll be going solo from here. Robert and she are about to embark on a fifteen-day Aegean cruise.

22

Coffee with Ari

Rocky Mountain sunshine streams through my bedroom window, Mother Nature's alarm clock. I slide from a mound of a downy quilt with anticipation building over my visit with Ari.

Although his manner is welcoming, I sense a reserve in his demeanor toward me. I'll need to tread lightly if I hope to achieve my goal of learning the history of Isaiah and the Prophecy Mine.

Grandmater's Cookie Tin Lesson floats through my thoughts. "Trust, Nevy, is a precious gem to be earned, honored, and revered."

Edna is removing a tray of cinnamon rolls from the oven, filling the room with a smell close to heaven as I enter her kitchen.

"Good morning, Edna."

"Miss Nevy, what are you doing up at such an early hour?" Edna clucks good-naturedly.

"The sunshine was pouring though my window beckoning me to take advantage of this spectacular day. I'm joining Ari for coffee this morning," I explain.

"He is such an intriguing man, refined, not at all like the western cowboy I was expecting when I walked into his country store." I peek over her shoulder, inhaling deeply, then feigning a light-headed swoon act.

Edna chuckles, entertained by my antics and places a warm cinnamon roll into my open palms. "They're better when they are frosted," she advises.

"Not possible!" I protest through a mouthful of the delicious, flaky roll.

Edna circles back to Ari. "Ari is a true gentleman. Did you know that he was a professor at the University of Denver?"

"Ahh, that explains Ben's nickname for him, but he's originally from Blue Eagle, right?"

Edna settles on the barstool next to mine and reaches for the bowl of frosting and the rack of cooled cinnamon rolls.

"Yes, born and raised here, an only child. Jacob befriended him, becoming more like a big brother to Ari. Jacob understood what it was like to be an only child. His passing caused much heartache for Ari."

"I hope my mention of the fishing camp to Ari that day I stopped to ask for directions didn't bring back sad memories for him."

"No, those would be fond memories. That's where Ari developed his love for fishing. You see, Ari has two loves: fishing and books. Papa Jake told us that when Ari was a kid, you would either find him sitting on the dock with a fishing pole in his hand or sitting under a tree with a book in his hand." Edna smiles in remembrance.

"Then when Ari went away to college out of state, he fell in love with the world of academia. His visits home became infrequent as he pursued his advanced degrees. By then, both of his parents had passed. Jacob attended each of his graduation ceremonies, so proud he was of Ari."

Edna pauses to fill the spatula with another scoop of frosting, then continues her story. "When Ari was hired for the position at the University of Denver, they were ecstatic because they could resume their close relationship. Ari never married, but Elizabeth and Jacob adopted him into their family. He shared every holiday at the ranch and his summer vacation helping with the fishing camp."

"So he really is a part of the family, like Charlie and you."

"Oh, even more so, I would say. We love him dearly."

"I am guessing that when he retired, he decided to return to Blue Eagle?"

Edna chuckles. "That was Jacob's doing. He gave Ari the piece of land the store sits on as a retirement gift and enticement to move back home."

I catch a glimpse at the wall clock and scramble from the barstool. "Oh, my gosh, I'm going to be late."

"He won't mind. Nothing much flusters Ari. Wait one second, sugar, and I'll wrap some cinnamon rolls to go with your coffee. They are his favorites."

As Edna busies herself with her task, my thoughts wander to Ari's discomfort when I asked about Ruby. I've broached a sensitive subject with this man known for his gentle manner.

The pan of warm rolls that I cradle in my arms is a welcome warmth on this cool morning as I follow the shortcut to town that Jake pointed out to me. A chorus of Aspen leaves flutters in the soft breeze, accompanied by the sound of the flowing creek.

The discordant clunk of the cowbell announces my arrival, and Athena prances from behind the counter to investigate, her black hair glistening to a glossy shine. Ari trails behind with brush in hand.

"Athena, stay girl," he issues a gentle command, and she screeches to a halt.

"Good morning, beautiful Athena. Don't you look gorgeous."

Athena whimpers and wags her tail, peering adoringly at Ari, who relents, nodding his okay for her to respond.

I kneel on one knee, and I'm enveloped in doggy licks to the face that I repay with a scratch behind the ears while attempting to balance the pan of rolls with my other hand.

I rise and offer a greeting to Ari. "Good day, Ari. I bring you scrumptious morsels from the manor in trade for a cup of java." I present the tray of cinnamon rolls.

"Ahh, if my nose does not deceive me, that's a tray of Edna's cinnamon rolls. I dare say you have the better of the trades." He smiles broadly. "Allow me to show you to the best table in the house, mindful, of course, that it's the only table in the house." He turns with Athena at his side and proceeds to the rear of the store.

While I unwrap the tray of rolls, Ari disappears into the back room, reappearing with a tray containing a coffee pot, sugar bowl, cream pitcher, a delicate china cup and a heavy mug. Athena settles at the foot of her master as Ari sits in the chair across from mine.

He waits until I've doctored my coffee with cream, then raises his mug to offer a toast. "An official welcome to Blue Eagle, Miss Nevy. I hope your visit goes well."

"How nice of you to make me feel so welcome, Ari."

He turns his attention to the tray of cinnamon rolls. "One for the lady," he pauses, "and the rest for me." He playfully pulls the tray in his direction.

"Edna did say they're your favorite. Bon appétit!"

Ari licks the last of the frosting from his fingertips and confesses. "This far exceeds my usual fare of commercially prepared cupcakes from the store's shelves. Please convey my sincere thanks to Edna." He holds the coffee pot mid-air. "Would you care for a refill of your coffee before we discuss the purpose of your visit? I assume there is another reason than to satiate my sweet tooth?"

I hold my hand up, "no thanks, I've had my quota for the morning. I do confess to an ulterior motive for my visit though, but foremost, is my joy in sharing your company."

Ari nods but makes no comment, instead folding his hands and looking in my direction.

I launch into my explanation. "As I mentioned during my first visit, the purpose of my trip to Colorado and Blue Eagle is to gather research for an article I'm writing for a travel guide venture we've decided to call *Sharing Discoveries.*

"It's my boss's dream to create a guide where others can share information about places and hidden gems they have chanced upon along their journeys. Contessa, my boss, found the article I shared with you about Prophecy. She believes it's a sign to begin with Prophecy as the site chosen for the first publication."

Ari folds his arms across his chest but remains silent. I fidget in my chair under his scrutiny and try to elaborate on my purpose. "The photograph of Ruby's lone cabin contrasted against the backdrop of the formidable mountains piqued my curiosity to learn more about the brave individuals who first settled here. Who were these people, where did they come from, what inspired them or drove them to pursue their dreams, and what were their dreams. Was it to find their fortune, or perhaps something more?"

I pause to catch my breath. "You see, Ari, I am a student of the human condition. It's in my blood. My grandmother, Alma Mater—"

He casts an inquisitive eye in my direction but allows me to finish.

"She was a wonderfully wise woman and writer for our hometown newspaper in Ohio. She nurtured my natural curiosity about people. I have a passion for learning their real-life stories."

Ari rests his elbows on the table, tenting his fingers and resting his chin on them while he contemplates my words.

I retrieve the library book from my backpack and open it to the bookmarked pages devoted to Prophecy. I slide it across the table. "I discovered this at the library yesterday."

Ari studies the photographs.

"Ben has given me twenty-four hours to return it. It's due back at eleven thirty-seven a.m. today, period, dot...or the guillotine!"

A tiny smile appears on his face. "That would be Ben. He takes his position as chief librarian very seriously."

"Have you seen this book before, Ari?"

"Yes, years ago." He sighs. "You are quite a sleuth to unearth it."

"I have a knack for these things, although it was Jake who brought it to my attention."

"May I ask what you intend to do with the information you've uncovered?"

I squirm under his gaze, remembering what it felt like years ago in a lecture hall when asked by my professor to expound on an answer I had given.

"My purpose is to make the story about Prophecy come alive by relating their real-life stories. I have bits and pieces of information, and I was hoping that you might help me tie it all together."

"Yes, I see," Ari stares in my direction with a faraway look in his eyes. "I must warn you, Nevy, to open the story of the Prophecy Mine is to open Pandora's box. I can see no good that would come by the telling of this tale," he warns.

Defeated, I ask, "So you won't help me?" I slump in my chair.

"Will not and cannot, my dear. To do so would be to betray a trust that I have sworn to keep."

He slides the book to me and stands.

Dismissed, I scramble to gather my belongings and stow the treasured book in my backpack, I extend my hand toward him. "Thank you, Ari, for sharing your morning. I hope I haven't offended you in any way."

"No, but I do hope you'll take my words seriously, Miss Nevy." He guides me toward the door. "Give Edna my thanks for the cinnamon rolls. Tell her I'll return the pan later in the week. Have a good day." He opens the door, and the clanking cowbell signals my departure.

I decide to drop the book off at the library on my way back to the lodge so I will be in Ben's good graces. He scrutinizes his timepiece giving me a nod of approval as he stamps the word "RETURNED" on the index card, then turns to toss the card into the wastebasket. Straight-faced, I exit the library.

The walk back to the lodge is filled with emotion. My mind is a jumble of thoughts with no coherent theme. How am I to tell the story of Prophecy now?

The renovation is underway as I return. To my surprise, I catch sight of Jake dragging a piece of two by four lumber to Chris, who waits patiently at the saw table.

Jake spots me and beams with pride. "Nevy, come and see. I'm helping Chris with the renovation!" he shouts in my direction.

Chris has traded his meeting clothes from yesterday for workman's clothes today. Gone is the fine western dress shirt, now replaced with a blue denim work shirt. His sleeves are rolled to his elbows, exposing a pair of muscular arms, and the jeans he wears are faded and worn. A leather tool belt containing a multitude of tools has replaced the crafted leather belt. A pair of scuffed workman's boots and backward-facing ball cap complete the outfit.

"Hi, guys, hope I'm not interrupting?"

"Not at all. Good morning, Nevy." Chris shares an infectious smile.

"Look at the pile of lumber we have already cut, Nevy," Jake boasts.

"That's awesome! I bet Chris is happy to have your help."

"It's my pleasure, ma'am," he replies in a slow western drawl.

"You two make a great pair, but I should let you get back to work." I leave them with heads bent together measuring a piece of lumber to be cut, a background symphony of hammers and saws filling the air.

I observe a puzzling scene when I return to the lodge. A cloud of dust follows a sleek luxury car bouncing down Miners' Alley and entering the lodge driveway. What would a fancy car like that be doing on the mountain road?

It's too beautiful a day to remain inside. I enter my room, grab a bottle of water, retrieve my journal and pen, and exit the French doors to my private garden. I sink into the mound of sun-warmed pillows decorating the glider and soon fall asleep.

An hour later, I awaken to the clanging of Edna's lunch bell, still clutching the unused pen and journal in my hands.

The combination of mountain air and the hike to Ari's this morning has left me feeling famished. I scramble to respond to Edna's call.

I shower my face with a quick splash of cold water and run my hands through my hair in a futile attempt to calm the curls and exit the room.

Charlie, Chris, and Jake are seated at the family table when I enter the kitchen. Edna bustles about in her usual efficient manner, delivering trays laden with sliced meats and loaves of homemade bread. A tureen brimming with tasty soup provides the centerpiece.

"Mm, Edna, what wizardry have you concocted today?" I ask.

Charlie grins at my praise of Edna's cooking. "This here is Edna's Colorado Venison Stew, best in the west. Ain't that right, Jake?"

"Best in the west," he mimics with a loving smile in Edna's direction.

Chris stands to offer a chair at the table for me, as Charlie does the same for Edna.

Edna turns to Jake. "Would you like to say the blessing?"

"Yes, ma'am, but do you think we should wait for Mom?"

"No." Edna shakes her head, appearing a bit flustered by his question. "Your mom said to go ahead without her."

"But where—"

Edna stops Jake mid-sentence with an end-of-discussion look. "She's having a business meeting, that's all I know."

Jake bows his head in prayer, and we follow his lead. Platters are passed, and soup bowls are filled. Charlie and Chris are quick to finish, anxious to return to work. Jake follows in their footsteps leaving Edna and me alone.

"So, Nevy, how was your visit with Ari today? Did you learn anything new about Prophecy?"

I twirl the wooden napkin ring around my finger, biding time for my response. I decide to avoid a retelling of my meeting with Ari. "Not much. It's a mystery how little written information there is about Prophecy. Why is that, do you suppose?"

Edna ignores my evasion and responds, "Yes, you would think that there would be more of a written record. But, you see, these old mining towns were so short-lived. There are several in our area, Montezuma, Saint John, Masontown, to name a few. It was the era of boom and bust for most. The reason Prophecy lives on is because of Pappy Young's legend. If it wasn't for the cattle business, I imagine Blue Eagle would have suffered the same fate." Edna pauses, then adds, "And where would that leave Charlie and me?"

"Fate, Edna. I think this is exactly where you're meant to be." I stand and kiss the top of her head. "I think I'll head back to my room for some writing."

As I leave Edna, I reconsider my plans. A good part of the day remains. It's a good time to take a solo trip to Prophecy to visit the cemetery. I stop in my room to grab my backpack, jacket, and keys, then exit into the hallway heading toward the foyer. Halfway down the hallway, the sound of an unfamiliar voice causes me to pause.

"I hope you'll give my offer some thought, Miss McLean," a high-pitched, grating male voice replies.

Leigh responds, "It's a big decision, Mr. Dunlow. When would you need an answer?"

"A week max; the sooner the better," the man replies in a clipped response.

"Only a week?" Leigh's voice betrays her concern.

"My clients are very motivated and impatient to get started. They have other sites under consideration. I would advise you to act quickly. You have my card, don't hesitate to call. A pleasure to meet you, Miss McLean."

The sound of the entrance door opening and footsteps receding is followed by the sound of Leigh's office door opening and closing.

I experience a moment of premonition accompanied with an uneasy feeling about the purpose of Mr. Dunlow's visit. The image of his car bouncing down Miners' Alley reminds me of the cars I've observed driven by realtors, as did the content of his conversation with Leigh. What could be going on?

Perplexed, I decide the ride to Prophecy might help to clear my thoughts.

23

A Walk in the Cemetery

An eerie silence pervades the scene aided by an overcast sky as I stand in the shadow of yesteryear.

"Whatcha doing?" Ruby's voice cackles from behind me, nearly sending me toppling off the ridge.

"Scared ya, didn't I?" Her face twists into a half-smile.

"You sure did. I had no idea you were behind me."

"Been panning down at the creek. Came up the back way."

I study her ensemble of the day. It's a combination of flamboyance and practicality. She wears bib overalls over a purple-flowered shirt with a down vest overtop, a pair of wader boots, and a fur-lined leather trapper's hat with earflaps. Around her neck, she's tied a jaunty yellow silk scarf knotted at the side. A pair of gray woolen gloves with the fingertips cut out complete the costume. A worn khaki canvas bag carrying a small dirt-encrusted shovel and pickaxe hangs from her shoulder.

"Been out since early morning. Heading home now. What're you up to?" She leans on her walking stick giving me the once over.

Her scrutiny puts me on the defensive. "I'm contemplating a walk to the cemetery," I counter and wait for her disapproval.

Ruby shakes her head in dismay. "Ain't much to it, just some fallen down headstones and a few piles of rocks markin' some of the old-timers' graves. Most of the wooden markers are long gone, decayed, and blown away. Paupers' graveyard 'cept for Pappy's grave."

"What do you mean, 'paupers' graveyard'?"

"Miners, prospectors, folks down on their luck who had no one to give 'em a proper burial."

"That's so sad."

"What's so sad about it? Chose to live that way. Some folks like living alone, don't make 'em bad or sad," she blurts defensively.

"You're right, Ruby," I rush. "I never thought of it that way. Still, I think I'd like to take a look at the cemetery."

"If you ask me, what I think is that people should respect other people's privacy, dead or alive! Be careful you don't go falling into no holes up there, ain't no one gonna hear ya yellin' if you do."

Ruby turns and hesitates while shaking her head. She looks back in my direction. "Just stick to the worn path behind the boardinghouse, and you'll be okay. Wouldn't dilly dally." She glances at the sky. "Got some dark clouds starting to form." She turns and continues her way down Miners' Alley, hunched over, toting her bag of miner's tools, and I am reminded of Jake's story of his friend's sighting of Old Pappy's ghost.

The sunshine is intermittently blocked by the clouds skittering across the sky as I follow the familiar path to the boardinghouse. I take a last break on its steps before tackling the final assault up the steep slope leading to the cemetery.

The trees are much thinner here with an occasional pine tree that has somehow managed to push its way through the rocky and inhospitable terrain.

Stopping frequently to catch my breath, I arrive at the pitiful remains of the Prophecy Cemetery. Like the town itself, the cemetery is fading into history, exposed and subject to the elements as Ruby has described.

Dark clouds rolling across the sky create an ominous feeling as I walk among the gravesites. Rock piles cover the width and length of some of the graves, the wooden markers disintegrated beyond recognition. "Dust to dust," I whisper.

I stoop, resting on one knee to take a closer look at a small stone cross standing upright, unlike the few headstones that lean precariously or completely fallen over. The faded inscription on the rough-hewn rock base reads simply: "Baby Boy," a sorrowful epitaph for a too brief life.

A low rumble overhead creates a warning sound, sending me scrambling to the top of the hill.

The grand monument towers over all. It's carved from a single piece of granite. The memorial is inscribed with the words:

In Memory Of

Old Pappy Young

The Richest Man in Prophecy

RIP

Curious, I say to myself, "Care to share your secrets, Pappy?" I ask but receive no reply.

A cold wind whips across the barren landscape, accompanied by more rumbles growing closer. I glance at the darkening sky and realize I've overstayed my visit and hurry back the way I came.

Raindrops are falling by the time I dive into the protection of Red and begin the drive down Miners' Alley.

The pounding rain makes visibility poor; the road feels more like slush than gravel under the tires. Braking for the final switchback with fists visor-like on the steering wheel, I overcompensate and take the curve too sharply. Red slides sideways out of my control. A horrible scraping sound, followed by a great thud, ends with an abrupt and tilted stop.

I pull the hoodie over my head, although in this rain, I doubt that it will give me much protection, and open the door clinging to the running board for a closer look at the damage. Red has come to rest atop a pile of fallen rocks and a small boulder. The right front wheel hangs suspended in the air, making escape impossible.

Rain pelts my body, and I hurry back inside. "Geneva Evelyn Ellis! What have you done?!" I whimper and rest my head on the steering wheel, not knowing what else to do.

Frantic pounding upon my window rouses me from my self-pity. I look at the frightening sight of a bat-like figure peering through my window.

"You okay in there?" Ruby shouts from under the cover of a canvas tarp she holds over her head.

I give her a thumbs up, opening the door and taking shelter under the protection of the tarp as we stumble our way to her cabin.

Ruby holds the door open as I dash inside. She follows, dropping the tarp onto the porch as we enter the dark cabin lit only by the kerosene lantern that sits on the kitchen table. Rain is falling sideways from the fierce wind, striking the windows with angry force.

A small puddle of water forms at my feet as I shiver from the cold rain, shaken by the accident. I must be a pathetic sight standing before Ruby. "There's a blanket on the cot you can wrap up in. I'll get some coffee for us. Have a seat at the table; I'll just be a second," she says and hobbles off.

I wrap myself in the warmth of the woolen blanket and totter across the room. A worn leather Bible rests on the weathered table as I settle onto one of the two chairs. Ruby returns, carrying two cups of steaming coffee.

I hurry to clear room for the coffee mugs, sliding the Bible to one side. It teeters on the edge of the table and crashes, scattering a collection of photographs across the floor.

"Oh, my!" I throw off the blanket and lurch to the floor on bended knees, nearly knocking heads with Ruby, who swoops down to gather all but the lone photo I clutch in my hand.

"I...I was trying to make room for the coffee mugs when the Bible..." I struggle to apologize.

Ruby snatches the photo from my grasp and snaps, "Get a good look? Recognize anyone?"

She's right. I did get a look. "Yes," I whisper meeting her gaze. "There's a photograph of him in a book in the library when he was much younger. He was very handsome. The little girl bears a strong resemblance to you." I brave her wrath for confirmation.

"Heard you been snoopin' around."

"Whoa, Ruby." I hold my hands up in defense. "I've been very honest with everyone about my intentions. If I've stumbled on something best left untold, then that's where it'll remain."

Ruby glares and shakes her head. "Guess I figured I would be found out some day."

I stand and offer my hand. "Come, let's have some coffee before it gets cold." Ruby brushes my hand away and reaches up to steady herself on the table as she stands. I pick up the Bible and take my seat.

She slumps in her chair, her hands around the coffee mug, eyes downcast. I remain silent, unsure of what to say.

She breaks the silence. "Ari says it's time for me to share my story. Says it would help me get over my hurt, help me to move on. He's worried I can't make it through another winter taking care of Sass and Dolly and myself. I got down this spring; wouldn't have made it without Ari. He says we need a new plan; neither of us is getting any younger. Seems to think I can trust ya."

"If you would like to share your story, Ruby..." I place my hand upon the Bible. "I swear it will go no farther than these four walls if that's your wish."

Ruby considers my offer. "Swear on the Bible?"

"I swear. One of the most important lessons of life my grandmother taught me was to always respect the privacy of others, and when someone confides in you, never betray their confidence. I promise, Ruby."

Ruby studies me, conflict written across her face. Her thoughts are not in the moment but beyond in another time and place.

She seems to come to a resolution. "First off, you was right." Ruby lays the photo on the table. "That's me in the photograph with my grandmam and granddad, Ida and Jonah LaPierre, taken back in the fifties in Nome, Alaska, where I grew up. They raised me from the time I was a little girl. My momma, their daughter Irene, left me in their care when my daddy was killed in a bulldozer accident working to build the Alaska Highway. Momma went in search of work in California and never came back until she was old and gray and needing my help."

Ruby studies the photo and her voice softens. "My granddad was the best man that ever lived. Each night at bedtime, he would tell me a story about his gold mining days in Prophecy, Colorado, with his best friend Isaiah McLean."

I remain silent, fearful of stopping her tale.

"Them two was as different as day and night. Granddad was a handsome devil and a darling with the ladies. Had a head of thick curly black hair he inherited from the French-Canadian side of the family and dark eyes that twinkled with mischief. He was known for his tall tales, such a jokester! Isa was his opposite, tall and gangly, flaming-red hair, freckle-faced, and awkward as they came, especially with the ladies."

Curious, I ask, "If they were so different in character, how did they become partners?"

"It's a funny story how they first met if ya want to hear it?" Ruby's face lights with animation. Jake was right when he said she had a pretty smile.

"I would be delighted to hear it." I can't believe my good fortune.

"You see, Jonah was already workin' at the Portland Mine, a big commercial operation, in Cripple Creek when Isaiah arrived into town. Granddad had been on his own since he was fourteen years old, kicked out of his home by a mean stepfather. He worked doing odd jobs for a few years until he could earn a grubstake for the gold fields of Cripple Creek. Hitched his way there from Minnesota."

Ruby takes a sip of coffee pausing to consider her next words.

"I'll tell it like my granddaddy used to tell me at bedtime." Ruby straightens, clasps her hands together, and begins her tale. "The year was nineteen hundred when Isaiah, a poor farm boy from Missouri arrived in The District with his head spinning full of dreams to find his El Dorado like all the thousands before him chasing the same dream. The streets was filled with ever' kind of conveyance and folks of ever' kind. Buckboards rumbling down the streets, ore wagons loaded with mined rock heading for the stamp mills, stagecoaches bringing new folks into town, mule trains loaded with new supplies, lone prospectors with their burros heading for the high country. You get the picture." She nods.

I'm captivated by her storytelling and nod my head, urging her to continue.

"And the noise! Boom, boom, boom!" Ruby shouts. "Go the underground mine explosions filling the air along with the construction and daily livin' sounds taking place above ground." Ruby's voice rises an octave higher as if to compete with the noise in the scene she describes.

I can't contain my laughter. "Ruby, you are an amazing storyteller. Please go on."

"Take after my granddaddy, I reckon. Anyway, poor Isa was so flummoxed by all the commotion and unusual sights going on around him that a flock of painted ladies exiting a saloon stopped him in his tracks as he was crossing the street. He never seen the loaded ore wagon thundering in his direction."

"Oh, no!" I yelp, clasping my hand over my mouth.

"Jonah, seeing the greenhorn's dilemma, jumps from the boardwalk and grabs Isa by the suspenders." Ruby reaches out with two hands, imitating the scene. "And pulls Isa out of the way just in time. He lands on his behind, staring up into Granddaddy's face. His first words to Isa was, 'new in town'?" We erupt into laughter at the vision of Isa sprawled in the street before Jonah.

"By coincidence, Jonah was in need of a new roommate to share expenses, his last roommate having taken up residence in Mt. Pisgah Cemetery, shot dead in a gambling dispute."

"It really was the wild, wild west."

"Yes, indeed. It was Jonah who got Isa a job working at the Portland Mine, taught him the ropes of hard rock mining, became one of the best double-jacking teams in the mine."

"Double-jacking? What's that?"

"Why, one of the most dangerous jobs in the mine, takes two men working as a team. One holds the drill bit as the other one swings the sledgehammer striking the steel bit. It's the way they drilled holes into the side of the rock. Ambitious they was, working all day at the mine and spending ever' free moment working their own claim, saving ever' penny they made. That was their life, workin' together and building a friendship, Jonah spinning his tales about the fortune they would make one day, and Isaiah keeping them focused on reaching their dreams. But then... things got scary in The District." The sound of Ruby's voice becomes ominous.

"How so?"

A knock on Ruby's door breaks the spell.

"Who in the..." Ruby shuffles across the room, swinging the door open with a crash.

A startled Jake peers into the cabin.

"Jake, what you doin' out in this storm?" Ruby motions for him to enter.

"Um," he hesitates, looking over his shoulder. "Chris is outside. We got your SUV off the rocks, Nevy. The rain has stopped. Uh... I hung the tarp over the porch rail to dry out." A sweet smile fills his face.

"That is so thoughtful, Jake." I join Ruby at the door. "I'm sorry we didn't hear you out there." I turn to Ruby. "I better go, Ruby. I hope we can continue this another day?"

"Reckon so," she obliges.

Disappointed to end Ruby's storytelling, but elated at the news of Red's liberation, I follow Jake's lead to where Chris is busy unhitching his tow line.

"Am I in big trouble?" I grimace.

Chris chuckles. "No, ma'am, Jake and I saw you heading up earlier. When you didn't return after the storm, we thought we had better check on you."

"I'm so grateful to both of you. Did I do much damage?"

"Nah, a little bumper damage; makes you look like a local now."

"I slid on the wet gravel. Ruby offered me cover from the storm. You're so kind to come and check on me."

"Glad to help. You should be good to go now. If you would like, we'll lead the way down. The storm left some sizable gullies in the road."

"Good idea. Thanks."

I turn to give Ruby, who stands in the doorway, a final wave. She surprises me with a wave in return.

We separate at the entrance to the lodge, Chris and Jake returning to the cabins while I park in the guest lot.

As I enter the lodge, I hear Leigh's muffled voice behind her closed office door in animated agitation. I hurry down the hallway toward Edna's kitchen, not wanting to be caught eavesdropping.

Edna stands at the chopping block dicing a colander of vegetables.

"Knock, knock," I announce my arrival.

"Hi, Nevy. Come in and keep me company. I hope you had a restful afternoon. That was some storm."

"Edna, you would not believe my afternoon!"

She turns with a puzzled look.

"I decided to clear my head and take a ride up the mountain to the cemetery after I left you."

Edna covers her heart with her hand. "Don't tell me you got caught in that storm! Wait, one second. I want to hear it all." She empties the board of vegetables into a simmering pot on the stove and gives it a quick stir, then hurries to the sink, rinses her hands, and wipes them dry upon her apron. She turns to the cupboard and reaches for a coffee cup, raising it in the air and asks, "Care to join me?"

"You read my mind." I grin.

She places the steaming cup before me and settles onto the next barstool, cocking an eye in my direction. "So, tell me about your afternoon."

"I learned a good lesson today, Edna, to be more mindful of Colorado's changing weather."

"Yes, these summer storms can pop up from nowhere. Did you get caught in the rain?"

"Yes, and then some." I begin my tale, my eyes growing wider as the details of my adventure emerge. "The dark clouds were starting to roll in about the time I reached the cemetery. It was very eerie with the storm moving in, thunder rumbling overhead and walking among the graves."

"It gives me the chills." Edna hugs her arms. "Is the cross for the baby boy still standing?" Her expression grows sad.

"Yes, unlike most of the others. Can you imagine having to bury your baby there?"

"There are lots of sad stories on that hill, Nevy."

"Yes, but I'm afraid that Ari and Ruby are correct. There isn't much information to be learned. Most of the headstones have fallen over, wiped clean as a slate from exposure to the elements, except for Pappy Young's. His monument is huge!"

"The headstone was Isa's idea, from what I understand, his way of honoring Pappy for all he had done for Jonah and him, leading them to that first claim."

"I am curious about the epitaph engraved on the stone, and the words 'The Richest Man in Prophecy.'"

Edna chuckles, "That, I can explain. It was well known that Pappy used to claim one day he would be the richest man in Prophecy. According to legend, he did find the mother lode and had a map to prove it, but no one has ever found the map. So, in a sense, Pappy's prophecy came true. He is the richest man among all those poor souls buried in Prophecy."

"Hmm, that makes sense. Sure makes for a good story to tell!"

"I see the writer's wheels spinning in that pretty head." Edna laughs.

A whisper in my ear reminds me to keep my promise to Ruby, so I avoid any discussion about my visit with her. A wave of exhaustion sweeps over me as I stretch my arms, and give a great uncontrolled yawn. "I think I'll retire to my room for the siesta I missed, Edna. My adventures have caught up with me."

"Sweet dreams, sugar."

Rose René peers from her portrait in hushed silence as I enter the room. "What a beauty you are," I say and think to myself what a mismatched pair Isaiah and she made. What is your story? I wonder. There is so much yet to discover, but fatigue overtakes my curiosity, and I crawl into the soft heaven of my bed, falling blissfully asleep.

24

Cookout Under the Stars

Fading sunlight and a cool breeze tempt me out of bed. I cross the room to open the French doors, and step into my private garden.

The rainstorm has renewed the outdoor world, and I inhale a deep breath of intoxicating mountain air.

Distant voices pique my curiosity. I follow the animated chatter to observe Chris, Leigh, and Jake returning from the lake area with fishing poles and a bucket in hand. I pause, wondering whether to proceed when Mogul bounds in my direction, alerting them to my presence.

"Nevy!" Jake whoops.

"Hi, guys, I hope I'm not intruding." I bend to scratch the pup's ear.

Leigh shares a lighthearted greeting with a smile covering her face. "Not at all, Nevy, but please rescue me from these tall tale fish stories these two are sharing," she declares, shaking her head at their antics as Chris and Jake feign innocence.

"Evening, Miss Nevy." Chris tips his hat.

"What a glorious evening," I say.

"Yes, ma'am, it was a much-needed rain, settled the dust and freshened everything."

I nod in agreement before asking, "So, did you catch any fish?"

"That's why they're picking on me." Leigh fakes a pout and points to the bucket. "I'm the only one who caught a fish!" She breaks into a grin.

Jake tips the bucket, revealing a large trout inside. "After we had to bait your hook."

"Still counts. Remember, you're the one who talked me into joining you," Leigh chides her son. "Hey, tell Nevy our surprise for tonight."

"We're having a cookout with s'mores and hot dogs and lots of other good stuff to eat. Ari and Athena are coming, and Chris is staying for it, too, right Chris?"

"Wouldn't miss it," Chris responds with a subtle glance in Leigh's direction. She nods and lowers her eyes, her lips forming a tiny smile.

Hmm, do I sense a budding romance in the air? How sweet is that?

"But first..." Leigh looks at her son.

"I know, I know. Wash up and help Edna and Charlie."

"I would be glad to help also," I offer.

"No, this is our treat. Tonight you're our special guest," Leigh informs. "You'll need a jacket, though. Once the sun goes down, it'll get pretty chilly, even with the campfire. You can meet us down at the barbecue area."

We separate, and I return to my suite and decide on a quick shower to freshen up after my rain soaked day on the mountain.

Refreshed, I grab my new polar fleece jacket and exit the French doors at the moment the dinner bell clangs.

The fragrant smell of burning piñon wood floats through the air as I approach the campfire. Leigh chats with Chris, her lovely face alight with animation. Charlie holds a platter of steaks in one hand while stoking the charcoal on the grill. Jake sits at the crackling fireside under the watchful eyes of his mother and Chris while carving a fine point on a stick for roasting marshmallows.

We all turn at the sound of Edna's laughter to see Ari and Edna laden with trays of food following the path from the lodge.

"Ari, Athena!" Jake shouts and bounds in their direction with Mogul in hot pursuit.

Athena pauses for Ari's permission. He nods, and she races to join her friends.

"Jake, don't go too far. Charlie is about to put the steaks on the grill."

He comes to a full stop to peer at his mother. She anticipates his response, and laughs. "Yes, you can roast hot dogs instead."

His shout of delight follows him along the lake path, his two companions close behind.

Charlie turns from the grill and rubs his hands. "Let's get this party started! Ladies, can I interest you in a glass of wine?"

"Let me do the honors," Chris offers, his long legs covering the space to the picnic table in a few strides while Leigh assists by passing out the wineglasses.

Charlie, Ari, and Chris opt for a cold brew.

The scene is so heartwarming that I raise my glass in a spontaneous toast. "To my newfound friends, your warmth and hospitality will never be forgotten," I say with genuine gratitude, as we click our glasses and bottles.

Leigh raises her glass high and adds, "And to Nevy, may this be the first of many visits to Meadow View. You will always hold a special place in our hearts."

Touched, I place my hand over my heart and whisper, "And you in mine."

"Everybody, grab a seat at the table," Charlie commands. "Them steaks is just about ready."

Following dinner, we collapse into the padded log chairs that circle the campfire, content in our silence as we watch Jake roast marshmallows.

"Hot dogs, roasting marshmallows, and s'mores, all your dreams come true. What more could you want?" Leigh smiles at her son.

Jake turns to his mother with a serious look, and replies, "There is one more wish I have. Next time, could we invite Ruby?"

An awkward silence ensues. "I think Jake and Ruby are becoming friends after our visit with her. Isn't that right, Jake?" I ask.

Focused on his task of roasting marshmallows, he nods. "I think she's sad living by herself, and she loves your cooking, Edna." He smiles in her direction.

Edna sputters a reply, "Why, of course, we'll invite Ruby next time, Jake. That's very thoughtful of you to think of her."

While Charlie mutters under his breath, "That ain't never gonna happen."

I rest my head against the chair back and point to the sky. "Look at that night sky. It's a kaleidoscope of shimmering stars and galaxies. "I've never seen anything so spectacular!"

"Yes," Ari responds, "we locals tend to take it for granted. We're spoiled seeing it every night."

Firelight dances from the campfire, casting light and shadow around each of us seated in the circle. Only the sound of the crackling fire is heard above the night sounds as we settle in to watch the display of the universe above.

Jake rests his back against his mother's legs, his head lolling to one side. "I think," Leigh whispers, peering at her son, "I had better get my son to bed."

Chris springs into action swooping the sleeping boy into his arms. "Let me carry him for you, Leigh. You lead the way."

She murmurs a shy thank you and proceeds up the path toward the lodge, followed by Chris and the sleeping boy with Mogul trailing behind.

"How does a little nightcap of hot buttered rum to round out the night sound?" Edna offers.

"Devine!" I squeal. "May I help?" I ask already knowing the answer.

"No, ma'am, you keep Ari company. We got this handled." Charlie places his arm around his wife's shoulder as they walk to the lodge.

I turn to Ari. "I'm glad we have a moment alone, Ari. I've been wanting to share the news of my visit with Ruby today."

Ari straightens in his chair. "Is that right?" he asks, surprise clear on his face.

"I got caught in the rainstorm, and she offered me refuge in her cabin." I pause, choosing my next words carefully. "I chanced upon an old photograph of Ruby and her grandparents while I was there."

"So," he nods, "her secret was revealed."

"She told me you had suggested that she share her story with me."

"I did. I've been very worried about Ruby making it through another winter on the mountain. It's past time that she comes down, but she is as stubborn as that goat of hers. She's isolated herself to the point that there's no one but me she can turn to for help. I think telling her story would be good therapy and perhaps a way of finding a solution."

"I've made a pledge on the Bible that I'll abide her wishes and guard her confidence."

"You can do no more. Let me know if I can be of help."

Edna and Charlie return with four steaming mugs of buttered rum garnished with cinnamon sticks and topped with whipped cream.

"I didn't think the night could get any better." I swoon over the heavenly aroma.

"It's just the four of us," Edna advises. "The kids said to go ahead without them. Chris needs to get home, and Leigh doesn't want to leave Jake alone." Edna chuckles. "I think they want a little private time together. Don't they make a sweet couple?" She crosses her fingers.

"Now, Edna, don't you go trying to be a matchmaker. Let nature take its course." Charlie waves his finger at his wife.

"Shush." Edna giggles.

We sip our mugs in silence and watch the fire dwindle to embers as the night air turns cooler.

"Gracious." Edna shudders, jumping to her feet and hugging her arms. "I think it's time to call it a night."

It's the impetus we need to bring this memorable evening to a close.

25

A Tale of Woe

A new morning dawns as I exit my room and tiptoe into the kitchen.

"Good morning, Edna. I see my timing is perfect," I chirp.

Edna stands before the cooling racks, checking off the selection of cookies before her. "Snickerdoodles for Jake, peanut butter for Charlie, and can't go wrong with chocolate chip, always a crowd pleaser. What's your pleasure this morning, Miss Nevy, or perhaps bacon and eggs first?"

I cross the room and take a seat at the counter. "Not after that feast last night! It's granola and fruit for me this morning...but, there's always room for one of your homemade cookies." I grin and snatch a cooled chocolate chip cookie from the rack.

The timer on the oven signals that the next batch of cookies is ready to be removed. Edna looks from the oven to me with a perplexed look on her face.

"Go tend to your baking, Edna. I can help myself," I reassure her.

"I hope our future guests are as accommodating as you, Nevy." She hurries to the oven, mitt in hand. She carries the rack of oven-warm cookies to the counter and turns to ask, "What's on your agenda for today?"

I evade a direct answer and reply, "Not sure yet. I may take another walk to the cemetery. The storm cut my visit short yesterday. I may stop for a visit with Ruby. I think she is warming to my company, thanks to your homemade goodies."

"Really?" Edna turns a furrowed brow in my direction. "You would be one of the first. I do feel sorry for her, but she hasn't made it easy on herself remaining so isolated all of these years. I'll pack a container of cookies for you to share with her."

"I was hoping you would say that." I smile in gratitude.

I exit through the deck and across the property to access Miners' Alley. The cabin Chris and Jake have been working on is silent, unusual for this time of day. Just then, Chris's truck turns down Miners' Alley off Main Street approaching from town. His broad shoulders and western hat fill the driver's side. A miniature silhouette sits in the passenger seat. Mogul sits in between.

Chris slows the truck as Jake lowers his window.

I place my foot on the running board and lean in. "Good morning, guys. Looks like you got an early start on things." The bed of the truck is loaded with lumber.

"Yes, ma'am. Morning." Chris tips his hat in greeting.

"Hi, Nevy, where you going?" Jake's nose peeks over the window frame.

Feeling a sense of guilt, I explain, "I promised Ruby I would return for a visit today. I need to talk to her in private about some things. It looks like you two have a full day of work ahead of you."

"That's right, partner," Chris interjects. "I'm counting on your help putting the final touches on the cabin."

Jake's face brightens with a grin. "Mom is going to be so surprised, Nevy. We finished ahead of schedule."

"That's awesome! I can't wait to see it, too. I better let you guys get to work, then. I'll see you later."

They tip their hats in unison and proceed to the rear entrance of the lodge as I continue my trek up Miners' Alley.

Sweet Dolly and Sassy Pants, my nickname for the obstinate goat, peek around the corner of the cabin from their pen as I approach. I reach into my backpack and retrieve the treats I've brought. I scratch Dolly's nose and offer her an apple which she takes gently from my hand.

The goat has turned his back to me but sneaks a sly peek as I offer an apple for him. He races toward me, snatches the apple from my hand, and prances away with a sassy backward kick in defiance.

"You're welcome, Mr. Sassy Pants." I giggle at his antics.

Ruby hobbles around the corner of the cabin. "Sassy Pants." She cackles. "I'll have to remember that. Suits him better, that's for sure."

I display the container of cookies. "Edna sent you special treats, too."

"That's mighty nice of her. Come on inside then. I reckon you've returned to hear the rest of the story. Didn't tell no one about it, did ya?"

"Only Ari. He joined us for a cookout last night. I mentioned our visit. I hope that was okay since he was the one who encouraged you to talk with me."

Ruby nods her head and motions for me to follow.

I place the container of cookies in the middle of the table, cautious not to disturb the Bible.

"Have a seat. I'll be back with some coffee."

She plunks the heavy mug before me and settles into her chair, and lurches into the story where she left off, catching me off-guard. She shares her tale as if it were a first-hand account after all the years of listening to her grandfather's bedtime stories.

"August nineteen oh three, and the situation in The District is getting serious. The WFM," she clarifies at my puzzled look, "Western Federation of Miners, has called for a second strike of the mines. But this time...they is calling for all fifty mines to strike instead of the twelve before. Tensions is running high with all kinds of intimidations happening on both sides of the issue."

I frown wondering what she means. "What kind of intimidations?"

She leans her elbows on the table and rests her chin on her clenched fists. She raises her head to peer at me with a serious look and explains, "For starters, the mine owners is bringing in non-union men to work the mines with the promise they can keep the jobs if they break the strike."

"You mean take the jobs of the striking miners?"

"Yes, ma'am. There has also been a report of a union member's house being burned to the ground. In retaliation, a shaft house at one of the mines is set afire. Gunfire, fistfights, and beatings is becoming an ever' day occurrence. There's talk that the governor is planning to call out the National Guard like he done in Colorado City a couple of months earlier."

"It must have been a very scary time for your granddaddy and Isa."

Ruby nods. "Things is looking real bad for the boys. Their claim is played out, money is running low, and the merchants is only accepting cash payment for their goods."

"That's when they decide to move to Blue Eagle," I jump to a conclusion.

Ruby waves her finger at me. "Not until the night there comes a pounding on their cabin door. A gang of rabble- rousers at the Portland Mine is planning to dynamite the shaft house, and they want Jonah and Isaiah to join them."

"Is that when they decide to head for Blue Eagle?"

"Sure enough, but first, the boys tell these fellers they have to think on it for a night. They leave, but with a warning to Isaiah and Jonah that they'll be in deep trouble if their plan gets out."

"How did they leave without these men finding out?" I ask, knowing that the two made it to Blue Eagle successfully.

"Packed their meager belongings and tools in the dead of night and caught a ride with another feller doing the same thing, only he was heading for Colorado Springs. From there they took the train into Leadville and the narrow gauge into Silver Plume. They walked the rest of the way to Blue Eagle, then on up to the creek to do some panning. That's when they met Pappy Young. Reckon you know the rest of the story."

"Bits and pieces, Ruby. I know they found the ancient riverbed which contained a treasure of gold ore deposits."

"Some of the richest deposits ever found in Clear Creek County," Ruby boasts. "Provided the funds they needed to launch the claim that became the Prophecy Mine. The discoveries at Prophecy created a stampede of miners and prospectors. Soon the town of Prophecy was under construction. Isaiah built his boardinghouse and Granddaddy built his saloon. Ain't that just like him." Ruby laughs.

Her demeanor turns serious. "But over the years, all that money and different ideas about how to spend it caused conflict between Isaiah and Jonah. Other things too," she says with a raised eyebrow.

I sense that I shouldn't ask for clarification.

"Just as the situation between the two of 'em was gettin' real bad, word of the Alaska gold discoveries hit the news. Gave my granddaddy a reason for leaving and striking out on his own."

"So that's the Alaska connection. I wondered."

"Yep. It's where he met my grandmam who was workin' at the boardinghouse where he was staying in Nome. Granddaddy told me she was the best thing that ever happened to him.

"Married her, he did. She convinced him to invest the money he had left into buying the boardinghouse. It provided an income for the rest of their lives. Worked there myself, helping wherever I could, mostly cookin' for the restaurant." Ruby heaves a great sigh. "I think I'd like to take a break."

The grief on her face reveals the sadness these memories have brought back. "We can stop anytime, Ruby. It must be heartbreaking repeating these stories and remembering times shared with your grandparents."

"Yes and no, but I wanna finish this, get it out in the open. Just need to take a break, get some fresh air."

She rises slowly, holding onto the table with both hands, the storytelling having robbed her of energy. She crosses the room to open the door, filling the room with sunlight and fresh mountain air.

I join her and take in the spectacular view of the valley below. "Beautiful beyond words," I say in awe.

"Million-dollar view, they call it. I can't imagine living without it," her voice quivers.

I rest my arm on her slight shoulders. "Come, let's sample Edna's cookies."

With spirits renewed by Edna's tasty cookies, and the sunlight and fresh air flowing through the open doorway, Ruby embarks on the final chapter of her story.

"Just before my granddaddy passed, he told me I was old enough to hear the rest of his story."

A sadness has settled once again upon Ruby. I can't imagine what sorrow she's about to share.

"A few years after my granddaddy moved to Nome, he bumped into a feller from Prophecy. They was shocked to see each other. After some small talk, the man asked my granddaddy a strange question. He wanted to know how Miss Rose René was. Granddaddy was puzzled and asked how would he know as he hadn't seen the McLeans since he left Prophecy.

"The conversation grew awkward until the man blurted out that word in town was that my granddaddy and Rose René had run off together. Folks had seen them boarding the same train to Denver that day. The man said Isaiah nearly went crazy over the news. The man left Prophecy soon after, so that was all he knew."

Ruby shakes her head in disgust. "Granddaddy had no idea Rose René was on the same train. It pierced his heart that Isaiah would believe such a thing about him. He had loved him like a brother. He considered returning to Prophecy to confront Isaiah, but Grandmam talked him out of it. Thank the Lord."

"Is that why you decided to visit Blue Eagle, Ruby?"

Ruby raises her head to look into my eyes. "Maybe, in the beginning. I wanted to set the record straight. I was angry at Isaiah for thinking my granddaddy would betray his best friend like that. I didn't know what rumors was still circulating through town after all those years, but I wanted to make sure the truth was known."

"Yes, I can understand why it would be important for you. I would do the same."

"When I got to Blue Eagle, the bus from Denver dropped me off at the edge of town, and I wandered into Ari's. It was a shock to find out that the only place in town that offered rooms to rent was the McLean Fishing Camp. I must have shown my distress at this news. Ari explained that the McLeans was going through some tough times with Miss Elizabeth's illness, but he was sure his good friend, Jacob, would accommodate my needs."

"That must have been so awkward for you, Ruby."

She winces. "Things sure wasn't going as planned, but I had no other option. Ari drove me out to the fishing camp, and I stayed in the truck while Ari went in to talk to Jacob. Then, to my surprise, both Jacob and Miss Elizabeth, a frail little wisp of a lady, came out to welcome me to Blue Eagle, her so weak she had to hold tight onto Jacob to walk."

Ruby wipes a tear from her cheek as my eyes fill with tears as well.

"They invited me to stay in one of their fishing cabins as long as I needed. Them was some of the happiest days of my life." Ruby's face fills with a rare smile.

"I can't imagine how all of this is going to end."

"You could never guess." Ruby slowly shakes her head, her hands tightly clasping her coffee mug. "Ari and I struck up a friendship after that when we discovered our love for fishing. Spent a lot of afternoons sitting in his boat fishing out on the lake. One day, he told me his suspicions about who he thought I was, knowing I was from

Alaska and aware of the history of Isaiah and Jonah. He promised to keep my secret."

"He's a good man."

"That he is. Then one day, when I was hiking up in Prophecy, I got the idea of moving into the cabin where my granddaddy and Isaiah had first lived. Wasn't no inconvenience for me after living in Alaska especially with the convenience of running water piped in. So, all I needed was a few household items, which Ari supplied. Jacob never said a word when I shared my plans to move into the cabin. Maybe Ari told him my story, maybe he figured it out hisself. I don't know."

"I wish I could have met Papa Jake. He must have been a remarkable man."

"None better." Ruby nods her head in agreement.

"And now, Miss Nevy, I come to the end of my story. I confess I still harbored some anger at Isaiah. That is until I discovered Isaiah's Bible hidden in a rusty tackle box shoved in a dark corner in the shed."

I watch wide-eyed as Ruby picks up the tattered Bible and removes folded sheets of yellowed paper, bookmarking the chapters of Ecclesiastes, and slides the Bible across the table to me.

"That there," Ruby says, reaching across the table, tapping the Bible pages with a gnarled finger, "is a tormented man. I reckon he's paid for his sins."

As I fan the chapters of Ecclesiastes, I see margin after margin filled with handwritten notes of personal lament asking for God's forgiveness.

I glide my hand over the verses. "What sadness, Ruby."

Her attention is focused on the folded sheets of paper she holds in her hands. She slides the pages across the table to me. "This is what was markin' those chapters in the Bible. Explains a lot."

With great care, I unfold the fragile, creased sheets of aged paper. It's a letter.

Dear Jonah,

I write these words with a heavy heart guilty of blaming you for an act you never committed.

When Rose René informed me she was planning a trip to visit her Aunt Lillian in Denver for a few weeks, I agreed, thinking some distance between us might help remedy the anger over the situation with her father and our unhappiness together.

But then, the sin of gossip overtook my good senses when a rumor circulated that Rose René and you had run off together. Some folks testified they had seen you both boarding the same train to Denver. My attempts to contact her were unsuccessful. I confess my jealousy over the friendship you shared with her over these many years also jaded my conclusion.

When she returned home unexpectedly bursting with the news that she was with child, I assumed the worst knowing how unsuccessful we had been in bringing a child into this world.

I went crazy, filled with rage, never letting her explain and banishing her from our home. Consumed with anger, I set our beloved home on fire and watched it burn to the ground.

But now, the truth has been revealed. I have been wallowing in self-pity, isolating myself in our old cabin, until I received a letter from Lillian.

She told me that Rose René had died giving birth to my son.

She said she could no longer care for the baby, and I needed to come and claim him, and that I would have no doubt that he is my son.

I knew Lillian to be a trustworthy woman, so I caught the next train to Denver.

By the time I arrived in Denver, my sorrow and anger was so overflowing I near pounded her door down. When Aunt Lillian met me at the door, she shoved the squalling red-haired, blue-eyed babe into my arms.

I have a son, Jonah, with my rooster red hair and the same troublesome corkscrew cowlick.

I brought him home, along with the portrait of his beautiful mother that she had commissioned to be painted for me to make amends for the sadness between us over the business with her father, her true purpose of her trip to Denver. It is the reason I could not reach her due to the many appointments it required to complete.

I do not deserve the joy I feel over the birth of my son, but I truly deserve the deep sorrow over my loss of Rose René and the supposed betrayal of my best friend.

I write this not knowing where to send it, but with the hope of someday delivering it to you in person to ask for your undeserved forgiveness.

Isaiah

I turn my tear-filled eyes to Ruby. "This is so sad, knowing that Jonah never got to see it."

"Makes me ponder my own feelings of anger and distrust," she confesses with tears streaming down her face.

"I'm so honored that you would share your story with me, Ruby."

"Remember that when you write your article. Don't need to stir up old memories or stories most folks here don't even know or remember. No good will come of it."

I reach across the table and place my hands over hers. "I would never do that, Ruby. There's a right way to share the history of Prophecy. That's my intent."

Giving her hands a gentle squeeze, I say, "I think it's time for me to head back to the lodge. Would it be okay if I returned and brought Jake with me next time? He has become quite fond of you."

"That would be real nice," she whispers.

Ruby joins me on the porch as I follow the steps down and turn to wave a final goodbye from Miners' Alley. She sits in her rocker, deep in thought, the looming mountains forming an ominous backdrop to her tiny, solitary figure.

I retreat down Miners' Alley in silent contemplation of all that has been revealed.

As I enter the front door of the lodge, I nearly collide with Leigh, who is exiting her office at the same time in an agitated manner.

"Whoa!" I exclaim taking a step back. "Excuse me, Leigh, I didn't see you."

"I, I didn't see you either," she snaps defensively. It's obvious that something has upset her, this behavior so uncommon to her usual self-controlled demeanor.

She steadies herself against the reception desk, misery covering her face.

Realizing she is on the verge of a meltdown, I ask in an alarmed voice, "Leigh, what is it? Has something bad happened?"

Her eyes fill with tears as she confesses, "I've gotten myself into a real mess, Nevy."

"Let's go into your office where we have some privacy," I suggest, glancing at the entrance door.

With a tight grimace, she replies, "Yes, good idea. I don't want anyone to see me like this."

I lead the way into her office, surprised to see her take a seat on the Victorian settee used for guests rather than her own chair behind the desk. She huddles into its protective curve, clasping her hands into a tight knot as I sit down beside her.

She raises her eyes to mine. "I don't know what to do, Nevy. I'm at my wit's end." She winces. "I've underestimated everything. The renovation project is too big for the opening date I set, even with Chris's help. I underestimated the help Edna will need in the kitchen, and the additional staff we will need to provide all of the services we hope to offer. Worst of all..." Tears begin to stream down her face. "The bank loan is short term. I could lose the lodge, everything my grandparents worked for their whole lives."

I gently grasp her twisting hands as she continues, "And now, just when I thought I had the solution, a huge problem has come up."

I look at her tormented face with a sympathetic smile. "I don't mean to pry, but if you would like to share your problem, maybe I can help."

She gives a dismissive shrug. "I think it's beyond your help, Nevy. Recently, I was visited by a realtor who represents some wealthy clients who are interested in purchasing a piece of property to build a mountain home."

"And you own the property?" I ask with a feeling of dread.

"I thought I did, but there's a question about the deed. It's the parcel of land where Ruby is living." Leigh holds her hand up to silence my reply. "I know, I know, how can I do this to Ruby? But it's the only solution to saving the lodge. I have no other option. They're offering a small fortune." Her voice quivers an octave higher in self-defense.

"What about the deed?" A premonition of what she's about to say flitters through my thoughts.

Leigh explains. "When the realtor ran a title search, he discovered that the deed is titled in the name of both Isaiah McLean and Jonah LaPierre." She shakes her head in despair. "I never thought to check it; there was never any need...until now." She heaves a heavy sigh. "Rocky Dunlow, the realtor, his clients," Leigh stumbles through her explanation, "they are very persistent and eager to get started. The whole deal could fall through."

"I see," I reply as my thoughts reflect upon how devastating this news will be to Ruby.

"Nothing seems to be going my—"

Jake bursts into the room. "Mom, guess what?" he exclaims, his joy turning to concern when he observes his mother's tear-stained face.

"Mom! What's wrong?" He races to her side, placing a protective arm around her shoulder.

Leigh raises her hand to caress his face. "I'm okay, buddy, just having a sad moment. Everything is fine," she assures him.

"Are you thinking about Papa again?" Sympathy fills his face.

"Maybe a little, but Nevy has been a big help to comfort me. Don't you worry." Changing subjects, Leigh asks, "So what's all the excitement about?"

"Oh yeah," his joy returns. "Chris says he needs you down at the cabin. We have a surprise for you." He casts a quick conspiratorial glance at me.

I take the opportunity to leave them alone and jump to my feet. "You better not keep him waiting then. We can talk later, Leigh." I nod and exit the office and return to my room to reflect on the day's revelations.

A beam of sunlight highlights the portrait of Rose René as I enter the room, causing me to pause and study it. Her beauty is mesmerizing. The artist has posed her beside an ornate Victorian chair, her right hand resting gently on the wingback, a half-opened fan held between her delicate fingers. She wears a high-necked lace gown, the collar ruffling daintily beneath her uplifted chin, a single strand of pearls around her neck. A pink silk sash encircles her tiny waist. A garland of miniature pink roses adorns her head of thick golden-brown hair, swept into a pompadour style with escaping tendrils gracing her upraised face.

Her gaze is direct, not challenging, but more in a teasing, flirtatious way as evidenced by the impish smile on her upturned lips. It's in contrast to the somber, expressionless portraits that were popular at the time. It's obvious she is a woman aware of her beauty and charm.

The sunlight shifts, casting the portrait in a shadow, as if Rose René has chosen this moment to silence anymore of her secrets from being revealed. I can't imagine how devastated Isaiah must have been when he saw this portrait for the first time.

Although the bed beckons to me for a nap, I decide a visit with Ari will help to tie up loose ends to Ruby's story.

26

The Missing Piece

I follow the shortcut through the meadow, too occupied by thoughts of Leigh's predicament to appreciate the grandeur of the beauty that surrounds me.

A car with an out-of-state license plate is parked in the lot of Ari's store. I enter, and Ari mouths a silent hello as I busy myself, browsing the magazine rack while he assists the customer. The sound of the cowbell alerts me to the patron's exit.

"Good day, Nevy." Ari peeks around the rack with Athena at his side.

"Hi, Ari," my voice overflows with fake enthusiasm.

"I take it this is not a shopping venture," the astute professor replies, punctuated with raised eyebrows.

"Do you have time to talk? I just returned from a visit with Ruby," I blurt.

Ari waves his hand in the direction of the wooden table and leads the way.

With a forlorn look, I confess, "Ari, I don't know where to begin."

He takes the lead. "You say you had a visit with Ruby?"

"Yes, this morning, when I returned to hear the rest of her story." I pause and look into his compassionate eyes. "She shared Isaiah's letter with me, too."

Ari leans into his chair, his fingers tapping the edge of the table. "My, my. You've achieved quite a feat earning Ruby's confidence."

I clasp my hands on the table and continue, "I'm honored that she has confided in me, but there are some missing parts to her story. I didn't want to press her for information, but I'm hoping you can fill in the blanks."

"Let me preface my response by reminding you that I remain allegiant to Ruby's privacy. However, it would appear that her sharing of this tale has opened the door for further discussion."

"Mm, okay, please don't hesitate to let me know if I overstep my bounds, Ari. It's truly not my intent. You see, when Ruby shared her story, she mentioned that the relationship between Isaiah and Jonah had deteriorated over the years due to conflict over money issues and a vague reference to other things happening, too. Then, in the letter, Isaiah writes that the portrait of Rose René was to make amends for the situation with her father."

Ari studies me. "I don't know how much more of the intricacies of the story Ruby actually knows except for what's been revealed in Isaiah's letter and the stories Jonah shared with her as a child. The missing puzzle piece is the role the Cordell family played."

"The Cordell family?" I ask. "I haven't heard of these people before."

"Not by the name of Cordell, perhaps." Ari continues, "Each day brought new people to the boom town of Prophecy. One day, a new family by the name of Cordell moved to town. Mr. Cordell was an assayer by trade, having last worked in Cripple Creek. He brought with him his wife and beautiful daughter—"

"Rose René," I whisper.

Ari nods and shifts in his chair. "What folks did not know about Mr. Cordell is that he had been chased out of Cripple Creek due to a high-grading scheme he was discovered operating."

"High grading?"

"It was a common scheme created by devious miners and assayers to steal gold from the mines. The miners would carry out gold ore from the mine stuffed in their shoes, pants, lunch boxes, and so on. But they needed a middleman, a corrupt assayer, who would sell it to the smelter. It was a lucrative scheme. News of the good fortune of

The Prophets had spread across Cripple Creek, and Mr. Cordell set his sights on Isaiah as his next victim."

"I have a terrible feeling where this story is leading." I frown.

Ari shakes his head. "It wasn't long before Isaiah received an invitation to dinner with the Cordells, who introduced him to their daughter, Rose René. Inexperienced with women, Isaiah was immediately smitten with the beautiful Rose René. A marriage proposal followed not long after that. In truth, I believe both Isaiah and Rose René were pawns in her father's scheme. According to Jacob, my source, the wedding was a lavish affair. Isaiah transported all of his family from Missouri to attend so that he could display his beautiful wife and boast of his great success. But rather than impress his family, it created a wedge of jealousy and permanent estrangement."

"Because he had pursued his father's and uncles' dream and became a rich man." I sigh.

"No doubt, that was at the center of it," Ari confirms. "As a wedding gift, Isaiah built his bride a grand home in the meadow where the lodge now stands."

I gasp. "The home he burned to the ground."

Ari nods. "For the first few years, everything was bliss. Although Isaiah returned to his habit of working long hours at the mine, his young bride and her mother kept busy decorating and shopping for new furnishings for her home."

"In the meantime, Mr. Cordell had finagled his way into a position of importance at the mine. Isaiah mistook Jonah's warnings about the true character of Mr. Cordell as jealousy over Isaiah's good fortune in life. This created a deep rift in their friendship and business dealings."

I shake my head. "What a tangled web."

"Yes, indeed. When the profits of the mine began to suffer, Isaiah finally discovered that Mr. Cordell had been embezzling from the mine's profits."

"What did he do?"

"He confronted Cordell and gave him an ultimatum to make good or face prosecution. The Cordells, being well- versed in ultimatums of this type, chose to leave town, abandoning their daughter to pay for their sins while Isaiah buried himself in his work at the mine."

"Poor Rose René and Isaiah...and Jonah! What happened to Jonah after all of this?"

"Jonah retreated to his saloon, his friendship with Isaiah irreparably damaged. When word of a new gold rush in Alaska reached Prophecy, Jonah jumped at the opportunity to leave town."

"What became of the Prophecy Mine, Ari?"

"When Isaiah returned home from Denver with his son, he wanted nothing more to do with the mine. It had brought only heartache to him. So he boarded up the Prophecy forever. He used his profits to build a ranch house on the site of the original home and created a new life for his son, René, and himself in the cattle ranching business."

"René," I whisper. "He named his son after his mama." I slump in my chair overwhelmed by all I've learned.

"I'll make the rest of this tale short as I fear you're becoming fatigued by all of this...me too." Ari sighs.

"No, no, I want to hear it all. It's just a lot to take in," I assure him. "So then René would be Jacob's father? And his mother...?"

Ari fills in the blanks. "Faith, a local girl who moved to the ranch with Isaiah and René after they were married. A year later, Jacob was born, filling the household with joy, but it would be short-lived."

"No, Ari, not more bad news!" I shake my head in disbelief.

"Yes, I'm afraid so. When Jacob was only eight years old, his parents were killed in an automobile accident driving over Loveland Pass in a spring blizzard, returning home from Denver from their anniversary celebration."

"What a tragedy for everyone."

"So once again, Isaiah assumed the responsibility of raising a child on his own. To his dying day, he carried the misguided belief that it was God's wrath that took his René and Faith for the sins he had committed against Rose René and Jonah."

"Oh, Ari!"

"Perhaps now, you'll understand why Ruby and I have conspired to keep this story secret all these years."

"I do understand, Ari." I pause to choose the right words to make my case. "But I believe there is a way to tell the story of Prophecy without sharing this part of its history. Think of the business it could generate for Meadow View! That would be good, right?" My enthusiasm does not match his.

Avoiding my question, he asks, "How was Ruby doing when you saw her today?"

"She broke my heart, Ari. She seemed much more fragile today. I noticed that she needed more support to get around the cabin. She was quite wobbly on her feet. A couple of times, I thought I was going to have to help her, but she waved me off each time."

Ari nods his head in agreement. "That's what I've been noticing as well. The illness she suffered earlier this year has weakened her considerably. I wish I could move her off the mountain."

An idea enters my thoughts. "I wonder if there was a solution, would you consider going with me to talk to Ruby about it?"

"Of course, but I can't imagine what that might be. My advice to you is that you tread very carefully around Miss Ruby. You've gained her confidence. I wouldn't do anything to jeopardize her trust in you."

"No, I would never do that. Trust is sacred," I reply as Grandmater's words fill my thoughts.

I leave Ari in the company of his beloved Athena with a promise to follow his advice.

27

A Solution

As I exit Ari's store, the sign for Miss Liddy's beckons to my hunger pangs. I haven't had a bite to eat since the cookies I shared with Ruby.

The high school girl behind the counter fills my order, happy to have a customer. I escape to the outdoor picnic table and the privacy it offers to sort through my thoughts.

The warmth of the sun and murmur of the flowing creek nearby create a tranquil space as I seek a solution from my muse. An answer surfaces. If Ruby could be convinced to move into one of the lakeside cabins in exchange for her mountain cabin, then maybe things—

The sound of a speeding car interrupts my thoughts.

"What the heck!" I jump to my feet as the realtor's black car careens down the street, heading for the interstate and throwing gravel in every direction.

With a foreboding feeling, I discard the rest of my meal into the trash can and head for the lodge. As I cross the meadow, I catch a glimpse of Leigh's truck bouncing down Miners' Alley. We reach the parking lot at the same time.

Leigh jumps from the truck with an accusing finger pointed in my direction. "Have you known all along?" Her voice quivers with anger.

My mind races to defuse the volatile situation. "Ruby swore me to secrecy, Leigh. I've been trying to figure out a way to convince Ruby to tell you who she really is without betraying her trust."

"Too late now! Mr. Dunlow went behind my back and approached Ruby on his own. He traced her identity through an address change she made years ago when she moved here from Alaska. He figured out the connection to Jonah when he discovered both had resided in Nome."

"Oh, no. How did Ruby take the news?"

"Not the way he expected. When he presented his offer, she chased him off her property with her twelve-gauge shotgun. He stopped here on the way out of town, madder than a hornet. He says the deal is off unless I can talk some sense into her. I just came from Ruby's. She won't talk to me, slammed the door in my face!"

I look past Leigh and spot Jake standing behind the truck. "Hey, Jake," I call to the frightened boy to alert Leigh of his presence.

She whirls in his direction. "Jakie, how long have you been standing there? What's up, buddy?"

"I, uh," he hesitates, realizing he has stumbled into the midst of an argument. "Nah, nothing, Mom. I was just gonna get the guys some of Edna's cookies, that's all."

Leigh takes a step back, seeing the concern on his face. "Of course, you can get some cookies for the guys."

"Save some cookies for me," I tease with a fake smile, succeeding in my subterfuge.

"Snickerdoodle or chocolate chip?" he asks, his sweet smile returning to his face.

"One of each!"

"Deal." He turns toward the lodge.

"Wait up, Jake," his mother calls. "I'll come with you."

"We can talk later, Nevy," she informs tersely, pivoting on her heels and turning her back to me before I can reply.

Dismayed, I return to my room, drained from the emotions of the day. I let the backpack drop at my feet, and burrow into the mound of quilts on the bed.

But sleep is elusive with so many conflicting thoughts swirling through my mind. I surrender and prop myself into a sitting position and reach for my laptop on the bedside table. What was the name of that realtor Leigh has been dealing with? "Dunlop, Duncan,

Dunlow," I whisper aloud. That's it. I enter the name of "Dunlow" along with the words "realtor" and "Denver" into the search bar.

The first result lists an ad for Dunlow Real Estate Company, specializing in residential, commercial, and luxury properties. But more interesting is the next listing linking a Mr. Rocky Dunlow to a newspaper article. The article describes a controversy between Mr. Dunlow and the National Park Service over his purchase of a parcel of land referred to as a wilderness inholding. The rest of the article blurs into a mumbo jumbo of legal complexity. My weary mind refuses further input as I slide into the bed's comfort and a deep slumber.

I awake the next morning with remnants of a dream of my airplane ride with Jess, her blonde hair cascading from her cowboy hat, still fresh in my mind.

"Jess?" I sit on the side of the bed, rubbing my forehead in confusion when thoughts of yesterday's events flitter through my mind. I jump from my bed in search of my purse and rummage through its contents looking for the business card Jess's father gave me at the airport. In frustration, I dump the contents into the middle of the bed but to no avail.

"Think Nevy." I mumble aloud while considering how else I might track down Mr. Sheely. I know he works for Jefferson County, but where do I begin?

Perhaps a fresh shower will help to clear the cobwebs.

Freshly laundered and wrapped in the comfort of the plush lodge bathrobe, a thought tickles my memory. I cross the room to the armoire and search the pockets of the linen jacket I was wearing at the airport.

"Success!" I yelp as my fingers close around the card. I grab my cell phone and settle into the oak rocker. The card is embossed with the department name of Jefferson County Open Space. My fingers fly across the keypad as I enter the phone number listed on the card, glancing at the clock and hoping it's not too early to find him at work.

"Jeffco Open Space, Tom Sheely speaking." He answers on my first try.

"Hi, Tom, this is Nevy Ellis, Jessica's friend on the plane from Chicago. We met at the airport when Jessica returned home from a visit with her grandparents."

"Sure, I remember. How are you, Nevy?" His welcoming voice sets me at ease. "Are you still in our beautiful state of Colorado?"

"Yes, I'm calling from Blue Eagle where I've been researching the town of Prophecy."

"Gosh!" His exuberant voice booms. "I haven't been there since I was a kid. Is there anything left of the old town?"

"Yes, the boardinghouse, jail, and saloon are still standing, as well as a number of semi-intact structures."

"Brings back fond memories of hiking up there with my dad. What can I do for you, Nevy?"

"So, Tom, I've fallen into a situation concerning a land sale. I'm hoping you can clarify some questions I have."

"Not my area of expertise," he replies, "but I would be glad to help if I can."

"Thanks." I begin with a summary of Leigh's dilemma as he listens attentively, interrupting only to ask clarifying questions until I mention the name of Mr. Dunlow.

"Whoa! Rocky Dunlow?" He stops me mid-sentence. "I'll be damned."

Taken by surprise, I stutter, "You, you know him?"

"Not personally, but his reputation is well known by my peers in Open Space. He is quite the controversial subject."

"How do you mean, Tom?" I nervously ask.

"Mr. Dunlow is notorious for buying up parcels of private land and old mining claims, inholdings they call them, located in the middle of public land. Then he holds onto the land as a kind of ransom to the highest bidder, public and private, often selling it to the National Park Service who's eager to preserve these wilderness areas."

"Oh, gosh, this is worse than I thought."

"Yeah, not the kind of person you want to be doing business with, Nevy. These inholdings create all kinds of problems by exploiting the natural resources, blocking access to backcountry recreation trails and sometimes resulting in the construction of huge luxury homes in the middle of these wilderness areas requiring access in by helicopter. You can imagine the havoc that creates!"

"I don't know how I'm going to break this news to my friend. She's counting on the sale of her property."

"My suggestion to your friend is to get in touch with Open Space in Clear Creek County before she signs anything on the dotted line with Mr. Dunlow. They may be interested in purchasing the property. You can pull up their website, and it'll give you a description of their activities."

"Tom, you've been a blessing. I'm so glad I called you first."

"I sure hate to see these developers swallowing up our land. Programs like Open Space work to preserve the beauty, history, and natural resources for all to enjoy. Let me know if I can be of further help to you."

"I will. Be sure to say hello to Jess and Mrs. Sheely for me, and thanks again, Tom."

"Will do. Good luck, Nevy."

I reach for my laptop and locate the website Tom referenced and review the Open Space annual report. My heart fills with hope as I read the section devoted to land acquisitions, detailing their efforts to purchase private property for the "preservation of the natural environment."

"If only," I say aloud.

With renewed hope, I quickly dress and exit the room, heading for Leigh's office. My knock at the closed door receives a clipped response. "Who's there?"

I flinch. "It's Nevy, Leigh." I open the door and peek inside to see a look of displeasure covering her face.

She issues a sharp reply. "What do you want, Nevy?"

"Just a few minutes of your time, I promise. I might have some good news for you." I force a smile.

She raises her hand to her forehead and shakes her head as I tiptoe inside.

Before she has a chance to object, I share a brief synopsis of my discussion with Mr. Sheely. A deep frown burrows across her forehead at the mention of the controversy involving Mr. Dunlow.

"What part of this is good news?" she asks in a sarcastic tone.

"Mr. Sheely suggested that you contact the Clear Creek County Open Space. Here, I'll show you." Hesitantly, I approach her computer as she grudgingly allows me its use. Entering the website, I scroll to the annual report and its description of the county's land acquisitions. "This explains it better than I can." I back away from the computer.

As her eyes scan the screen, her demeanor shifts, changing from agitated to excited. She straightens in her chair, leaning closer for a better view of the annual report. Glancing up from the screen with a hopeful look, she asks softly, "Nevy, do you think this could be the solution?"

"Worth a call." I give her an encouraging smile with my fingers crossed as she picks up the phone. "I'll give you some privacy," I whisper, and exit her office.

<h1 style="text-align:center">28</h1>

<h1 style="text-align:center">A Trade</h1>

I wander into the kitchen hoping it's not too late for breakfast. I'm starving having missed dinner last night.

Edna is clearing the breakfast table as I enter.

"Good morning, Edna," I chirp.

"Miss Nevy," Edna twirls from the table with a worried look. "Where have you been? We missed you at dinner last night. Leigh said you wouldn't be joining us. It was very quiet at the dinner table." Her face fills with concern.

"I'll fill you in, but first, I'm dying for a cup of coffee."

"Sit yourself down at the snack bar this second, sugar." Edna bustles about, ushering me to the barstool. "Where did you have dinner last night?"

"I stopped at Miss Liddy's for a sandwich," I offer meekly.

Edna tsks and wipes her hands on the kitchen towel thrown over her shoulder. She fills a coffee cup with a splash of cream and sets it before me. "Bacon and eggs, coming up!" she exclaims and turns to the stovetop before I can utter a weak protest.

In no time, she sets a mouthwatering platter before me and settles onto a barstool with a cup of coffee for herself.

"Enjoy your breakfast. We can talk after."

"Thank you, Edna. I'm famished!"

Edna sips her coffee while I devour my breakfast and turn with an appreciative grin. "You're a lifesaver, Edna."

She brushes off my compliments. "So..." She arches an inquisitive brow in my direction.

"There's a lot I can't tell you right now."

Leigh rushes into the kitchen, startling us, her face beaming with a smile. "There you are, Nevy. I've been looking for you."

"Good news?" I swivel on the barstool to face her.

"I hope so. I have an appointment for today with them. They seem very interested." Her voice rises with excitement.

Edna looks from Leigh to me, perplexed. "I don't know what the two of you have cooked up, but it sure is good to see those smiles."

"Can't share yet, Edna." Leigh places her index finger to her mouth. "Mum's the word, even to Charlie for right now," she whispers and crosses the room, wrapping Edna in a gentle hug. "I promise to tell you soon. It could be very good news, thanks to Nevy."

Glancing in my direction, Leigh asks, "Join me for a walk by the lake?"

"Absolutely." I turn a guilty look at the dirty dishes before me, but Edna ushers me out the door.

Leigh remains silent until we reach the path. She squeezes my arm and whispers, "Guess what, Nevy?"

Before I can respond, she blurts, "The lady I spoke with seems very interested in hearing more about Mr. Dunlow's offer. She advised me to talk with them first before I commit to anything he's offering. That's why she scheduled the appointment for today."

"Really? I can't wait to hear what she has to say."

"Yes, she told me that most likely, Mr. Dunlow doesn't have a client, but that he's interested in purchasing the property for his own development. I can't thank you enough, Nevy."

Excited as I am for Leigh, I can't help but wonder what Ruby's reaction will be.

"It sounds very promising, Leigh, but it still doesn't solve your issue with Ruby." I wince at my words, hating to dampen her excitement. "I wonder," my thoughts swirl, "if you would consider a trade in property that might sweeten the deal."

"I don't understand. What do you mean?"

"A mountain cabin in trade for a lake cabin. Ari says it's time for Ruby to move off the mountain. Last year was a very rough year for her. She might be agreeable to signing the deed in trade for a renovated lake cabin."

Leigh stops walking. "It would mean one less cabin to rent, but if it would seal the deal, I think it's something I could live with." She pauses in thought. "I have a big favor to ask, Nevy. While I'm at this meeting, would you consider talking with Ari to ask for his help in convincing Ruby to agree to a meeting with me...so that I can explain the situation and offer this idea of a trade to her?"

I realize that I'm in too deep to refuse and wonder how I got myself into the middle of these things. If Contessa only knew!

"Of course, I'll talk with Ari, but please don't get your hopes up."

Relief floods her face. "Thank you, Nevy." She glances at her watch. "I have to run. I don't want to miss this appointment. I'll talk with you when I get back."

Looking toward the heavens, I say a prayer to Grandmater for her guidance.

My heart is pounding as I follow the familiar shortcut, ducking under the wood rail fence, crossing the flower-filled meadow, and following the gravel pathway into town.

Athena bounds to my side, eager for a scratch behind the ears. "Good morning beautiful lady." I greet her, bending to reach into her deep silky fur with my fingers as Ari watches from behind the counter.

"So soon?" he asks with a questioning look.

"Lots happening, Ari. Do you have a moment?"

"Let us adjourn to the conference table." He leads the way.

"So, Miss Nevy, what troubles you this morning?" he asks in a compassionate but cautious manner.

I reach for the plastic bag tie abandoned on the tabletop, twisting it to-and-fro as my mind searches for the perfect words to convey my request.

I take a deep breath before I begin. "I've come at the request of Leigh, seeking your help with Ruby. So much has happened in the last twenty-four hours. Some good, some not so good," I attempt to explain.

"You see, after I left your store yesterday, I decided to stop at Miss Liddy's for a bite to eat. I was sitting at a table when I spotted Mr. Dunlow's car speeding out of town. He's the realtor who's been talking with Leigh."

Ari winces. "A realtor?"

I nod in confirmation and dive into the full tale of Leigh's dilemma, ending with Ruby slamming the door in Leigh's face.

Silence envelops the room as Ari digests all that I've shared.

He frowns. "I didn't realize how dire the finances have become for Leigh. She is as stubborn as Ruby about accepting help from anyone."

"No one knows, Ari. She's been shouldering the whole burden. Her meeting with Clear Creek County Open Space today could be the solution if we can convince Ruby to go along."

"I see." Ari folds his hands and looks deeply into my eyes. "And that's the purpose of your visit with me?"

"Yes, before Leigh left for her meeting, she asked if I would seek your help to convince Ruby to give Leigh a chance to explain the situation. She has an offer she'd like to make to Ruby."

"And that offer would be?"

"A trade, an exchange of property. Ruby's mountain cabin for one of the renovated lake cabins. It would be the solution to everything. Ruby moves off the mountain to the security of a lake cabin, and Leigh receives the funding she needs to keep the lodge running."

"You realize that Ruby may not reach the same conclusion?"

"But it's worth a try, isn't it?"

Ari places both hands flat on the table and nods. "Let me give Ben a call to ask if he might cover the store while we take a ride to Ruby's."

"Thank you, Ari!" My face fills with relief.

29

Pappy's Map

An hour and several of Ben's fish tales later, we arrive at Ruby's cabin. His knock on the door and calls to Ruby go unanswered.

"She must not be home." I teeter on my tiptoes for a look over his shoulder.

Ari holds his hand up to still my impatience as he knocks again and calls her name. "Ruby, it's Ari. Please open the door."

Minutes pass, but then the door cracks open a few inches, and Ruby peeks out.

"Ain't interested in talking to nobody, Ari, 'specially that one!" Ruby points an accusing finger in my direction.

Ari continues in a soft, placating manner. "You have a right to be angry, Ruby."

"Damn right I do!" she spits out.

"Just a moment of your time, that's all we ask, my friend," Ari replies to the defiant woman.

Ruby hesitates, caught between the dilemma of turning away her friend or including me if she honors his request.

"Only because of our friendship." Ruby opens the door to allow our entrance.

She turns to cross the room, a tiny, shriveled figure with drooping shoulders and labored gait.

"Have a seat at the table, Ari," she commands. "You," she says, pointing in my direction, "can sit there on the cot, I suppose."

Meekly, I follow her instructions as Ari crosses to the table and offers a chair to Ruby.

"Stop your fussing. I'm still capable of sitting down at my own table," she scolds.

Unruffled by her reply, Ari responds, "A gentleman always holds a chair for a lady."

Ruby grumbles and sits in the chair. "Not much to talk about, so you might as well save your breath. Maybe you don't understand what's going on here, Ari." Anger and torment fill her face. "They're trying to steal my property out from under me, the last plot of land still belonging to my granddaddy! That's the McLean way, don't you know? No allegiance to anyone, much less their best friend in the whole world." Ruby heaves a great sigh as she spews forth her pent-up emotions and feelings of wrongs done to her revered grandfather.

Ari bows his head, then looking into Ruby's eyes, he chooses another approach. "Ruby, we both know what a difficult year this has been for you on this mountain."

"That's not the point." Ruby squirms, clenching her teeth in a tight grimace.

Silently, he raises his hand, asking permission to continue.

Ruby straightens in her chair, assuming a defensive posture, with arms crossed and a scowl covering her face.

Ari, nonplussed, continues in a soft voice, "I don't know what Mr. Dunlow, the real estate developer, said to you, but I do know that he went behind Miss Leigh's back by talking with you first before she had a chance to explain. That was the purpose of her visit here."

Ruby shakes her head and mumbles under her breath as Ari continues. "You see, Ruby, Leigh is in jeopardy of losing the lodge. Then who knows what might happen? A developer like Mr. Dunlow could turn the lodge and its holdings into one big subdivision or worse. We just don't know what his true intent is. All I'm asking, is that you give Leigh a chance to explain."

The door shudders with the sound of frantic pounding.

Without thinking, I jump from the cot and race to the door with Ari and Ruby on my heels.

As I open the door, Leigh stands with her fist raised in mid-air, anxiety and fear covering her face. Chris, who's standing behind her, places his hands gently on her shoulders in an attempt to calm her.

Leigh blurts out, "Is Jakie with you?" She peers desperately into the cabin.

Chris intercedes to explain. "Jake and Mogul are missing. We've searched everywhere and can't find them. Ben told us where you had gone."

Leigh interjects, "Edna called me in the middle of my meeting upset because she couldn't find Jake or Mogul. She hasn't seen them since just after breakfast assuming Jake had gone to help at the cabins. He's been gone for hours."

"We left Edna and Charlie in town searching and drove here with the hope that he had followed you." The worried expression on Chris's face betrays his calm demeanor.

I turn to look at Ari and Ruby who shake their heads in confirmation and turn back to advise that we haven't seen him.

Ruby whispers from behind, "You don't 'spose he might have gone up to Prophecy, do you?"

"Prophecy?!" Leigh turns a wild-eyed look at Ruby. "He knows he's not allowed up there by himself. Why would you say that?" she asks accusingly.

Ruby squirms her body between the door and me and grasps the frame for support. "Well, now, he visited me a few days ago, filled with questions about the legend of Pappy Young. He was 'specially curious about the map to the gold mine Pappy was supposed to have hid somewhere in Prophecy. Wanted me to tell him the story all over again."

"You foolish old woman!" Leigh screeches. "Filling his head with nonsense."

"Take a breath, Leigh," Chris pleads. "We'll find him."

She turns to face him. "But what if he's fallen into one of those abandoned shafts?!"

"He knows the danger of those shafts. More than likely, he's lost track of time. We can take my truck up to Prophecy. It can handle the terrain—"

Before he can finish his sentence, Leigh hops from the porch and runs to the truck, and Chris follows.

I turn an anxious look at Ari, who replies, "We can follow in my SUV. It's a stock four wheel drive and can handle these mountains."

"I'm coming, too," Ruby states in a tone preventing argument.

Ari helps Ruby into the front seat as I climb into the back, and we follow Chris's lead. Ari pauses at the ridge to allow Chris a safe distance to maneuver his truck down the ravine. Conversation is limited due to the lurching movement and straining sounds of the vehicle as we dodge the boulders and rocks on our way down and our ascent up to the boardinghouse.

We arrive to hear Leigh's pitiful pleas as she calls out her son's name. "Jake, Mogul, where are you?! Answer me!" she desperately shouts.

We gather in a huddled group on the wooden porch of the boardinghouse to make an action plan.

Chris takes command. "Leigh and I can search the boardinghouse and general store; Ari, Nevy, you can search the saloon and adjacent building."

Ruby hasn't joined us. Instead, she walks to the end of the porch and stands with hands raised to her eyes as she peers up the mountainside.

I join her as the others trail behind me. "What are you thinking, Ruby?" I ask softly, understanding how upsetting this is for her.

Ruby shakes her head and turns to me with a troubled look covering her face. "Ain't gonna find him here. My guess is he's gone up to the mine."

Leigh steps between us, grabbing Ruby by the arm. "Why would you say that? Jake knows he's forbidden to go anywhere near that mine."

Ruby jerks away from Leigh's grasp and replies, "Jake knows I've searched ever' part of Prophecy over the years looking for that map. Only place left to look is up at the mine where Pappy spent his last years sharing stories with the miners."

Leigh turns a pleading look toward Chris.

He responds, "We can pick up the fire trail above the cemetery, but it's going to be rough going until we reach it. That hill gets steeper as you go, so we need to switchback slowly across it. Follow my lead, Ari."

Ruby and I scramble into Ari's SUV as he takes the driver's seat. "Buckle up, ladies," he warns.

Chris pulls into the rutted remains of the old road, passing in front of the saloon and adjacent buildings. His truck disappears behind the last of the buildings as we follow and begin the slow ascent, switching back and forth in order to traverse the steep hill.

I brace my hands on the back of Ruby's seat in futile support as we rock along the rugged terrain. The SUV clings at a perilous angle, defying gravity, the drive testing its capabilities.

An eternity later, we pass by Pappy's monument and reach the fire trail. We heave a collective sigh of relief as the tires dig into the gravel surface, and we begin our final ascent to the Prophecy Mine.

Suddenly, Chris's truck comes to a stop. He motions with a raised arm through the open window for us to do the same.

"What is he doing?" I ask.

Ari opens his window and turns to me. Placing his index finger to his mouth, he whispers, "Listen."

The muted sound of Mogul's bark can be heard in the distance.

Chris motions us forward as Leigh leans from her open window frantically calling her son's name. It's a heartbreaking sound.

We arrive at the clearing located below the Prophecy Mine. Mogul prances impatiently on the hilltop. The distraught dog disappears and reappears over and over again.

Leigh jumps from the truck and scrambles up the hillside before we can exit the SUV.

Chris follows closely behind, calling in a soothing voice to the distressed dog. "It's okay, boy. Settle down; we're coming."

Ari waves for me to follow Chris and Leigh. "You go ahead, Nevy. It's too steep for us. We'll wait for you here."

I nod and follow the path Chris and Leigh have taken. I stop to catch my breath at the top of the hill, relieved to see that the boarded entrance to the mine remains untouched.

Mogul paces in front of a decaying log cabin a short distance from the mine's entrance, entering and exiting the dark cavity of its doorway as Leigh and Chris run, calling Jake's name.

It's then that we hear Jake's distinctive high-pitched whistle coming from the depths of the building.

Chris pauses at the entrance, holding an arm across it to prevent Leigh from entering. "Let me go in first, Leigh. Too many of us in there can bring this whole thing down. See how the bracing has rotted?" He points to the precariously leaning cabin wall.

Before she can reply, Chris removes his hat and hands it to her, bends his tall frame, and enters the dark building as we pace outside.

I grab Mogul's trailing leash to restrain the pup from following. "Mogul, stay!" I command the reluctant dog, who's torn between obedience to my command and allegiance to his owner.

Moments pass. Sounds of shuffling come from inside as we listen to Chris's soft voice and his reassurances to Jake.

There is a loud sound of wrenching wood and Jake's sharp cry of pain.

Leigh gasps and disappears into the cabin, only to back out seconds later as Chris emerges, carrying Jake.

She hovers over her son as Chris explains. "He fell through the floorboards, a common accident in these old buildings filled with dry rot. I think he sprained his ankle; he may have broken it. He can't stand on his own. Pretty painful, huh, buddy?"

"Hurts like hell!" Jake curses, bringing a relieved smile to all of our faces at the realization of how much worse it could have been.

Mogul whimpers at my side as Jake catches sight of his pup.

"Mogul!" he shouts. I inch closer as Chris bends on one knee for the two to reunite.

"It was Mogul who helped us find you, Jake," I tell him.

He gives the adoring pup a hug. "Good dog, Mogul."

Leigh brushes the hair from Jake's eyes with relieved tears streaming down her face.

"Mom, stop your fussing." He gently pushes her hand away.

"I have a right to be concerned, Jake," she snaps. "You scared us to death! What were you thinking?"

"I was only trying to help you," he replies defensively. "I knew if I could find Pappy's map, it would solve all your money problems, but I fell through the floor before I had a chance to search."

"Oh, Jakie," Leigh responds, crestfallen.

Chris stands. "Time enough for that conversation, I reckon. We need to get him to the ER for a look at his ankle."

Chris peers in my direction. "Nevy, can you handle Mogul down the hillside? Best if you two go first."

"Good idea, Chris." I shorten the leash securing it tightly in my clinched fist as the reluctant dog and I descend the hillside stopping frequently as Mogul pauses to confirm that the others are following.

Ari and Ruby lean against the SUV, watching our progress. At the sight of Ruby, Jake holds his hand out, and she steps forward, enclosing his hand with both of hers. Tears streak her weary face.

Leigh steps forward defensively. "We need to get you to the ER, Jake." She pauses to look at Ruby and adds, "You've done enough harm for the day."

A pained look covers Jake's face as Ruby releases his hand and steps away. "It's not Ruby's fault!" he shouts in her defense. "She warned me to stay away from the mine. She said it was nothing but bad luck and heartache. But I thought I could help you with your troubles, Mom. I've heard you talking with that mean man. I see how sad he makes you feel."

Leigh stands stoically at her son's side with all eyes on her. "Well, you don't have to worry anymore, Son. I've solved my own problems." She looks at Ruby. "You can keep that damn cabin. I don't need it. Open Space made me a better offer. Turns out they did their own search for land rights. They discovered that each time a claim or land was placed for sale, Isaiah purchased it. Over the years, he ended up owning all of the abandoned townsites and properties, nearly a hundred acres. When Papa Jake passed, Jake and I inherited it all!"

"Oh, my," I gasp.

Leigh continues, "The folks at Open Space are excited to acquire such a large piece of property out from under Dunlow and his dirty tricks. They told me this purchase will allow them to preserve and protect a large piece of the river basin backcountry as well as the historical site of Prophecy. It's a win-win! I secure the money to keep the lodge in business as well as preserve Prophecy's legacy."

The news has caught us all by surprise.

"Come on, Chris, let's get this boy to Georgetown." Leigh marches stiff-necked toward the truck.

Chris glances in our direction and shakes his head in dismay. He shrugs his shoulders in defeat and follows Leigh. Jake casts a sorrowful look at Ruby, and we hear him ask Chris, "Please talk to my mom. This was all my fault. Ruby had nothing to do with it."

Ruby turns to Ari, drained and defeated. "Please take me home," she whispers.

Ari and I share a look of resignation. He helps Ruby into the SUV while I follow behind, urging Mogul into the back seat.

We retrace our path descending the mountainside. Pappy's headstone emerges, signaling our return to Prophecy.

"Your legend lives on, Pappy," I whisper as we pass his grave.

The exhausted pup stretches across the seat, his furry head propped on my lap, his eyes searching mine for reassurance. I scratch his ears in an attempt to calm his worries, wishing someone could calm my worries as well.

As we near her cabin, Ruby turns to Ari and issues a short command. "Drop me off at the road, Ari. I can handle it from there."

He ignores her and pulls off the road, driving, instead, to her porch. He exits the SUV to assist her into the cabin. She doesn't protest. The fight has gone out of Ruby.

As Ari returns to the SUV, I utter a sigh of despair. "Ari, what can we do?"

He shakes his head and looks in my direction. "Only time will put this fire out, Nevy. It's best to let the embers settle. There are too many inflamed feelings right now."

We follow Miners' Alley down the mountain in silence.

As we enter the driveway, Mogul rouses and stands with his front legs balanced on the back of Ari's seat. He gives a great "woof" at the sight of his home. Ari reaches behind to give the pup a gentle pat as I attach the leash and exit the SUV and bid goodbye to Ari.

"I'll visit Ruby tomorrow," he promises.

I murmur a small thanks, my voice choking with emotion.

Mogul pulls at the leash when we enter the lodge and leads me toward the familiar muffled voices in the kitchen.

Edna and Charlie sit side by side at the family table, their conversation cut short by our appearance.

I linger hesitantly at the doorway, straining to hold the whimpering pup who dances at my side.

Charlie is quick to come to my rescue and jumps from his chair. "I'll take Mogul to the barn for now. Be back shortly." He turns to give Edna's shoulder a gentle squeeze.

"I take it you've heard the news about Jake?" I ask.

"Leigh called on their way to Georgetown and filled us in." Edna pats the chair beside her. "Come, sit. You look done in."

"Ah, Edna, I think I'll rest for a bit." I grimace at my futile attempt to escape.

Edna nods her head in understanding. The hallway leading to my room seems a mile long to my leaden feet. I enter the solitude of my private suite, closing off the outside world and look into the accusing gaze of Rose René.

Beyond tired, I cannot believe the time showing on the clock. It's only 5:45 p.m., too early for bed.

The oak rocking chair calls to me. I settle into its welcoming arms and comforting sway and snuggle into the quilt, hoping for solace and a solution from my faithful muse. "What are we to do, Grandmater? How can I make this right?" My eyelids grow heavy with fatigue, and I lean my head on the headrest and quickly fall asleep.

A soft tapping on my door rouses me from my sleep. "Just a moment," I call out as I untangle from the quilt, turn on the table lamp, and hurry to the door.

Edna bustles into the room carrying a dinner tray. The delicious smell wafts through my room and reminds me of how famished I am.

"I thought you might be a little hungry, Nevy." She crosses the room and sets the tray on the table next to the rocker.

"I'm starving! Bless you, Edna," I follow in her wake. "Did Leigh and Jake make it home yet?"

Edna turns and pats my shoulder in a reassuring manner. "Yes, the good news is that there's no break, just a badly sprained ankle. The bad news is that he'll be on crutches for a while. He's tuckered out and fast asleep. Leigh is with him."

"I'm so glad to hear that."

Edna taps the rocker. "Sit now and eat while your dinner is hot." She removes the linen napkin, and I feast my eyes on a heaping platter of a fried chicken dinner, Jake's favorite.

Unable to contain my emotions, my eyes fill with tears. "Oh, Edna, I think this is all my fault."

"Nevy, why would you ever think such a thing?"

I shrug my shoulders in despair and confess, "If I hadn't encouraged Ruby to share her story, she would've remained silent and wouldn't have told Jake more about the legend of Pappy Young."

Edna pats my back. "Sugar, Jake was desperate to help his momma. He's been curious about that legend ever since he heard his buddies talking about it. You saw how excited he got the evening you first arrived when Charlie shared the story with you."

Feeling less guilty at her words, I wrap Edna in a bear hug and kiss her on the cheek.

"Wipe those eyes now and eat my dinner before it gets cold. I'm going to join Charlie in the kitchen to share dinner together."

30

A Cabin by the Lake

I'm awakened by the silence. In my tiredness, I forgot to turn on the little fan, my noise maker, that lulls me to sleep each night. Nor did I close the drapes; the room was dark by the time I slipped into bed, but is now bathed in bright sunshine.

But I'm in no hurry. For the first time since my arrival, I have no plan for the day ahead of me. So I take my time showering and dressing, purposely delaying my appearance at the family table, wondering what kind of reception I'll receive from Leigh.

To my surprise, the kitchen bustles with activity. I pause at the doorway to observe the scene before me.

Edna stands at the eight-burner gas stove, overseeing a sizzling pan of bacon and a skillet of sunny side eggs.

Charlie mans the toaster, building a tower of toasted bread, which he slathers with butter.

Jake sits at the family table, his foot in a fiberglass cast propped on the adjacent chair. A pair of crutches leans on the counter nearby. Mogul rests in peaceful contentment under Jake's raised leg.

"Come on, Edna girl, this toast is gonna go cold before you finish them bacon and eggs," Charlie teases in a giddy manner.

Edna giggles and replies, "You make me break these eggs, and you're going to be real sorry, Mister."

He turns to Jake, feigning a scared look behind Edna's back, tweaking a crooked grin from the somber-faced boy.

Mogul is the first to notice my presence, He raises his head to issue a welcoming bark.

Edna turns in my direction. "Good morning, Nevy. You're just in time for breakfast. Come, join Jake at the table." She waves her spatula in his direction.

Charlie hurries to the table to offer a chair. "Allow me, Miss Nevy."

Bewildered by all the attention, I shrug and look to Jake for an explanation, but his mood reflects more of the one I had expected to find.

He shakes his head in annoyance at their antics and mumbles a soft, "Morning, Nevy."

Charlie carries the mountain of toast to the table and explains. "Well, now, it seems that our Leigh hit the lotto when she followed your friend's advice to get in touch with Clear Creek County Open Space. We owe your friend a world of gratitude."

Hesitantly, I reply, "Yes, Leigh mentioned their offer yesterday, but it was a bit confusing to understand all that she was saying."

Charlie grasps the back of the empty chair across from me and explains. "We always thought of Prophecy as an old abandoned town not worth anything with the mine boarded up and closed off as it is. We had our hands full taking care of the lodge and our sadness over Jacob's passing."

Edna adds, "That and the fact that Prophecy was always a taboo subject around Isaiah and Jacob. We wonder now if Isaiah bought up all the property rights and claims for the purpose of sealing it and the mine off forever." She turns to Charlie. "Help me dish up these bacon and eggs so we can fill Nevy in on all the details."

Charlie hurries to the stove, returning to the table carrying two dishes, placing them before Jake and me.

"I'm not really hungry, Charlie," Jake mumbles. "Toast is all I want." He leans a weary head on his propped arm.

"Give it a try, son," Charlie pleads, looking down on the despondent child.

Edna follows with the remaining two dishes, setting them on the table and reaching for Jake's hand. "Just try a few bites, Jake," she says softly. "It'll make you feel better. You didn't eat much of my fried chicken dinner last night. You must be hungry."

"Anyway," Charlie continues, "looks like Meadow View Lodge is back in business thanks to you, Miss Nevy." Charlie raises his coffee cup in my direction. "A toast to Nevy."

Edna raises hers and adds, "For saving Meadow View."

I protest, embarrassed by their praise. "I did nothing. Truly, it was all Leigh's doing."

It's then that I realize she's missing. "Where is Leigh this morning?"

"She had another meeting with Clear Creek County, but she promised to be home soon to celebrate," Edna exclaims, filled with joy.

Through all of this, Jake has remained silent. I look across the table and catch his eye. "This is good news, right, Jake?" I ask in an attempt to include him in the conversation.

He peers in my direction with a sorrowful look. "Yeah, I guess, but what about Ruby? What's going to happen to her?" he asks with concern written across his face.

I search my thoughts and remember Ari's promise. "When Ari and I dropped Ruby off at her cabin, he promised he would return today to check on her."

"He did?" Jake sits a little straighter in his chair, a glimmer of hope brightening his eyes.

"Yes, he did, and if anyone can fix this situation, Ari can. He and Ruby have a special friendship. So let's see what Ari's visit with Ruby turns up, okay?" I share an encouraging smile.

"Sure," he murmurs.

Charlie takes a last sip of coffee and pushes away from the table. "I bet Chris is down at the cabins, Jake. You want to go along with me? I can drive you down in the pickup."

Even the mention of Chris doesn't elicit a response from Jake, who shifts his foot off the chair.

"No, I can make it there on my own." He reaches for the crutches as Mogul stands guardedly by his side.

"Here now, let me grab them crutches for you." Charlie comes to his aid as I cross the room to open the door for their exit.

"Stop your fussing, guys." Jake accepts the crutches grudgingly from Charlie.

Halfway across the deck, Jake stops and points toward the road. "Is that Mom's truck coming down Miners' Alley?"

"Sure is, but who is that with her?" Charlie squints into the morning sun.

Edna has followed us onto the deck. "Why, that's Ari, but who have they got with them?"

"Ruby!" Jake shrieks and hobbles down the steps and waits for his mother to park the truck.

Leigh hops from the truck and runs to her son's side while Ari helps Ruby from the truck.

Jake turns a stunned look from his mother to Ruby.

"I've invited Ari and Ruby to join us for our celebration." Her face beams with a look of achievement that I haven't seen before.

All eyes turn to Ruby in stunned silence. Ruby's eyes rest on Jake.

"Reckon I'd like to take a look at that cabin you been so excited to tell me about, Jake. You up for a walk?" A smile reserved only for Jake fills her face.

"You bet! It's down the lake path, not too far," he promises.

We watch as Jake balances on his crutches and the old woman leans on her cane, their heads bent in each other's direction in a loving friendship as they follow the lake path to the cabin.

"Well, I'll be." Charlie shakes his head. "How in the world did you two accomplish that?" He looks from Ari to Leigh.

Ari raises both hands. "It was all Leigh's doing. I just went along as the mediator."

"Not fair, Ari. If it wasn't for your help I wouldn't have gotten my foot in the door." Leigh wraps her arms around his waist and leans her head on his chest. "I'm forever indebted to you," she whispers.

"But how? What did you say to her to change her mind?" Edna asks, bewildered by the scene that has just taken place.

"I started off by asking if she would share Isaiah's letter to Jonah and his notes in the Bible that Nevy told me about."

"Thank you," she whispers, glancing in my direction.

"We sat together on the cot and shared our grief over Isaiah's words. Then she gave me a chance to tell my part of the story about my dealings with Mr. Dunlow and the offer from Open Space. I asked for her forgiveness. The fact that I was sobbing probably helped." Leigh blinks back the tears hovering on her eyelids.

"Ruby said she would consider the offer from Open Space after she takes a look at the lake cabin."

"By the looks of those two," I reply, "I don't think you have much to worry about." We turn to watch Jake and Ruby. Their laughter carries on the mountain breeze as they disappear inside the cabin.

31

Homecoming

It's the morning of my departure. I have been awake since the first sign of daybreak, nestled in the oak rocker.

I purposely booked an early afternoon flight. I don't wish to prolong my goodbyes of yesterday. They asked me to stay longer, but I know it's the perfect time for me to leave.

This weekend is all about Ruby, as it should be. She and Leigh signed the final sales contract with Open Space yesterday. They'll move Ruby off the mountain and into her new home.

There is a lightness and softness about Ruby now that the decision has been made. A part of it is the move, which will make her life much easier. She could hardly contain her pleasure at the thought of moving to the lovely renovated cabin when she returned from her inspection with Jake.

"It'll be good for Sass and Dolly to get off the mountainside," she reasoned.

But I think the true reason for her inner happiness is the satisfaction of accomplishing her goal of restoring the name and reputation of her beloved grandfather, Jonah LaPierre.

Open Space has suggested a role as a docent in Prophecy for Ruby when they begin running tours in the old town. There, she can relive the stories shared by her grandfather and, perhaps, include a few of Jonah's whale tales in the process. She walks with her head held high these days, proud of her heritage, a secret no more.

I cast my eyes about the suite one last time. I'll miss this lovely sanctuary. My life in Chicago seems foreign to me now, attached as I've become to Meadow View Lodge and its inhabitants.

I stand before the portrait of Rose René, sunlight illuminating her mesmerizing image. I've chosen this moment to say my farewell to this woman I've come to know so intimately.

"I promise to honor your family and you, Rose René McLean. Your legacy lives on at Meadow View," I whisper softly, her image and story forever imprinted in my memory.

Shouldering the backpack, I pick up the suitcases to stifle the sound that the wheels would make on the wooden floor and tiptoe across the room. I exit through the French doors and follow the wraparound porch to the front of the house.

"Caught ya!" Jake giggles as I spy Leigh and him ensconced on the swing and wrapped in a quilt.

"No fair, you guys." I fake a pout.

Jake hobbles across the porch to wrap his arms around my waist in a tight hug as Leigh follows to join us.

"We are going to miss you, Nevy. Promise you'll come back." His words are muffled through the group hug.

"I promise." I reach to tousle his lush brown curls one last time, trying to hold back my tears.

"We have a going-away present for you." Leigh reveals a wrapped gift from behind her back.

She gives it to her son, who offers it to me, his beautiful face filled with the smile I have come to love and will never forget.

"Open it now!" he shouts.

"Yes, please open it," Leigh encourages me.

"Oh, my," I murmur, and with trembling fingers, peel away the delicate wrapping paper. My heart leaps as I peer at the smiling faces of each of my new friends.

They stand together in a group under the Meadow View Lodge sign. Charlie, Chris, and Ari form the back row with Charlie resting his hands on Edna's shoulders as Chris does with Leigh and Ari with

Ruby. Jake stands next to Ruby holding her hand. Mogul and Athena sit as bookends with adoring eyes turned toward their masters.

"Do you like the frame, Nevy?" Jake asks, his eyes wide and voice filled with excitement. "Chris and I carved it special for you. See the flowers in the corners? They were the hardest part." He points with a stubby finger. "This is the one I carved all by myself. It's a wild rose. That was Mom's idea." He turns a loving look toward his mother.

I trace the flower with my fingers, loving its imperfection in the exquisitely carved frame and hold it closer to scrutinize the inscription, which I read aloud. "Friendship, the true hidden treasure at Meadow View Lodge."

I choke back the tears and whisper, "I love you guys."

"We love you, too, Nevy," Jake and Leigh say in unison.

"Time to hit the road," I sputter. Reluctantly, I climb into Red to begin the journey home, stopping beneath the Meadow View sign to wave a final goodbye.

As I pass by Ari's, I give a short tap on my horn, and picture him seated at the wooden table, his mug of coffee before him and the lovely Athena at his side as the sound of Pachelbel's Canon fills the air.

I pause at the yield sign to the entrance of I-70 and roll my window down for one last deep breath of mountain air. I accelerate and enter the world I left behind.

The drive to Denver is anticlimactic as the majestic Rocky Mountain range fades like a disappearing mirage into my rearview mirror.

I've built extra time into my schedule, anticipating possible delays along the route, but I make the seventy-three-mile drive in record time, exiting off I-70 onto Peña Boulevard.

It's with a nostalgic heart that I bid goodbye to my trusty steed, the last tangible connection to my Colorado adventure. I remove my luggage and sign off with the car rental agent who, to my surprise, dismisses the slight damage to the bumper with a shrug.

I head outside to wait for the airport shuttle. A young man stands alone at the shuttle bus stop.

"Have you been waiting long?" I greet him as the roar of a plane overhead momentarily curtails further conversation.

He nods. "Shuttle should be here soon. I've been waiting quite a while. Just missed the last one," he replies, combing his fingers through his head of disheveled hair.

I nod in return, and we settle into a silent wait, each of us lost in our private worlds, strangers crossing each other's paths for a moment in time.

The shuttle bus appears. He slings his heavy backpack over his shoulder and steps inside, but quickly turns back to pick up my bags. "My mom would be all over me for that!" He grins sheepishly.

I scramble on board murmuring my thanks and taking a seat across from him. "Looks like you've been doing some hiking," I say, glancing at his hiking boots.

"Yeah, my college roommate is from Denver. He invited me out to climb Mount Bierstadt with him. It's supposed to be the easiest of the fourteeners, but the elevation still kicked my butt. Guess I'm not in as good of shape as I thought. Heading home today."

"Where's home?"

"McMinnville, Oregon, elevation one hundred and fifty-seven feet. Guess I had better do some high elevation training. He invited me out again next summer." He laughs at his own expense. "How about you?"

"Heading home, too, only in the opposite direction, Chicago."

He nods as we again settle into a comfortable silence, my own thoughts shifting to the article I'll write.

I remember the articles Grandmater wrote for the *Girdham Free Press* and pledge to make it Alma-Mater-worthy, to encourage others to visit Meadow View and Prophecy and make their own discoveries.

The shuttle bus changes course exiting off Peña Boulevard in the direction of Jeppesen Terminal, interrupting my thoughts. I glance up and catch a view of a massive cobalt blue sculpture of a wild horse rearing on its hind legs.

"Whoa! That is some piece of art," I yelp.

The young man turns his head in the direction of the sculpture and chuckles. "The locals call it 'Blucifer' for its demon-like appearance. It even has glowing red eyes! My friend tells me it's created quite a bit of controversy."

"Hmm, yes, we have one of those ourselves," I confess. An image of a giant owl perched atop the Harold Washington Library Center flashes through my thoughts, turning my focus towards home.

We disembark then, each of us uttering safe travel wishes to the other and fading into the anonymous throng of travelers entering the terminal.

After checking in and clearing security, I have an abundance of time, several hours to fill before my 2:40 p.m. departure, and an opportunity to continue working on the draft for my article.

A quick trip on the automated train takes me to Terminal B. Jostled among the disparate passengers, I narrowly miss colliding with a giggling tot mounted atop a rolling duffle bag being pushed by an older sibling.

The emotion of the day and travel fatigue have begun to take their toll. A search for a restaurant leads me to a cafe advertising sandwiches served on a variety of freshly baked breads. The smell sends me into a swoon and a momentary flashback of Edna's kitchen while I stand in line to place my order.

Sandwich in hand, I scan the premises and spot a lone table being cleared in an isolated corner. Perfect, I think to myself, the challenge being to claim it before anyone else does. I dodge the way through fellow travelers, carry-on luggage, and crowded tables in a predatory fashion, reaching my destination just before a young woman with eyes focused a bit too long on her cell phone.

"Sorry," I murmur, plopping my backpack on the table to stake my claim.

She walks away, uttering the word "rude" under her breath as I gratefully settle into my secluded corner.

A parade of travelers passes by the entrance of the cafe, a microcosm of the world only footsteps away from my table, but I'm lost in my own world of remembered thoughts and experiences.

Time passes quickly as I'm absorbed in the activity of writing. It's time to find my gate for the flight home.

Seated in my window seat, I bury my nose into the neck cushion purchased at the airport. A wise investment, I discover, as it allows me to escape the bickering couple sharing my row. I fall asleep immediately.

I arrive at O'Hare a little after 6:00 p.m. and send Bob a quick message, advising that I'll text again when I have my luggage in hand.

He responds immediately. "Welcome home, Miss Nevy. We've missed you."

A smile creeps across my lips at his warm welcome.

Swept into the mass of exiting passengers, I make my way to the baggage area, experiencing a brief conflicted feeling of melancholy over the absence from sight of a single cowboy hat or pair of western boots.

My bags finally arrive, and I send Bob a text. He replies that he's ten minutes away.

I step outside, and I'm momentarily disoriented by the blast of humid summer air and the frenzy that greets me. There's a cacophony of honking horns, jockeying vehicles vying for parking spaces, and people-filled sidewalks. It's with great relief when I spot Bob's limo weaving through the traffic.

The gleaming limo glides to the sidewalk. After a quick hug with Bob, I relax into the comfort of the deep leather seats and blessed air conditioning, thinking how surreal coming back to Chicago feels.

Even the thought of home strikes an illusory image. Home? I'd been in the carriage house for such a short time before leaving for Colorado. Mixed emotions leave me feeling unsettled.

The scene outside my window is a blur of passing vehicles on this busy Friday evening as revelers travel into the city for a night of entertainment. The closer we get to the city, the slower the traffic becomes assuming a bumper-to-bumper pace.

The sun has begun its slow descent in the west as the city lights rise, twinkling on the horizon.

It's past 7:30 p.m. when we reach the entrance gates to Summer Hill. A short pause allows Bob to enter the security code I share, signaling the ornate iron gates to open.

The tree-lined drive offers a tranquil refuge after the busy city streets and recalls to mind my first visit to this enchanted forest. My heart leaps with unexpected joy at the sight of the carriage house, its twinkling interior lights welcoming me home.

Bob coasts to a stop as my trembling fingers search inside my purse for the keys to my home. "Home," I whisper.

He waits patiently with my luggage as I fumble to open the massive door.

"You can set the bags here in the hallway, Bob. I can take it from there. I can't tell you how happy it made me feel to see your welcoming face tonight." We share another quick hug before he leaves.

Excitement builds as I close the door and turn to behold my surroundings.

The French grandfather clock greets me like an old friend, its rhythmic ticking a warm reminder of all my cherished treasures waiting to be rediscovered.

I pause, overwhelmed by the beauty before me. The crystal chandelier shimmers with light above the pedestaled round vintage dining table.

A handwritten note has been left on the table. The elegant gold-embossed card with the initials "C&R" reads:

Welcome Home, Nevy.

We're sorry we're not here in person to greet you. You'll find the refrigerator fully stocked and a lovely chilled white waiting for you. We're excited to hear about your adventure and discoveries.

Love, Contessa and Robert

I'm moved by their warm welcome and feel a sliver of guilt at the knowledge that Contessa and Robert won't return from their travels for many days yet. But I do relish this private time of my homecoming.

A loud knock on the door interrupts my thoughts. "Who in the world..." I mutter, perturbed by the interruption. I cross the room and stand on tiptoes to peek through the peephole, but my full view is obstructed by a large floral arrangement.

I crack the door an inch to hear an unfamiliar male voice ask, "Miss Nevy?"

I respond with a timid, "Yes?"

"It's Shan, Robert's son." A handsome face peers from around the flowers.

"So sorry, it's a gift from Dad's garden. I was supposed to have it waiting for you beside their note."

At a loss for words, I open the door wider. I invite him in, blaming jet lag for my slow response.

"Totally understand. I won't stay. Let me set this on the table for you." He turns, his brown eyes dancing with mischief under the light of the chandelier, and whispers, "Don't tell Dad I was late with my delivery."

Charmed, I chuckle and reply, "Your secret is safe with me."

"I'm staying at the house until Tessa and Dad return. If you need anything. Maybe we could share lunch at the gazebo someday?"

I commit before thinking. "I, um, yes that would be lovely."

"Great! I'll let you get settled in then."

I follow him to the door. "Talk soon, Nevy, and welcome home." His face fills with an infectious grin.

I watch as he follows the path leading to Summer Hill. He turns to give a final wave, and I attempt a wave in return and stumble back through the doorway.

Disconcerted, I retrace my steps to the foyer and busy myself by retrieving the notebooks from my backpack. I carry them to the side table next to Grandmater's rocker, light the globe lamp, then take a step back, and murmur, "Yes, that'll do."

As tempting as a glass of wine sounds, exhaustion sweeps over me, propelling my path upstairs. I open the window to breathe in the summer night's air.

After a quick change into my nightgown, I sink into the sublime comfort of my own bed, a sojourner no more. "Home, at last, Grandmater." I fall soundly asleep.

The early morning song of the cardinal perching atop the blue spruce floats on the lake breeze and through my open window. It's music to my ears as I awake to the joyful awareness of my homecoming.

I sit up in bed and survey the room filled with treasured objects as recognition turns darkened forms into shape. I reach to light the Tiffany lamp, and my gaze rests on Dad's writing desk nestled in the space created by the dormer window.

I delight at the sight of the oak coat rack strung with my collection of colorful silk purses. Each one hangs from a wooden peg by its fragile golden chain like a delicate Christmas tree ornament. The one from James, with its hidden treasure, graces the top.

My survey continues to the brick wall and the hand-carved wooden bookcase now filled with a collection of daguerreotype photos. It's the perfect spot to place the framed photo given to me by Jake and Leigh, a forever reminder of the love and friendship of my friends at Meadow View Lodge.

The chimes of the French grandfather clock hasten my decision to leave the comfort of my nest. I slip from my cocoon and onto the aged wooden flooring, using memory and touch to guide my path down the loft staircase.

A halo of golden lamplight encircles the stack of notebooks I placed on the side table, beckoning for my attention, but that will come later. I gather Grandmater's heirloom quilt that adorns the arm of the rocking chair into a loving embrace. Its touch on my cheek feels like worn silk, soft and smooth from decades of Ellis use, its warmth like a gentle hug welcoming me home.

I settle into the oak rocking chair, a memory keeper like the Ellis quilt. Although the spectacular image of the Rocky Mountains will remain imprinted in my memory and in my heart, I realize that nothing will compare to the sunrise over Lake Michigan that heralds my homecoming and reconnection to all that is familiar and meaningful in my life.

"Welcome home, Nevy," Grandmater's voice floats upon the whispers of the angels.

32

Nevy's Article

As sunrise turns to sun-filled morning, I reach for the stack of notebooks to begin the process of writing the article for our new endeavor, *Sharing Discoveries*.

A Visit to Prophecy, Colorado

I traveled to the gold mining town of Prophecy, Colorado to discover a hidden treasure and hit the mother lode!

The abandoned gold mining town of Prophecy lies at an elevation of 10,400 feet, located above the town of Blue Eagle.

A late bloomer, Prophecy evolved from the dreams of two young men, Isaiah McLean and Jonah LaPierre, better known to the locals as "The Prophets," each bearing the name of a prophet in the Bible.

Strangers to each other, they first met during the boom days of the 1890s in the renowned Cripple Creek District of Colorado, where they learned the skills required for hard rock mining.

The Labor Wars of 1903-1904 in The District propelled Isaiah and Jonah to pursue their dreams of finding their own hidden treasure. Their destination was Blue Eagle, Colorado, where Isaiah's father and uncles had chased their dreams with the original 49ers, only to join the "go-backers" when their funds and supplies ran out. It was Isaiah's quest to fulfill his father's dream.

Lady Luck smiled on The Prophets when they chanced upon Pappy Young, an old-time miner returning from the high country. He pointed them in the direction of a suspected ancient river channel he had spotted on his way out of the mountains.

Single-minded, Pappy had no interest in it himself, having spent the past forty years searching for the gold described in a legend about a lost gold mine that contained a vein of gold as wide as a man's arm, the mother lode they called it.

261

Isaiah and Jonah found the ancient river channel and named the mine and the town that grew up around it, Prophecy.

There's more to this story and much to see. I encourage you to visit the site yourself, where you can listen to the story as told by Jonah's own granddaughter, Miss Ruby, who volunteers as a docent for Clear Creek County Open Space.

When you visit, I recommend a stay at Meadow View Lodge in Blue Eagle, owned and operated by Leigh McLean, the great-great-granddaughter of Isaiah McLean, and her son, Jake. If you're game for a walking tour of Prophecy, Jake is sure to entertain you with stories about the ghost of Old Pappy Young and the Legend of Pappy's Promise.

Fish rainbow trout off the deck of one of the renovated fishing cabins, or you may wish to choose one of the lovely suites in the lodge. My personal favorite is the Wild Rose, where you'll meet the beautiful Rose René, the matriarch of the McLean family, whose portrait graces the suite.

Blue ribbon gourmet meals prepared by the lodge's chef, Edna, and her staff await your arrival. Her husband, Charlie, grills a freshly caught rainbow trout specialty on Friday night cookouts, as well as steaks and tasty barbecue. Jake is in charge of hot dogs and marshmallow roasting.

At Meadow View Lodge, you will be surrounded by the beauty of the Colorado Rockies, soaring mountain peaks, quaking Aspen trees, glimmering freshwater lakes, and wildflower-filled meadows all under the canopy of an unblemished powder blue sky during the day and a star-studded sky beyond your imagination at night.

These are just a few treasures waiting to be discovered at Meadow View Lodge and the historic gold mining town of Prophecy, Colorado.

Epilogue

Two friends sit facing each other with fishing poles in hand as the boat drifts upon the tranquil water of Lake Meadow View, content in each other's silence.

Jake is the first to speak. "I was listening to you yesterday, Ruby, talking to the visitors in Prophecy."

The old woman casts a loving smile in the boy's direction. "You was?"

"Yeah, you tell the stories real good. I'm learning a lot about storytelling from you."

She smiles. "Why, that's real nice of you to say, Jake."

"I could see that the people were interested in what you were saying." He pauses. "You even scared some of them a little when you were describing how the ghost of Old Pappy Young still roams the town of Prophecy. I could see them looking over their shoulders like Old Pappy was going to jump out into the middle of them!" They chuckle over their shared conspiracy about the Legend of Old Pappy Young.

"Learned my storytelling from my granddaddy. Ever' night he would tell me a tale about his days in Colorado, 'specially up in Prophecy."

A puzzled look appears on the boy's face. "It made me curious about something, though."

She turns a concerned look towards Jake. "What's bothering you?" she asks, encouraging him to explain.

"Listening to you tell that story made me wonder all over again where you think Pappy might have hid that map." A wistful look covers his face.

"What?!" Ruby squawks. "After all you been through, you're still wondering about that old legend?"

"I can't help thinking about it. I promise I learned my lesson when I fell through the floor and scared all of you so bad. I just want to know if Old Pappy ever did find the mother lode after chasing his dreams all them years. I sure hope he did!"

Ruby studies the wishful expression on Jake's upturned face. "You promise if I finish telling you the story, you ain't never gonna look for that map again? 'Cause you ain't never gonna find it, that's for sure!"

Jake nods his head excitedly placing his hand on his heart. "I swear, Ruby."

"Gotta wet my whistle then." She takes a slow sip of coffee from her thermos while staring into the mountains, her eyes searching for guidance. She cocks her head, nods, and begins the familiar tale. "Some folks say Pappy did find that vein of gold, the mother lode, the source of all the gold them fellers been sifting out of the stream bed in Prophecy all these years. He named his claim, 'Pappy's Promise,' after his promise that he would be the richest man in Prophecy someday. Pappy said he hid the map real safe in Prophecy where no one would ever find it." Ruby nods her head in confirmation.

"He didn't tell nobody where he hid it?" Jake squints in disbelief into Ruby's eyes.

Ruby pauses to consider his question. An ornery smirk creeps across her face. "Maybe he did and maybe he didn't. We'll never know for sure. You see, Old Pappy started gettin' funny in the head, Granddaddy said, real forgetful-like. One day he would know you, and the next day not. Happens sometimes when you get real old, Jake." Ruby reaches across to pat his hand. "Nothing for you to worry about. Probably all them years spent alone finally took a toll on Pappy, I figure.

"Isaiah and Granddaddy was afraid that Pappy would go into the high country one day and never find his way back down. So they talked him into staying in Prophecy. Gave him a job at the mine checking in the miners coming to work each day. Couldn't have been happier, sittin' there all day, visiting with the miners and telling his stories." Ruby chuckles. "My granddaddy and Pappy had a lot in common, they did.

"Granddaddy reckoned that Pappy did find the mother lode and was content knowing he had achieved his goal. Wasn't ever about the money to Pappy. No sir, it was all about chasing the dream. He had finally caught up to it."

"Yes!" Jake pumps his arm in triumph. "I knew he found it!"

Ruby chuckles at his antics, but her voice turns serious. "But then, Pappy got real sick."

"Oh, no." His eyes fill with tears.

"Never did recover from his illness, even through all of Isaiah's doctoring. He buried him on the top of the hill, king of the mountain. Ordered that fancy rock for him, so fond he was of Old Pappy."

"What do you think happened to the map to Pappy's Promise, Ruby?" Jake asks, wide-eyed.

"Most folks say it never existed 'cept in Pappy's imagination."

Undeterred, Jake asks, "What do you think, Ruby?"

A chill wind ripples across the still waters. Ruby straightens, her gaze lingering on the faraway mountains of the high country.

Silently, she nods her head in agreement with her decision to put this legend to rest. "Well, now, Jake, what I think is that Isaiah saw to it that Old Pappy went to his grave resting on a pillow of fulfilled dreams, the richest man in Prophecy."

Jake cocks his head, a puzzled look on his face. "But..."

"End of story, Jake," Ruby whispers.

About the Author

Diana Bartol was born and raised in a small town in northwest Ohio five miles from the Toledo Express Airport. As a child, she watched the planes flying overhead and dreamed of traveling to faraway places. A job with the airlines fulfilled her dreams. Later, corporate moves with her husband, Dan, provided many more travel experiences in homes located in cities from the East Coast to the West Coast, the Rockles to the Midwest, and to their current home in Tucson, Arizona. It is from these experiences that *Lessons from My Alma Mater*, her first book, evolved.

www.ingramcontent.com/pod-product-compliance
Lightning Source LLC
Chambersburg PA
CBHW061429150726
47987CB00001B/147